GOLDFINGER

'It takes a genius to make gold exciting for twenty-five pages of a novel. The game between Bond and Goldfinger is one of the most sustained pieces of descriptive writing I have ever read.' *Philip Kerr*

Also by the same author
and available from Coronet:

Casino Royale
Diamonds are Forever
Dr No
From Russia with Love
For Your Eyes Only
Live and Let Die
The Man with the Golden Gun
Moonraker
Octopussy *and* The Living Daylights
On Her Majesty's Secret Service
The Spy Who Loved Me
Thunderball
You Only Live Twice

Goldfinger

Ian Fleming

CORONET BOOKS
Hodder and Stoughton

Copyright © Glidrose Productions Ltd, 1959

The right of Ian Fleming to be identified as the Author of
the Work has been asserted by him in accordance with the
Copyright, Designs and Patents Act 1988.

First published in Great Britain in 1959 by Jonathan Cape Ltd.
First published in paperback in 1989 by Hodder and Stoughton
A division of Hodder Headline PLC
A Coronet Paperback

20 19 18 17 16 15 14 13 12 11

British Library Cataloguing in Publication Data

Fleming, Ian, *1908–1964*
Goldfinger
I. Title
823'.914[F]

ISBN 0 340 42568 7

Printed and bound in Great Britain by
Clays Ltd, St Ives plc

Hodder and Stoughton
A division of Hodder Headline PLC
338 Euston Road
London NW1 3BH

CONTENTS

*Goldfinger said, "Mr Bond, they have a saying in Chicago:
'Once is happenstance, twice is coincidence, the third time it's
enemy action.'"*

PART 1 · HAPPENSTANCE

PART 2 · COINCIDENCE

PART 3 · ENEMY ACTION

To
my gentle Reader
William Plomer

PART ONE : HAPPENSTANCE

CHAPTER I

REFLECTIONS IN A DOUBLE BOURBON

JAMES BOND, with two double bourbons inside him, sat in the final departure lounge of Miami Airport and thought about life and death.

It was part of his profession to kill people. He had never liked doing it and when he had to kill he did it as well as he knew how and forgot about it. As a secret agent who held the rare double-O prefix—the licence to kill in the Secret Service—it was his duty to be as cool about death as a surgeon. If it happened, it happened. Regret was unprofessional— worse, it was death-watch beetle in the soul.

And yet there had been something curiously impressive about the death of the Mexican. It wasn't that he hadn't deserved to die. He was an evil man, a man they call in Mexico a *capungo*. A capungo is a bandit who will kill for as little as forty pesos, which is about twenty-five shillings— though probably he had been paid more to attempt the killing of Bond—and, from the look of him, he had been an instrument of pain and misery all his life. Yes, it had certainly been time for him to die; but when Bond had killed him, less than twenty-four hours before, life had gone out of the body so quickly, so utterly, that Bond had almost seen it come out of his mouth as it does, in the shape of a bird, in Haitian primitives.

What an extraordinary difference there was between a body full of person and a body that was empty! Now there is someone, now there is no one. This had been a Mexican with a name and an address and an employment card and perhaps a driving licence. Then something had gone out of him, out of the envelope of flesh and cheap clothes, and had left him an empty paper bag waiting for the dustcart. And the difference, the thing that had gone out of the stinking Mexican bandit, was greater than all Mexico.

Bond looked down at the weapon that had done it. The cutting edge of his right hand was red and swollen. It would soon show a bruise. Bond flexed the hand, kneading it with his left. He had been doing the same thing at intervals through the quick plane trip that had got him away. It was a painful process, but if he kept the circulation moving the hand would heal more quickly. One couldn't tell how soon the weapon would be needed again. Cynicism gathered at the corners of Bond's mouth.

"National Airlines, 'Airline of the Stars', announces the departure of their flight NA 106 to La Guardia Field, New York. Will all passengers please proceed to gate number seven. All aboard, please."

The Tannoy switched off with an echoing click. Bond glanced at his watch. At least another ten minutes before Transamerica would be called. He signalled to a waitress and ordered another double bourbon on the rocks. When the wide, chunky glass came, he swirled the liquor round for the ice to blunt it down and swallowed half of it. He stubbed out the butt of his cigarette and sat, his chin resting on his left hand, and gazed moodily across the twinkling tarmac to where the last half of the sun was slipping gloriously into the Gulf.

The death of the Mexican had been the finishing touch to a bad assignment, one of the worst—squalid, dangerous and without any redeeming feature except that it had got him away from headquarters.

A big man in Mexico had some poppy fields. The flowers were not for decoration. They were broken down for opium which was sold quickly and comparatively cheaply by the waiters at a small café in Mexico City called the 'Madre de Cacao'. The Madre de Cacao had plenty of protection. If you needed opium you walked in and ordered what you wanted with your drink. You paid for your drink at the caisse and the man at the caisse told you how many noughts to add to your bill. It was an orderly commerce of no concern to anyone outside Mexico. Then, far away in England, the Government, urged on by the United Nations' drive against drug smuggling, announced that heroin would be banned in Britain. There was alarm in Soho and also among respectable doctors who wanted to save their patients agony. Prohibition is the trigger of crime. Very soon the routine smuggling

8

channels from China, Turkey and Italy were run almost dry by the illicit stock-piling in England. In Mexico City, a pleasant-spoken Import and Export merchant called Blackwell had a sister in England who was a heroin addict. He loved her and was sorry for her and, when she wrote that she would die if someone didn't help, he believed that she wrote the truth and set about investigating the illicit dope traffic in Mexico. In due course, through friends and friends of friends, he got to the Madre de Cacao and on from there to the big Mexican grower. In the process, he came to know about the economics of the trade, and he decided that if he could make a fortune and at the same time help suffering humanity he had found the Secret of Life. Blackwell's business was in fertilizers. He had a warehouse and a small plant and a staff of three for soil testing and plant research. It was easy to persuade the big Mexican that, behind this respectable front, Blackwell's team could busy itself extracting heroin from opium. Carriage to England was swiftly arranged by the Mexican. For the equivalent of a thousand pounds a trip, every month one of the diplomatic couriers of the Ministry of Foreign Affairs carried an extra suitcase to London. The price was reasonable. The contents of the suitcase, after the Mexican had deposited it at the Victoria Station left-luggage office and had mailed the ticket to a man called Schwab, c/o Boox-an-Pix, Ltd, WC1, were worth twenty thousand pounds.

Unfortunately Schwab was a bad man, unconcerned with suffering humanity. He had the idea that if American juvenile delinquents could consume millions of dollars' worth of heroin every year, so could their Teddy boy and girl cousins. In two rooms in Pimlico, his staff watered the heroin with stomach powder and sent it on its way to the dance halls and amusement arcades.

Schwab had already made a fortune when the CID Ghost Squad got on to him. Scotland Yard decided to let him make a little more money while they investigated the source of his supply. They put a close tail on Schwab and in due course were led to Victoria Station and thence to the Mexican courier. At that stage, since a foreign country was concerned, the Secret Service had had to be called in and Bond was ordered to find out where the courier got his supplies and to destroy the channel at source.

Bond did as he was told. He flew to Mexico City and

quickly got to the Madre de Cacao. Thence, posing as a buyer for the London traffic, he got back to the big Mexican. The Mexican received him amiably and referred him to Blackwell. Bond had rather taken to Blackwell. He knew nothing about Blackwell's sister, but the man was obviously an amateur and his bitterness about the heroin ban in England rang true. Bond broke into his warehouse one night and left a thermite bomb. He then went and sat in a café a mile away and watched the flames leap above the horizon of rooftops and listened to the silver cascade of the fire-brigade bells. The next morning he telephoned Blackwell. He stretched a handkerchief across the mouthpiece and spoke through it.

"Sorry you lost your business last night. I'm afraid your insurance won't cover those stocks of soil you were researching."

"Who's that? Who's speaking?"

"I'm from England. That stuff of yours has killed quite a lot of young people over there. Damaged a lot of others. Santos won't be coming to England any more with his diplomatic bag. Schwab will be in jail by tonight. That fellow Bond you've been seeing, he won't get out of the net either. The police are after him now."

Frightened words came back down the line.

"All right, but just don't do it again. Stick to fertilizers." Bond hung up.

Blackwell wouldn't have had the wits. It was obviously the big Mexican who had seen through the false trail. Bond had taken the precaution to move his hotel, but that night, as he walked home after a last drink at the Copacabana, a man suddenly stood in his way. The man wore a dirty white linen suit and a chauffeur's white cap that was too big for his head. There were deep blue shadows under Aztec cheek-bones. In one corner of the slash of a mouth there was a toothpick and in the other a cigarette. The eyes were bright pinpricks of marihuana.

"You like woman? Make jigajig?"

"No."

"Coloured girl? Fine jungle tail?"

"No."

"Mebbe pictures?"

The gesture of the hand slipping into the coat was so well

known to Bond, so full of old dangers that when the hand flashed out and the long silver finger went for his throat, Bond was on balance and ready for it.

Almost automatically, Bond went into the 'Parry Defence against Underhand Thrust' out of the book. His right arm cut across, his body swivelling with it. The two forearms met mid-way between the two bodies, banging the Mexican's knife arm off target and opening his guard for a crashing short-arm chin jab with Bond's left. Bond's stiff, locked wrist had not travelled far, perhaps two feet, but the heel of his palm, with fingers spread for rigidity, had come up and under the man's chin with terrific force. The blow almost lifted the man off the sidewalk. Perhaps it had been that blow that had killed the Mexican, broken his neck, but as he staggered back on his way to the ground, Bond had drawn back his right hand and slashed sideways at the taut, offered throat. It was the deadly hand-edge blow to the Adam's apple, delivered with the fingers locked into a blade, that had been the standby of the Commandos. If the Mexican was still alive, he was certainly dead before he hit the ground.

Bond stood for a moment, his chest heaving, and looked at the crumpled pile of cheap clothes flung down in the dust. He glanced up and down the street. There was no one. Some cars passed. Others had perhaps passed during the fight, but it had been in the shadows. Bond knelt down beside the body. There was no pulse. Already the eyes that had been so bright with marihuana were glazing. The house in which the Mexican had lived was empty. The tenant had left.

Bond picked up the body and laid it against a wall in deeper shadow. He brushed his hands down his clothes, felt to see if his tie was straight and went on to his hotel.

At dawn Bond had got up and shaved and driven to the airport where he took the first plane out of Mexico. It happened to be going to Caracas. Bond flew to Caracas and hung about in the transit lounge until there was a plane for Miami, a Transamerica Constellation that would take him on that same evening to New York.

Again the Tannoy buzzed and echoed. "Transamerica regrets to announce a delay on their flight TR 618 to New York due to a mechanical defect. The new departure time will be at eight am. Will all passengers please report to the

Transamerica ticket counter where arrangements for their overnight accommodation will be made. Thank you."

So! That too! Should he transfer to another flight or spend the night in Miami? Bond had forgotten his drink. He picked it up and, tilting his head back, swallowed the bourbon to the last drop. The ice tinkled cheerfully against his teeth. That was it. That was an idea. He would spend the night in Miami and get drunk, stinking drunk so that he would have to be carried to bed by whatever tart he had picked up. He hadn't been drunk for years. It was high time. This extra night, thrown at him out of the blue, was a spare night, a gone night. He would put it to good purpose. It was time he let himself go. He was too tense, too introspective. What the hell was he doing, glooming about this Mexican, this capungo who had been sent to kill him? It had been kill or get killed. Anyway, people were killing other people all the time, all over the world. People were using their motor cars to kill with. They were carrying infectious diseases around, blowing microbes in other people's faces, leaving gasjets turned on in kitchens, pumping out carbon monoxide in closed garages. How many people, for instance, were involved in manufacturing H-bombs, from the miners who mined the uranium to the shareholders who owned the mining shares? Was there any person in the world who wasn't somehow, perhaps only statistically, involved in killing his neighbour?

The last light of the day had gone. Below the indigo sky the flare paths twinkled green and yellow and threw tiny reflections off the oily skin of the tarmac. With a shattering roar a DC 7 hurtled down the main green lane. The windows in the transit lounge rattled softly. People got up to watch. Bond tried to read their expressions. Did they hope the plane would crash—give them something to watch, something to talk about, something to fill their empty lives? Or did they wish it well? Which way were they willing the sixty passengers? To live or to die?

Bond's lips turned down. Cut it out. Stop being so damned morbid. All this is just reaction from a dirty assignment. You're stale, tired of having to be tough. You want a change. You've seen too much death. You want a slice of life—easy, soft, high.

Bond was conscious of steps approaching. They stopped

at his side. Bond looked up. It was a clean, rich-looking, middle-aged man. His expression was embarrassed, deprecating.

"Pardon me, but surely it's Mr Bond . . . Mr—er—James Bond?"

CHAPTER 2

LIVING IT UP

B OND LIKED anonymity. His "Yes, it is" was discouraging. "Well, that's a mighty rare coincidence." The man held out his hand. Bond rose slowly, took the hand and released it. The hand was pulpy and unarticulated—like a hand-shaped mud pack, or an inflated rubber glove. "My name is Du Pont. Junius Du Pont. I guess you won't remember me, but we've met before. Mind if I sit down?"

The face, the name? Yes, there *was* something familiar. Long ago. Not in America. Bond searched the files while he summed the man up. Mr Du Pont was about fifty—pink, clean-shaven and dressed in the conventional disguise with which Brooks Brothers cover the shame of American millionaires. He wore a single-breasted dark tan tropical suit and a white silk shirt with a shallow collar. The rolled ends of the collar were joined by a gold safety pin beneath the knot of a narrow dark red and blue striped tie that fractionally wasn't the Brigade of Guards'. The cuffs of the shirt protruded half an inch below the cuffs of the coat and showed cabochon crystal links containing miniature trout flies. The socks were charcoal-grey silk and the shoes were old and polished mahogany and hinted Peal. The man carried a dark, narrow-brimmed straw Homburg with a wide claret ribbon.

Mr Du Pont sat down opposite Bond and produced cigarettes and a plain gold Zippo lighter. Bond noticed that he was sweating slightly. He decided that Mr Du Pont was what he appeared to be, a very rich American, mildly embarrassed. He knew he had seen him before, but he had no idea where or when.

"Smoke?"

"Thank you." It was a Parliament. Bond affected not to notice the offered lighter. He disliked held-out lighters. He picked up his own and lit the cigarette.

"France, '51, Royale les Eaux." Mr Du Pont looked eagerly at Bond. "That Casino. Ethel, that's Mrs Du Pont, and me were next to you at the table the night you had the big game with the Frenchman."

Bond's memory raced back. Yes, of course. The Du Ponts had been Nos 4 and 5 at the baccarat table. Bond had been 6. They had seemed harmless people. He had been glad to have such a solid bulwark on his left on that fantastic night when he had broken Le Chiffre. Now Bond saw it all again—the bright pool of light on the green baize, the pink crab hands across the table scuttling out for the cards. He smelled the smoke and the harsh tang of his own sweat. That had been a night! Bond looked across at Mr Du Pont and smiled at the memory. "Yes, of course I remember. Sorry I was slow. But that was quite a night. I wasn't thinking of much except my cards."

Mr Du Pont grinned back, happy and relieved. "Why, gosh, Mr Bond. Of course I understand. And I do hope you'll pardon me for butting in. You see . . ." He snapped his fingers for a waitress. "But we must have a drink to celebrate. What'll you have?"

"Thanks. Bourbon on the rocks."

"And dimple Haig and water." The waitress went away.

Mr Du Pont leant forward, beaming. A whiff of soap or after-shave lotion came across the table. Lentheric? "I knew it was you. As soon as I saw you sitting there. But I thought to myself, Junius, you don't often make an error over a face, but let's just go make sure. Well, I was flying Transamerican tonight and, when they announced the delay, I watched your expression and, if you'll pardon me, Mr Bond, it was pretty clear from the look on your face that you had been flying Transamerican too." He waited for Bond to nod. He hurried on. "So I ran down to the ticket counter and had me a look at the passenger list. Sure enough, there it was, 'J. Bond'."

Mr Du Pont sat back, pleased with his cleverness. The drinks came. He raised his glass. "Your very good health, sir. This sure is my lucky day."

Bond smiled non-committally and drank.

Mr Du Pont leant forward again. He looked round. There was nobody at the nearby tables. Nevertheless he lowered his voice. "I guess you'll be saying to yourself, well, it's nice to see Junius Du Pont again, but what's the score? Why's he so particularly happy at seeing me on just this night?" Mr Du Pont raised his eyebrows as if acting Bond's part for him. Bond put on a face of polite inquiry. Mr Du Pont leant still farther across the table. "Now, I hope you'll forgive me, Mr Bond. It's not like me to pry into other people's secre . . . er—affairs. But, after that game at Royale, I did hear that you were not only a grand card player, but also that you were—er—how shall I put it?—that you were a sort of—er—investigator. You know, kind of intelligence operative." Mr Du Pont's indiscretion had made him go very red in the face. He sat back and took out a handkerchief and wiped his forehead. He looked anxiously at Bond.

Bond shrugged his shoulders. The grey-blue eyes that looked into Mr Du Pont's eyes, which had turned hard and watchful despite his embarrassment, held a mixture of candour, irony and self-deprecation. "I used to dabble in that kind of thing. Hangover from the war. One still thought it was fun playing Red Indians. But there's no future in it in peacetime."

"Quite, quite." Mr Du Pont made a throwaway gesture with the hand that held the cigarette. His eyes evaded Bond's as he put the next question, waited for the next lie. (Bond thought, there's a wolf in this Brooks Brothers clothing. This is a shrewd man.) "And now you've settled down?" Mr Du Pont smiled paternally. "What did you choose, if you'll pardon the question?"

"Import and Export. I'm with Universal. Perhaps you've come across them."

Mr Du Pont continued to play the game. "Hm. Universal. Let me see. Why, yes, sure I've heard of them. Can't say I've ever done business with them, but I guess it's never too late." He chuckled fatly. "I've got quite a heap of interests all over the place. Only stuff I can honestly say I'm not interested in is chemicals. Maybe it's my misfortune, Mr Bond, but I'm not one of the chemical Du Ponts."

Bond decided that the man was quite satisfied with the particular brand of Du Pont he happened to be. He made no comment. He glanced at his watch to hurry Mr Du Pont's play of the hand. He made a note to handle his own cards carefully. Mr Du Pont had a nice pink kindly baby-face with a puckered, rather feminine turn-down mouth. He looked as harmless as any of the middle-aged Americans with cameras who stand outside Buckingham Palace. But Bond sensed many tough, sharp qualities behind the fuddyduddy façade.

Mr Du Pont's sensitive eye caught Bond's glance at his watch. He consulted his own. "My, oh my! Seven o'clock and here I've been talking away without coming to the point. Now, see here, Mr Bond. I've got me a problem on which I'd greatly appreciate your guidance. If you can spare me the time and if you were counting on stopping over in Miami tonight I'd reckon it a real favour if you'd allow me to be your host." Mr Du Pont held up his hand. "Now, I think I can promise to make you comfortable. So happens I own a piece of the Floridiana. Maybe you heard we opened around Christmas time? Doing a great business I'm happy to say. Really pushing that little old Fountain Blue," Mr Du Pont laughed indulgently. "That's what we call the Fontainebleau down here. Now, what do you say, Mr Bond? You shall have the best suite—even if it means putting some good paying customers out on the sidewalk. And you'd be doing me a real favour." Mr Du Pont looked imploring.

Bond had already decided to accept—blind. Whatever Mr Du Pont's problem—blackmail, gangsters, women— it would be some typical form of rich man's worry. Here was a slice of the easy life he had been asking for. Take it. Bond started to say something politely deprecating. Mr Du Pont interrupted. "Please, please, Mr Bond. And believe me; I'm grateful, very grateful indeed." He snapped his fingers for the waitress. When she came, he turned away from Bond and settled the bill out of Bond's sight. Like many very rich men he considered that showing his money, letting someone see how much he tipped, amounted to indecent exposure. He thrust his roll back into his trousers pocket (the hip pocket is not the place among the rich) and took Bond by the arm. He sensed Bond's resistance to the contact and removed his hand. They went down the stairs to the main hall.

"Now, let's just straighten out your reservation." Mr Du Pont headed for the Transamerica ticket counter. In a few curt phrases Mr Du Pont showed his power and efficiency in his own, his American, realm.

"Yes, Mr Du Pont. Surely, Mr Du Pont. I'll take care of that, Mr Du Pont."

Outside, a gleaming Chrysler Imperial sighed up to the kerb. A tough-looking chauffeur in a biscuit-coloured uniform hurried to open the door. Bond stepped in and settled down in the soft upholstery. The interior of the car was deliciously cool, almost cold. The Transamerican representative bustled out with Bond's suitcase, handed it to the chauffeur and, with a half-bow, went back into the Terminal. "Bill's on the Beach," said Mr Du Pont to the chauffeur and the big car slid away through the crowded parking lots and out on to the parkway.

Mr Du Pont settled back. "Hope you like stone crabs, Mr Bond. Ever tried them?"

Bond said he had, that he liked them very much.

Mr Du Pont talked about Bill's on the Beach and about the relative merits of stone and Alaska crab meat while the Chrysler Imperial sped through downtown Miami, along Biscayne Boulevard and across Biscayne Bay by the Douglas MacArthur Causeway. Bond made appropriate comments, letting himself be carried along on the gracious stream of speed and comfort and rich small-talk.

They drew up at a white-painted, mock-Regency frontage in clapboard and stucco. A scrawl of pink neon said: BILL'S ON THE BEACH. While Bond got out, Mr Du Pont gave his instructions to the chauffeur. Bond heard the words. "The Aloha Suite," and "If there's any trouble, tell Mr Fairlie to call me here. Right?"

They went up the steps. Inside, the big room was decorated in white with pink muslin swags over the windows. There were pink lights on the tables. The restaurant was crowded with sunburned people in expensive tropical get-ups— brilliant garish shirts, jangling gold bangles, dark glasses with jewelled rims, cute native straw hats. There was a confusion of scents. The wry smell of bodies that had been all day in the sun came through.

Bill, a pansified Italian, hurried towards them. "Why, Mr Du Pont. Is a pleasure, sir. Little crowded tonight. Soon fix you up. Please this way please." Holding a large leather-bound menu above his head the man weaved his way between the diners to the best table in the room, a corner table for six. He pulled out two chairs, snapped his

17

fingers for the maître d'hôtel and the wine waiter, spread two menus in front of them, exchanged compliments with Mr Du Pont and left them.

Mr Du Pont slapped his menu shut. He said to Bond, "Now, why don't you just leave this to me? If there's anything you don't like, send it back." And to the head waiter, "Stone crabs. Not frozen. Fresh. Melted butter. Thick toast. Right?"

"Very good, Mr Du Pont." The wine waiter, washing his hands, took the waiter's place.

"Two pints of pink champagne. The Pommery '50. Silver tankards. Right?"

"Vairry good, Mr Du Pont. A cocktail to start?"

Mr Du Pont turned to Bond. He smiled and raised his eyebrows.

Bond said, "Vodka martini, please. With a slice of lemon peel."

"Make it two," said Mr Du Pont. "Doubles." The wine waiter hurried off. Mr Du Pont sat back and produced his cigarettes and lighter. He looked round the room, answered one or two waves with a smile and a lift of the hand and glanced at the neighbouring tables. He edged his chair nearer to Bond's. "Can't help the noise, I'm afraid," he said apologetically. "Only come here for the crabs. They're out of this world. Hope you're not allergic to them. Once brought a girl here and fed her crabs and her lips swelled up like cycle tyres."

Bond was amused at the change in Mr Du Pont—this racy talk, the authority of manner once Mr Du Pont thought he had got Bond on the hook, on his payroll. He was a different man from the shy embarrassed suitor who had solicited Bond at the airport. What did Mr Du Pont want from Bond? It would be coming any minute now, the proposition. Bond said, "I haven't got any allergies."

"Good, good."

There was a pause. Mr Du Pont snapped the lid of his lighter up and down several times. He realized he was making an irritating noise and pushed it away from him. He made up his mind. He said, speaking at his hands on the table in front of him, "You ever play Canasta, Mr Bond?"

"Yes, it's a good game. I like it."

"Two-handed Canasta?"

"I have done. It's not so much fun. If you don't make a fool of yourself—if neither of you do—it tends to even out. Law of averages in the cards. No chance of making much difference in the play."

Mr Du Pont nodded emphatically. "Just so. That's what I've said to myself. Over a hundred games or so, two equal players will end up equal. Not such a good game as Gin or Oklahoma, but in a way that's just what I like about it. You pass the time, you handle plenty of cards, you have your ups and downs, no one gets hurt. Right?"

Bond nodded. The martinis came. Mr Du Pont said to the wine waiter, "Bring two more in ten minutes." They drank. Mr Du Pont turned and faced Bond. His face was petulant, crumpled. He said, "What would you say, Mr Bond, if I told you I'd lost twenty-five thousand dollars in a week playing two-handed Canasta?" Bond was about to reply. Mr Du Pont held up his hand. "And mark you, I'm a good card player. Member of the Regency Club. Play a lot with people like Charlie Goren, Johnny Crawford—at bridge that is. But what I mean, I know my way around at the card table." Mr Du Pont probed Bond's eyes.

"If you've been playing with the same man all the time, you've been cheated."

"Ex-actly." Mr Du Pont slapped the table-cloth. He sat back. "Ex-actly. That's what I said to myself after I'd lost —lost for four whole days. So I said to myself, this bastard is cheating me and by golly I'll find out how he does it and have him hounded out of Miami. So I doubled the stakes and then doubled them again. He was quite happy about it. And I watched every card he played, every movement. Nothing! Not a hint or a sign. Cards not marked. New pack whenever I wanted one. My own cards. Never looked at my hand—couldn't, as I always sat dead opposite him. No kibitzer to tip him off. And he just went on winning and winning. Won again this morning. And again this afternoon. Finally I got so mad at the game—I didn't show it, mind you—" Bond might think he had not been a sport—"I paid up politely. But, without telling this guy, I just packed my bag and got me to the airport and booked on the first plane to New York. Think of that!" Mr Du Pont threw up his hands. "Running away. But twenty-five grand is twenty-five grand. I could see it getting to fifty, a hundred. And I just couldn't stand another of these damned games and I couldn't stand not being able to catch this guy out. So I took off. What do you think of that? Me, Junius Du Pont, throwing in the towel because I couldn't take the licking any more!"

Bond grunted sympathetically. The second round of drinks came. Bond was mildly interested, he was always interested in anything to do with cards. He could see the scene, the two men playing and playing and the one man quietly shuffling and dealing away and marking up his score while the other was always throwing his cards into the middle of the table with a gesture of controlled disgust. Mr Du Pont was obviously being cheated. How? Bond said, "Twenty-five thousand's a lot of money. What stakes were you playing?"

Mr Du Pont looked sheepish. "Quarter a point, then fifty cents, then a dollar. Pretty high I guess with the games averaging around two thousand points. Even at a quarter, that makes five hundred dollars a game. At a dollar a point, if you go on losing, it's murder."

"You must have won sometimes."

"Oh sure, but somehow, just as I'd got the s.o.b. all set for a killing, he'd put down as many of his cards as he could meld. Got out of the bag. Sure, I won some small change, but only when he needed a hundred and twenty to go down and I'd got all the wild cards. But you know how it is with Canasta, you have to discard right. You lay traps to make the other guy hand you the pack. Well, darn it, he seemed to be psychic! Whenever I laid a trap, he'd dodge it, and almost every time he laid one for me I'd fall into it. As for giving me the pack—why, he'd choose the damndest cards when he was pushed—discard singletons, aces, God knows what, and always get away with it. It was just as if he knew every card in my hand."

"Any mirrors in the room?"

"Heck, no! We always played outdoors. He said he wanted to get himself a sunburn. Certainly did that. Red as lobster. He'd only play in the mornings and afternoons. Said if he played in the evening he couldn't get to sleep."

"Who is this man, anyway? What's his name?"

"Goldfinger."

"First name?"

"Auric. That means golden, doesn't it? He certainly is that. Got flaming red hair."

"Nationality?"

"You won't believe it, but he's a Britisher. Domiciled in Nassau. You'd think he'd be a Jew from the name, but he doesn't look it. We're restricted at the Floridiana. Wouldn't have got in if he had been. Nassavian passport. Age forty-two. Unmarried. Profession, broker. Got all this from his passport. Had me a peek via the house detective when I started to play with him."

"What sort of broker?"

Du Pont smiled grimly. "I asked him. He said, 'Oh, anything that comes along.' Evasive sort of fellow. Clams up if you ask him a direct question. Talks away quite pleasantly about nothing at all."

"What's he worth?"

"Ha!" said Mr Du Pont explosively. "That's the damnedest thing. He's loaded. But loaded! I got my bank to check with Nassau. He's lousy with it. Millionaires are a dime a dozen in Nassau, but he's rated either first or second among them. Seems he keeps his money in gold bars. Shifts them around the world a lot to get the benefit of changes in the gold price. Acts like a damn federal bank. Doesn't trust currencies. Can't say he's wrong in that, and seeing how he's one of the richest men in the world there must be something to his system. But the point is, if he's as rich as that, what the hell does he want to take a lousy twenty-five grand off me for?"

A bustle of waiters round their table saved Bond having to think up a reply. With ceremony, a wide silver dish of crabs, big ones, their shells and claws broken, was placed in the middle of the table. A silver sauceboat brimming with melted butter and a long rack of toast was put beside each of their plates. The tankards of champagne frothed pink. Finally, with an oily smirk, the head waiter came behind their chairs and, in turn, tied round their necks long white silken bibs that reached down to the lap.

Bond was reminded of Charles Laughton playing Henry VIII, but neither Mr Du Pont nor the neighbouring diners seemed surprised at the hoggish display. Mr Du Pont, with a gleeful "Every man for himself", raked several hunks of crab on to his plate, doused them liberally in melted butter and dug in. Bond followed suit and proceeded to eat, or rather devour, the most delicious meal he had had in his life.

The meat of the stone crabs was the tenderest, sweetest shellfish he had ever tasted. It was perfectly set off by the dry toast and slightly burned taste of the melted butter. The champagne seemed to have the faintest scent of strawberries. It was ice cold. After each helping of crab, the champagne cleaned the palate for the next. They ate steadily and with absorption and hardly exchanged a word until the dish was cleared.

With a slight belch, Mr Du Pont for the last time wiped butter off his chin with his silken bib and sat back. His face was flushed. He looked proudly at Bond. He said reverently, "Mr Bond, I doubt if anywhere in the world a man has eaten as good a dinner as that tonight. What do you say?"

Bond thought, I asked for the easy life, the rich life. How do I like it? How do I like eating like a pig and hearing remarks like that? Suddenly the idea of ever having another meal like this, or indeed any other meal with Mr Du Pont, revolted him. He felt momentarily ashamed of his disgust. He had asked and it had been given. It was the puritan in him that couldn't take it. He had made his wish and the wish had not only been granted, it had been stuffed down his throat. Bond said, "I don't know about that, but it was certainly very good."

Mr Du Pont was satisfied. He called for coffee. Bond refused the offer of cigars or liqueurs. He lit a cigarette and waited with interest for the catch to be presented. He knew there would be one. It was obvious that all this was part of the come-on. Well, let it come.

Mr Du Pont cleared his throat. "And now, Mr Bond, I have a proposition to put to you." He stared at Bond, trying to gauge his reaction in advance.

"Yes?"

"It surely was providential to meet you like that at the airport." Mr Du Pont's voice was grave, sincere. "I've never forgotten our first meeting at Royale. I recall every detail of it—your coolness, your daring, your handling of the cards." Bond looked down at the table-cloth. But Mr Du Pont had got tired of his peroration. He said hurriedly, "Mr Bond, I will pay you ten thousand dollars to stay here as my guest until you have discovered how this man Goldfinger beats me at cards."

Bond looked Mr Du Pont in the eye. He said, "That's a handsome offer, Mr Du Pont. But I have to get back to London. I must be in New York to catch my plane within forty-eight hours. If you will play your usual sessions tomorrow morning and afternoon I should have plenty of time to find out the answer. But I must leave tomorrow night, whether I can help you or not. Done?"

"Done," said Mr Du Pont.

CHAPTER 3

THE MAN WITH AGORAPHOBIA

THE flapping of the curtains wakened Bond. He threw off the single sheet and walked across the thick pile carpet to the picture window that filled the whole of one wall. He drew back the curtains and went out on to the sun-filled balcony.

The black and white chequer-board tiles were warm, almost hot to the feet although it could not yet be eight o'clock. A brisk inshore breeze was blowing off the sea, straining the flags of all nations that flew along the pier of the private yacht basin. The breeze was humid and smelt strongly of the sea. Bond guessed it was the breeze that the visitors like, but the residents hate. It would rust the metal fittings in their homes, fox the pages of their books, rot their wallpaper and pictures, breed damp-rot in their clothes.

Twelve storeys down the formal gardens, dotted with palm trees and beds of bright croton and traced with neat gravel walks between avenues of bougainvillaea, were rich and dull. Gardeners were working, raking the paths and picking up leaves with the lethargic slow motion of coloured help. Two mowers were at work on the lawns and, where they had already been, sprinklers were gracefully flinging handfuls of spray.

Directly below Bond, the elegant curve of the Cabana Club swept down to the beach—two storeys of changing-rooms below a flat roof dotted with chairs and tables and an occasional red and white striped umbrella. Within the curve was the brilliant green oblong of the Olympic-length swimming-pool fringed on all sides by row upon row of mattressed steamer chairs on which the customers would soon be getting their fifty-dollar-a-day sunburn. White-jacketed men were working among them, straightening the lines of chairs, turning the mattresses and sweeping up yesterday's cigarette butts. Beyond was the long, golden beach and the sea, and more men—raking the tideline, putting up the umbrellas, laying out mattresses. No wonder the neat card inside Bond's wardrobe had said that the cost of the Aloha Suite was two hundred dollars a day. Bond made a rough calculation. If he was paying the bill, it would take him just three weeks to spend his whole salary for the year. Bond smiled cheerfully to himself. He went back into the bedroom, picked up the telephone and ordered himself a delicious, wasteful breakfast, a carton of king-size Chesterfields and the newspapers.

By the time he had shaved and had an ice-cold shower and dressed it was eight o'clock. He walked through into the elegant sitting-room and found a waiter in a uniform of plum and gold laying out his breakfast beside the window. Bond glanced at the *Miami Herald*. The front page was devoted to yesterday's failure of an American ICBM at the nearby Cape Canaveral and a bad upset in a big race at Hialeah.

Bond dropped the paper on the floor and sat down and slowly ate his breakfast and thought about Mr Du Pont and Mr Goldfinger.

His thoughts were inconclusive. Mr Du Pont was either a much worse player than he thought, which seemed unlikely on Bond's reading of his tough, shrewd character, or else Goldfinger was a cheat. If Goldfinger cheated at cards, although he didn't need the money, it was certain that he had also made himself rich by cheating or sharp practice on a much bigger scale. Bond was interested in big crooks. He looked forward to his first sight of Goldfinger. He also looked forward to penetrating Goldfinger's highly successful and, on the face of it, highly mysterious method of fleecing Mr Du Pont. It was going to be a most entertaining day. Idly Bond waited for it to get under way.

The plan was that he would meet Mr Du Pont in the garden at ten o'clock. The story would be that Bond had flown down from New York to try and sell Mr Du Pont a block of shares from an English holding in a Canadian Natural Gas property. The matter was clearly confidential and Goldfinger would not think of questioning Bond about details. Shares, Natural Gas, Canada. That was all Bond needed to remember. They would go along together to the roof of the Cabana Club where the game was played and Bond would read his paper and watch. After luncheon, during which Bond and Mr Du Pont would discuss their 'business', there would be the same routine. Mr Du Pont had inquired if there was anything else he could arrange. Bond had asked for the number of Mr Goldfinger's suite and a pass-key. He had explained that if Goldfinger was any kind of a professional card-sharp, or even an expert amateur, he would travel with the usual tools of the trade—marked and shaved cards, the apparatus for the Short Arm Delivery, and so forth. Mr Du Pont had said he would give Bond the key when they met in the garden. He would have no difficulty getting one from the manager.

After breakfast, Bond relaxed and gazed into the middle distance of the sea. He was not keyed up by the job on hand, only interested and amused. It was just the kind of job he had needed to clear his palate after Mexico.

At half past nine Bond left his suite and wandered along the corridors of his floor, getting lost on his way to the elevator in order to reconnoitre the lay-out of the hotel. Then, having met the same maid twice, he asked his way and went down in the elevator and moved among the scattering of early risers through the Pineapple Shopping Arcade. He glanced into the Bamboo Coffee Shoppe, the Rendezvous Bar, the La Tropicala dining-room, the Kittekat Klub for children and the Boom-Boom Nighterie. He then went purposefully out into the garden. Mr Du Pont, now dressed 'for the beach' by Abercrombie & Fitch, gave him the pass-key to Goldfinger's suite. They sauntered over to the Cabana Club and climbed the two short flights of stairs to the top deck.

Bond's first view of Mr Goldfinger was startling. At the far corner of the roof, just below the cliff of the hotel, a man was lying back with his legs up on a steamer chair.

He was wearing nothing but a yellow satin bikini slip, dark glasses and a pair of wide tin wings under his chin. The wings, which appeared to fit round his neck, stretched out across his shoulders and beyond them and then curved up slightly to rounded tips.

Bond said, "What the hell's he wearing round his neck?"

"You never seen one of those?" Mr Du Pont was surprised. "That's a gadget to help your tan. Polished tin. Reflects the sun up under your chin and behind the ears—the bits that wouldn't normally catch the sun."

"Well, well," said Bond.

When they were a few yards from the reclining figure Mr Du Pont called out cheerfully, in what seemed to Bond an overloud voice, "Hi there!"

Mr Goldfinger did not stir.

Mr Du Pont said in his normal voice. "He's very deaf." They were now at Mr Goldfinger's feet. Mr Du Pont repeated his hail.

Mr Goldfinger sat up sharply. He removed his dark glasses. "Why, hullo there." He unhitched the wings from round his neck, put them carefully on the ground beside him and got heavily to his feet. He looked at Bond with slow, inquiring eyes.

"Like you to meet Mr Bond, James Bond. Friend of mine from New York. Countryman of yours. Come down to try and talk me into a bit of business."

Mr Goldfinger held out a hand. "Pleased to meet you, Mr Bomb."

Bond took the hand. It was hard and dry. There was the briefest pressure and it was withdrawn. For an instant Mr Goldfinger's pale, china-blue eyes opened wide and stared hard at Bond. They stared right through his face to the back of his skull. Then the lids drooped, the shutter closed over the X-ray, and Mr Goldfinger took the exposed plate and slipped it away in his filing system.

"So no game today." The voice was flat, colourless. The words were more of a statement than a question.

"Whaddya mean, no game?" shouted Mr Du Pont boisterously. "You weren't thinking I'd let you hang on to my money? Got to get it back or I shan't be able to leave this darned hotel," Mr Du Pont chuckled richly. "I'll tell Sam to fix the table. James here says he doesn't know much about cards and he'd like to learn the game. That right, James?" He turned to Bond. "Sure you'll be all right with your paper and the sunshine?"

"I'd be glad of the rest," said Bond. "Been travelling too much."

Again the eyes bored into Bond and then drooped. "I'll get some clothes on. I had intended to have a golf lesson this afternoon from Mr Armour at the Boca Raton. But cards have priority among my hobbies. My tendency to un-cock the wrists too early with the mid-irons will have to wait." The eyes rested incuriously on Bond. "You play golf, Mr Bomb?"

Bond raised his voice. "Occasionally, when I'm in England."

"And where do you play?"

"Huntercombe."

"Ah—a pleasant little course. I have recently joined the Royal St Marks. Sandwich is close to one of my business interests. You know it?"

"I have played there."

"What is your handicap?"

"Nine."

"That is a coincidence. So is mine. We must have a game one day." Mr Goldfinger bent down and picked up his tin wings. He said to Mr Du Pont, "I will be with you in five minutes." He walked slowly off towards the stairs.

Bond was amused. This social sniffing at him had been done with just the right casual touch of the tycoon who didn't really care if Bond was alive or dead but, since he was there and alive, might as well place him in an approximate category.

Mr Du Pont gave instructions to a steward in a white coat. Two others were already setting up a card table. Bond walked to the rail that surrounded the roof and looked down into the garden, reflecting on Mr Goldfinger.

He was impressed. Mr Goldfinger was one of the most relaxed men Bond had ever met. It showed in the economy of his movement, of his speech, of his expressions. Mr Goldfinger wasted no effort, yet there was something coiled, compressed, in the immobility of the man.

When Goldfinger had stood up, the first thing that had struck Bond was that everything was out of proportion.

Goldfinger was short, not more than five feet tall, and on top of the thick body and blunt, peasant legs, was set almost directly into the shoulders, a huge and it seemed exactly round head. It was as if Goldfinger had been put together with bits of other people's bodies. Nothing seemed to belong. Perhaps, Bond thought, it was to conceal his ugliness that Goldfinger made such a fetish of sunburn. Without the red-brown camouflage the pale body would be grotesque. The face, under the cliff of crew-cut carroty hair, was as startling, without being as ugly, as the body. It was moon-shaped without being moonlike. The forehead was fine and high and the thin sandy brows were level above the large light blue eyes fringed with pale lashes. The nose was fleshily aquiline between high cheek-bones and cheeks that were more muscular than fat. The mouth was thin and dead straight, but beautifully drawn. The chin and jaws were firm and glinted with health. To sum up, thought Bond, it was the face of a thinker, perhaps a scientist, who was ruthless, sensual, stoical and tough. An odd combination.

What else could he guess? Bond always mistrusted short men. They grew up from childhood with an inferiority complex. All their lives they would strive to be big—bigger than the others who had teased them as a child. Napoleon had been short, and Hitler. It was the short men that caused all the trouble in the world. And what about a misshapen short man with red hair and a bizarre face? That might add up to a really formidable misfit. One could certainly feel the repressions. There was a powerhouse of vitality humming in the man that suggested that if one stuck an electric bulb into Goldfinger's mouth it would light up. Bond smiled at the thought. Into what channels did Goldfinger release his vital force? Into getting rich? Into sex? Into power? Probably into all three. What could his history be? Today he might be an Englishman. What had he been born? Not a Jew—though there might be Jewish blood in him. Not a Latin or anything farther south. Not a Slav. Perhaps a German—no, a Balt! That's where he would have come from. One of the old Baltic provinces. Probably got away to escape the Russians. Goldfinger would have been warned—or his parents had smelled trouble and they had got him out in time. And what had happened then? How had he worked his way up to being one of the richest men in the world? One day it might be interesting to find out. For the time being it would be enough to find out how he won at cards.

"All set?" Mr Du Pont called to Goldfinger who was coming across the roof towards the card table. With his clothes on—a comfortably fitting dark blue suit, a white shirt open at the neck—Goldfinger cut an almost passable figure. But there was no disguise for the great brown and red football of a head and the flesh-coloured hearing aid plugged into the left ear was not an improvement.

Mr Du Pont sat with his back to the hotel. Goldfinger took the seat opposite and cut the cards. Du Pont won the cut, pushed the other pack over to Goldfinger, tapped them to show they were already shuffled and he couldn't bother to cut, and Goldfinger began the deal.

Bond sauntered over and took a chair at Mr Du Pont's elbow. He sat back, relaxed. He made a show of folding his paper to the sports page and watched the deal.

Somehow Bond had expected it, but this was no card-sharp. Goldfinger dealt quickly and efficiently, but with no hint of the Mechanic's Grip, those vital three fingers curled round the long edge of the cards and the index finger at the outside short upper edge—the grip that means you are armed for dealing Bottoms or Seconds. And he wore no signet ring for pricking the cards, no surgical tape round a finger for marking them.

Mr Du Pont turned to Bond. "Deal of fifteen cards," he commented. "You draw two and discard one. Otherwise straight Regency rules. No monkey business with the red treys counting one, three, five, eight, or any of that European stuff."

Mr Du Pont picked up his cards. Bond noticed that he sorted them expertly, not grading them according to value from left to right, or holding his wild cards, of which he had two, at the left—a pattern that might help a watchful opponent. Mr Du Pont concentrated his good cards in the centre of his hand with the singletons and broken melds on either side.

The game began. Mr Du Pont drew first, a miraculous pair of wild cards. His face betrayed nothing. He discarded casually. He only needed two more good draws to go out unseen. But he would have to be lucky. Drawing two cards doubles the chance of picking up what you want, but it also doubles the chance of picking up useless cards that will only clutter up your hand.

Goldfinger played a more deliberate game, almost irritatingly slow. After drawing, he shuffled through his cards again and again before deciding on his discard.

On the third draw, Du Pont had improved his hand to the extent that he now needed only one of five cards to go down and out and catch his opponent with a handful of cards which would all count against him. As if Goldfinger knew the danger he was in, he went down for fifty and proceeded to make a canasta with three wild cards and four fives. He also got rid of some more melds and ended with only four cards in his hand. In any other circumstances it would have been ridiculously bad play. As it was, he had made some four hundred points instead of losing over a hundred, for, on the next draw Mr Du Pont filled his hand and, with most of the edge taken off his triumph by Goldfinger's escape, went down unseen with the necessary two canastas.

"By golly, I nearly screwed you that time." Mr Du Pont's voice had an edge of exasperation. "What in hell told you to cut an' run?"

Goldfinger said indifferently, "I smelled trouble." He added up his points, announced them and jotted them down, waiting for Mr Du Pont to do the same. Then he cut the cards and sat back and regarded Bond with polite interest.

"Will you be staying long, Mr Bomb?"

Bond smiled. "It's Bond, B-O-N-D. No, I have to go back to New York tonight."

"How sad." Goldfinger's mouth pursed in polite regret. He turned back to the cards and the game went on. Bond picked up his paper and gazed, unseeing, at the baseball scores, while he listened to the quiet routine of the game. Goldfinger won that hand and the next and the next. He won the game. There was a difference of one thousand five hundred points—one thousand five hundred dollars to Goldfinger.

"There it goes again!" It was the plaintive voice of Mr Du Pont.

Bond put down his paper. "Does he usually win?"

"Usually!" The word was a snort. "He always wins."

They cut again and Goldfinger began to deal.

Bond said, "Don't you cut for seats? I often find a

change of seat helps the luck. Hostage to fortune and so on."

Goldfinger paused in his deal. He bent his gaze gravely on Bond. "Unfortunately, Mr Bond, that is not possible or I could not play. As I explained to Mr Du Pont at our first game, I suffer from an obscure complaint—agoraphobia— the fear of open spaces. I cannot bear the open horizon. I must sit and face the hotel." The deal continued.

"Oh, I'm so sorry." Bond's voice was grave, interested. "That's a very rare disability. I've always been able to understand claustrophobia, but not the other way round. How did it come about?"

Goldfinger picked up his cards and began to arrange his hand. "I have no idea," he said equably.

Bond got up. "Well, I think I'll stretch my legs for a bit. See what's going on in the pool."

"You do just that," said Mr Du Pont jovially. "Just take it easy, James. Plenty of time to discuss business over lunch. I'll see if I can't dish it out to my friend Goldfinger this time instead of taking it. Be seeing you."

Goldfinger didn't look up from his cards. Bond strolled down the roof, past the occasional splayed-out body, to the rail at the far end that overlooked the pool. For a time he stood and contemplated the ranks of pink and brown and white flesh laid out below him on the steamer chairs. The heavy scent of suntan oil came up to him. There were a few children and young people in the pool. A man, obviously a professional diver, perhaps the swimming instructor, stood on the high-dive. He balanced on the balls of his feet, a muscled Greek god with golden hair. He bounced once, casually, and flew off and down, his arms held out like wings. Lazily they arrowed out to cleave the water for the body to pass through. The impact left only a brief turbulence. The diver jack-knifed up again, shaking his head boyishly. There was a smattering of applause. The man trudged slowly down the pool, his head submerged, his shoulders moving with casual power. Bond thought, good luck to you! You won't be able to keep this up for more than another five or six years. High-divers couldn't take it for long—the repeated shock to the skull. With ski-jumping, which had the same shattering effect on the frame, high-diving was the shortest-lived sport. Bond radioed to the diver, "Cash in quick! Get into films while the hair's still gold."

Bond turned and looked back down the roof towards the two Canasta players beneath the cliff of the hotel. So Goldfinger liked to face the hotel. Or was it that he liked Mr Du Pont to have his back to it? And why? Now, what was the number of Goldfinger's suite? No 200, the Hawaii Suite. Bond's on the top floor was 1200. So, all things being equal, Goldfinger's would be directly below Bond's, on the second floor, twenty yards or so above the roof of the Cabana Club—twenty yards from the card table. Bond counted down. He closely examined the frontage that should be Goldfinger's. Nothing. An empty sun balcony. An open door into the dark interior of the suite. Bond measured distances, angles. Yes, that's how it might be. That's how it must be! Clever Mr Goldfinger!

CHAPTER 4

OVER THE BARREL

AFTER LUNCHEON—the traditional shrimp cocktail, 'native' snapper with a minute paper cup of tartare sauce, roast prime ribs of beef *au jus*, and pineapple *surprise*—it was time for the siesta before meeting Goldfinger at three o'clock for the afternoon session.

Mr Du Pont, who had lost a further ten thousand dollars or more, confirmed that Goldfinger had a secretary. "Never seen her. Sticks to the suite. Probably just some chorine he's brought down for the ride." He smiled wetly. "I mean the daily ride. Why? You on to something?"

Bond was non-committal. "Can't tell yet. I probably won't be coming down this afternoon. Say I got bored watching—gone into the town." He paused. "But if my idea's right, don't be surprised at what may happen. If Goldfinger starts to behave oddly, just sit quiet and watch. I'm not promising anything. I think I've got him, but I may be wrong."

Mr Du Pont was enthusiastic. "Good for you, boyo!" he said effusively. "I just can't wait to see that bastard over the barrel. Damn his eyes!"

Bond took the elevator up to his suite. He went to his suitcase and extracted an M3 Leica, an MC exposure meter, a K2 filter and a flash-holder. He put a bulb in the holder and checked the camera. He went to his balcony, glanced at the sun to estimate where it would be at about three-thirty and went back into the sitting-room, leaving the door to the balcony open. He stood at the balcony door and aimed the exposure meter. The exposure was one-hundredth of a second. He set this on the Leica, put the shutter at f 11, and the distance at twelve feet. He clipped on a lens hood and took one picture to see that all was working. Then he wound on the film, slipped in the flash-holder and put the camera aside.

Bond went to his suitcase again and took out a thick book—*The Bible Designed to be Read as Literature*—opened it and extracted his Walther PPK in the Berns Martin holster. He slipped the holster inside his trouser band to the left. He tried one or two quick draws. They were satisfactory. He closely examined the geography of his suite, on the assumption that it would be exactly similar to the Hawaii. He visualized the scene that would almost certainly greet him when he came through the door of the suite downstairs. He tried his pass-key in the various locks and practised opening the doors noiselessly. Then he pulled a comfortable chair in front of the open balcony door and sat and smoked a cigarette while he gazed out across the sea and thought of how he would put things to Goldfinger when the time came.

At three-fifteen, Bond got up and went out on to the balcony and cautiously looked down at the two tiny figures across the square of green baize. He went back into the room and checked the exposure meter on the Leica. The light was the same. He slipped on the coat of his dark blue tropical worsted suit, straightened his tie and slung the strap of the Leica round his neck so that the camera hung at his chest. Then, with a last look round, he went out and along to the elevator. He rode down to the ground floor and examined the shop windows in the foyer. When the elevator had gone up again, he walked to the staircase and slowly climbed up two floors. The geography of the second floor was identical with the twelfth. Room 200 was where he had expected it to be. There was no one in sight. He took out his pass-key and silently opened the door and closed it behind him. In the small lobby, a raincoat, a light camel-hair coat and a pale grey Homburg hung on hooks. Bond took his Leica firmly in his right hand, held it up close to his face and gently tried the door to the sitting-room. It was not locked. Bond eased it open.

Even before he could see what he expected to see he could hear the voice. It was a low, attractive, girl's voice, an English voice. It was saying, "Drew five and four. Completed canasta in fives with two twos. Discarding four. Has singletons in kings, knaves, nines, sevens."

Bond slid into the room.

The girl was sitting on two cushions on top of a table which had been pulled up a yard inside the open balcony door. She had needed the cushions to give her height. It was at the top of the afternoon heat and she was naked except for a black brassière and black silk briefs. She was swinging her legs in a bored fashion. She had just finished painting the nails on her left hand. Now she stretched the hand out in front of her to examine the effect. She brought the hand back close to her lips and blew on the nails. Her right hand reached sideways and put the brush back in the Revlon bottle on the table beside her. A few inches from her eyes were the eyepieces of a powerful-looking pair of binoculars supported on a tripod whose feet reached down between her sunburned legs to the floor. Jutting out from below the binoculars was a microphone from which wires led to a box about the size of a portable record player under the table. Other wires ran from the box to a gleaming indoor aerial on the sideboard against the wall.

The briefs tightened as she leant forward again and put her eyes to the binoculars. "Drew a queen and a king. Meld of queens. Can meld kings with a joker. Discarding seven." She switched off the microphone.

While she was concentrating, Bond stepped swiftly across the floor until he was almost behind her. There was a chair. He stood on it, praying it wouldn't squeak. Now he had the height to get the whole scene in focus. He put his eye to the viewfinder. Yes, there it was, all in line, the girl's head, the edge of the binoculars, the microphone and, twenty yards below, the two men at the table with Mr Du Pont's hand of cards held in front of him. Bond could distinguish the reds and the blacks. He pressed the button.

The sharp explosion of the bulb and the blinding flash of light forced a quick scream out of the girl. She swivelled round.

Bond stepped down off the chair. "Good afternoon."

"Whoryou? Whatyouwant?" The girl's hand was up to her mouth. Her eyes screamed at him.

"I've got what I want. Don't worry. It's all over now. And my name's Bond, James Bond."

Bond put his camera carefully down on the chair and came and stood in the radius of her scent. She was very beautiful. She had the palest blonde hair. It fell heavily to her shoulders, unfashionably long. Her eyes were deep blue against a lightly sunburned skin and her mouth was bold and generous and would have a lovely smile.

She stood up and took her hand away from her mouth. She was tall, perhaps five feet ten, and her arms and legs looked firm as if she might be a swimmer. Her breasts thrust against the black silk of the brassière.

Some of the fear had gone out of her eyes. She said in a low voice, "What are you going to do?"

"Nothing to you. I may tease Goldfinger a bit. Move over like a good girl and let me have a look."

Bond took the girl's place and looked through the glasses. The game was going on normally. Goldfinger showed no sign that his communications had broken down.

"Doesn't he mind not getting the signals? Will he stop playing?"

She said hesitatingly, "It's happened before when a plug pulled or something. He just waits for me to come through again."

Bond smiled at her. "Well, let's let him stew for a bit. Have a cigarette and relax," he held out a packet of Chesterfields. She took one. "Anyway it's time you did the nails on your right hand."

A smile flickered across her mouth. "How long were you there? You gave me a frightful shock."

"Not long, and I'm sorry about the shock. Goldfinger's been giving poor old Mr Du Pont shocks for a whole week."

"Yes," she said doubtfully. "I suppose it's really rather mean. But he's very rich, isn't he?"

"Oh yes. I shouldn't lose any sleep over Mr Du Pont. But Goldfinger might choose someone who can't afford it.

Anyway, he's a zillionaire himself. Why does he do it? He's crawling with money."

Animation flooded back into her face. "I know. I simply can't understand him. It's a sort of mania with him, making money. He can't leave it alone. I've asked him why and all he says is that one's a fool not to make money when the odds are right. He's always going on about the same thing, getting the odds right. When he talked me into doing this," she waved her cigarette at the binoculars, "and I asked him why on earth he bothered, took these stupid risks, all he said was, 'That's the second lesson. When the odds aren't right, make them right.'"

Bond said, "Well, it's lucky for him I'm not Pinkertons or the Miami Police Department."

The girl shrugged her shoulders. "Oh, that wouldn't worry him. He'd just buy you off. He can buy anyone off. No one can resist gold."

"What do you mean?"

She said indifferently, "He always carries a million dollars' worth of gold about with him except when he's going through the Customs. Then he just carries a belt full of gold coins round his stomach. Otherwise it's in thin sheets in the bottom and sides of his suitcases. They're really gold suitcases covered with leather."

"They must weigh a ton."

"He always travels by car, one with special springs. And his chauffeur is a huge man. He carries them. No one else touches them."

"Why does he carry around all that gold?"

"Just in case he needs it. He knows that gold will buy him anything he wants. It's all twenty-four carat. And anyway he loves gold, really loves it like people love jewels or stamps or—well," she smiled, "women."

Bond smiled back. "Does he love you?"

She blushed and said indignantly, "Certainly not." Then, more reasonably, "Of course you can think anything you like. But really he doesn't. I mean, I think he likes people to think that we—that I'm—that it's a question of love and all that. You know. He's not very prepossessing and I suppose it's a question of—well—of vanity or something."

"Yes, I see. So you're just a kind of secretary?"

"Companion," she corrected him. "I don't have to type

or anything." She suddenly put her hand up to her mouth. "Oh, but I shouldn't be telling you all this! You won't tell him, will you? He'd fire me." Fright came into her eyes. "Or something. I don't know what he'd do. He's the sort of man who might do anything."

"Of course I won't tell. But this can't be much of a life for you. Why do you do it?"

She said tartly, "A hundred pounds a week and all this," she waved at the room, "doesn't grow on trees. I save up. When I've saved enough I shall go."

Bond wondered if Goldfinger would let her. Wouldn't she know too much? He looked at the beautiful face, the splendid, unselfconscious body. She might not suspect it, but, for his money, she was in very bad trouble with this man.

The girl was fidgeting. Now she said with an embarrassed laugh, "I don't think I'm very properly dressed. Can't I go and put something on over these?"

Bond wasn't sure he could trust her. It wasn't he who was paying the hundred pounds a week. He said airily, "You look fine. Just as respectable as those hundreds of people round the pool. Anyway," he stretched, "it's about time to light a fire under Mr Goldfinger."

Bond had been glancing down at the game from time to time. It seemed to be proceeding normally. Bond bent again to the binoculars. Already Mr Du Pont seemed to be a new man, his gestures were expansive, the half-profile of his pink face was full of animation. While Bond watched, he took a fistful of cards out of his hand and spread them down—a pure canasta in kings. Bond tilted the binoculars up an inch. The big red-brown moon face was impassive, uninterested. Mr Goldfinger was waiting patiently for the odds to adjust themselves back in his favour. While Bond watched, he put up a hand to the hearing aid, pushing the amplifier more firmly into his ear, ready for the signals to come through again.

Bond stepped back. "Neat little machine," he commented. "What are you transmitting on?"

"He told me, but I can't remember." She screwed up her eyes. "A hundred and seventy somethings. Would it be mega-somethings?"

"Megacycles. Might be, but I'd be surprised if he doesn't

37

get a lot of taxicabs and police messages mixed up with your talk. Must have fiendish concentration." Bond grinned. "Now then. All set? It's time to pull the rug away."

Suddenly she reached out and put a hand on his sleeve. There was a Claddagh ring on the middle finger—two gold hands clasped round a gold heart. There were tears in her voice. "Must you? Can't you leave him alone? I don't know what he'll do to me. Please." She hesitated. She was blushing furiously. "And I like you. It's a long time since I've seen someone like you. Couldn't you just stay here for a little more?" She looked down at the ground. "If only you'd leave him alone I'd do—" the words came out in a rush— "I'd do *anything*."

Bond smiled. He took the girl's hand off his arm and squeezed it. "Sorry. I'm being paid to do this job and I must do it. Anyway—" his voice went flat—"I want to do it. It's time someone cut Mr Goldfinger down to size. Ready?"

Without waiting for an answer he bent to the binoculars. They were still focused on Goldfinger. Bond cleared his throat. He watched the big face carefully. His hand felt for the microphone switch and pressed it down.

There must have been a whisper of static in the deaf aid. Goldfinger's expression didn't alter, but he slowly raised his face to heaven and then down again, as if in benediction.

Bond spoke softly, menacingly into the microphone. "Now hear me, Goldfinger." He paused. Not a flicker of expression, but Goldfinger bent his head a fraction as if listening. He studied his cards intently, his hands quite still.

"This is James Bond speaking. Remember me? The game's finished and it's time to pay. I have a photograph of the whole set-up, blonde, binoculars, microphone and you and your hearing aid. This photograph will not go to the FBI and Scotland Yard so long as you obey me exactly. Nod your head if you understand."

The face was still expressionless. Slowly the big round head bent forward and then straightened itself.

"Put your cards down face upwards on the table."

The hands went down. They opened and the cards slid off the fingers on to the table.

"Take out your cheque book and write a cheque to cash for fifty thousand dollars. That is made up as follows, thirty-five you have taken from Mr Du Pont. Ten for my fee. The extra five for wasting so much of Mr Du Pont's valuable time."

Bond watched to see that his order was being obeyed. He took a glance at Mr Du Pont. Mr Du Pont was leaning forward, gaping.

Mr Goldfinger slowly detached the cheque and counter-signed it on the back.

"Right. Now jot this down on the back of your cheque book and see you get it right. Book me a compartment on the Silver Meteor to New York tonight. Have a bottle of vintage champagne on ice in the compartment and plenty of caviar sandwiches. The best caviar. And keep away from me. And no monkey business. The photograph will be in the mails with a full report to be opened and acted upon if I don't show up in good health in New York to-morrow. Nod if you understand."

Again the big head came slowly down and up again. Now there were traces of sweat on the high, unlined forehead.

"Right, now hand the cheque across to Mr Du Pont and say, 'I apologize humbly. I have been cheating you.' Then you can go."

Bond watched the hand go across and drop the cheque in front of Mr Du Pont. The mouth opened and spoke. The eyes were placid, slow. Goldfinger had relaxed. It was only money. He had paid his way out.

"Just a moment, Goldfinger, you're not through yet." Bond glanced up at the girl. She was looking at him strangely. There was misery and fear but also a look of submissiveness, of longing.

"What's your name?"

"Jill Masterton."

Goldfinger had stood up, was turning away. Bond said sharply, "Stop."

Goldfinger stopped in mid-stride. Now his eyes looked up at the balcony. They had opened wide, as when Bond had first met him. Their hard, level, X-ray gaze seemed to find the lenses of the binoculars, travel down them and through Bond's eyes to the back of his skull. They seemed to say, "I shall remember this, Mr Bond."

Bond said softly, "I'd forgotten. One last thing. I shall be taking a hostage for the ride to New York. Miss Masterton. See that she's at the train. Oh, and make that compartment a drawing-room. That's all."

CHAPTER 5

NIGHT DUTY

IT WAS a week later. Bond stood at the open window of the seventh-floor office of the tall building in Regent's Park that is the headquarters of the Secret Service. London lay asleep under a full moon that rode swiftly over the town through a shoal of herring-bone clouds. Big Ben sounded three. One of the telephones rang in the dark room. Bond turned and moved quickly to the central desk and the pool of light cast by the green shaded reading-lamp. He picked up the black telephone from the rank of four.

He said, "Duty officer."

"Station H, sir."

"Put them on."

There was the echoing buzz and twang of the usual bad radio connection with Hongkong. Why were there always sunspots over China? A sing-song voice asked, "Universal Export?"

"Yes."

A deep, close voice—London—said, "You're through to Hongkong. Speak up, please."

Bond said impatiently, "Clear the line, please."

The sing-song voice said, "You're through now. Speak up, please."

"Hullo! Hullo! Universal Export?"

"Yes."

"Dickson speaking. Can you hear me?"

"Yes."

"That cable I sent you about the shipment of mangoes. Fruit. You know?"

"Yes. Got it here." Bond pulled the file towards him. He knew what it was about. Station H wanted some limpet mines to put paid to three Communist spy junks that were using Macao to intercept British freighters and search them for refugees from China.

40

"Must have payment by the tenth."

That would mean that the junks were leaving, or else that the guards on the junks would be doubled after that date, or some other emergency.

Bond said briefly, "Wilco."

"Thanks. 'Bye."

"'Bye." Bond put down the receiver. He picked up the green receiver and dialled Q Branch and talked to the section duty officer. It would be all right. There was a BOAC Britannia leaving in the morning. Q Branch would see that the crate caught the plane.

Bond sat back. He reached for a cigarette and lit it. He thought of the badly air-conditioned little office on the waterfront in Hongkong, saw the sweat marks on the white shirt of 279, whom he knew well and who had just called himself Dickson. Now 279 would probably be talking to his number two: "It's okay. London says can do. Let's just go over this ops. schedule again." Bond smiled wryly. Better they than he. He'd never liked being up against the Chinese. There were too many of them. Station H might be stirring up a hornets' nest, but M had decided it was time to show the opposition that the Service in Hongkong hadn't quite gone out of business.

When, three days before, M had first told him his name was down for night duty, Bond hadn't taken to the idea. He had argued that he didn't know enough about the routine work of the stations, that it was too responsible a job to give a man who had been in the double-O section for six years and who had forgotten all he had ever known about station work.

"You'll soon pick it up," M had said unsympathetically. "If you get in trouble there are the duty section officers or the Chief of Staff—or me, for the matter of that." (Bond had smiled at the thought of waking M up in the middle of the night because some man in Aden or Tokyo was in a flap.) "Anyway, I've decided. I want all senior officers to do their spell of routine." M had looked frostily across at Bond. "Matter of fact, 007, I had the Treasury on to me the other day. Their liaison man thinks the double-O section is redundant. Says that kind of thing is out of date. I couldn't bother to argue"—M's voice was mild. "Just told him he was mistaken." (Bond could visualize the scene.) "However, won't do any harm for you to have some extra duties now you're back in London. Keep you from getting stale."

And Bond wasn't minding it. He was half way through his first week and so far it had just been a question of common sense or passing routine problems on down to the sections. He rather liked the peaceful room and knowing everybody's secrets and being occasionally fed coffee and sandwiches by one of the pretty girls from the canteen.

On the first night the girl had brought him tea. Bond had looked at her severely. "I don't drink tea. I hate it. It's mud. Moreover it's one of the main reasons for the downfall of the British Empire. Be a good girl and make me some coffee." The girl had giggled and scurried off to spread Bond's dictum in the canteen. From then on he had got his coffee. The expression 'a cup of mud' was seeping through the building.

A second reason why Bond enjoyed the long vacuum of night duty was that it gave him time to get on with a project he had been toying with for more than a year— a handbook of all secret methods of unarmed combat. It was to be called *Stay Alive!* It would contain the best of all that had been written on the subject by the Secret Services of the world. Bond had told no one of the project, but he hoped that, if he could finish it, M would allow it to be added to the short list of Service manuals which contained the tricks and techniques of Secret Intelligence.

Bond had borrowed the original textbooks, or where necessary, translations, from Records. Most of the books had been captured from enemy agents or organizations. Some had been presented to M by sister Services such as OSS, CIA and the Deuxième. Now Bond drew towards him a particular prize, a translation of the manual, entitled simply *Defence*, issued to operatives of smersh, the Soviet organization of vengeance and death.

That night he was half way through Chapter Two, whose title, freely translated, was 'Come-along and Restraint Holds'. Now he went back to the book and read for half an hour through the sections dealing with the conventional 'Wrist Come-along', 'Arm Lock Come-along', 'Forearm Lock', 'Head Hold' and 'Use of Neck Pressure Points'.

After half an hour, Bond thrust the typescript away from him. He got up and went across to the window and stood looking out. There was a nauseating toughness in the blunt prose the Russians used. It had brought on another of the attacks of revulsion to which Bond had succumbed ten days before at Miami Airport. What was wrong with him? Couldn't he take it any more? Was he going soft, or was he only stale? Bond stood for a while watching the moon riding, careering, through the clouds. Then he shrugged his shoulders and went back to his desk. He decided that he was as fed up with the variations of violent physical behaviour as a psychoanalyst must become with the mental aberrations of his patients.

Bond read again the passage that had revolted him: 'A drunken woman can also usually be handled by using the thumb and forefinger to grab the lower lip. By pinching hard and twisting, as the pull is made, the woman will come along.'

Bond grunted. The obscene delicacy of that 'thumb and forefinger'! Bond lit a cigarette and stared into the filament of the desk light, switching his mind to other things, wishing that a signal would come in or the telephone ring. Another five hours to go before the nine o'clock report to the Chief of Staff or to M, if M happened to come in early. There was something nagging at his mind, something he had wanted to check on when he had the time. What was it? What had triggered off the reminder? Yes, that was it, 'forefinger'— Goldfinger. He would see if Records had anything on the man.

Bond picked up the green telephone and dialled Records.

"Doesn't ring a bell, sir. I'll check and call you back."

Bond put down the receiver.

It had been a wonderful trip up in the train. They had eaten the sandwiches and drunk the champagne and then, to the rhythm of the giant diesels pounding out the miles, they had made long, slow love in the narrow berth. It had been as if the girl was starved of physical love. She had woken him twice more in the night with soft demanding caresses, saying nothing, just reaching for his hard, lean body. The next day she had twice pulled down the roller blinds to shut out the hard light and had taken him by the hand and said, "Love me, James" as if she was a child asking for a sweet.

Even now Bond could hear the quick silver poem of the

level-crossing bells, the wail of the big windhorn out front and the quiet outside clamour at the stations when they lay and waited for the sensual gallop of the wheels to begin again.

Jill Masterton had said that Goldfinger had been relaxed, indifferent over his defeat. He had told the girl to tell Bond that he would be over in England in a week's time and would like to have that game of golf at Sandwich. Nothing else— no threats, no curses. He had said he would expect the girl back by the next train. Jill had told Bond she would go. Bond had argued with her. But she was not frightened of Goldfinger. What could he do to her? And it was a good job.

Bond had decided to give her the ten thousand dollars Mr Du Pont had shuffled into his hand with a stammer of thanks and congratulations. Bond made her take the money. "I don't want it," Bond had said. "Wouldn't know what to do with it. Anyway, keep it as mad money in case you want to get away in a hurry. It ought to be a million. I shall never forget last night and today."

Bond had taken her to the station and had kissed her once hard on the lips and had gone away. It hadn't been love, but a quotation had come into Bond's mind as his cab moved out of Pennsylvania station: 'Some love is fire, some love is rust. But the finest, cleanest love is lust.' Neither had had regrets. Had they committed a sin? If so, which one? A sin against chastity? Bond smiled to himself. There was a quotation for that too, and from a saint— Saint Augustine: 'Oh Lord, give me Chastity. But don't give it yet!'

The green telephone rang. "Three Goldfingers, sir, but two of them are dead. The third's a Russian post office in Geneva. Got a hairdressing business. Slips the messages into the right-hand coat pocket when he brushes the customers down. He lost a leg at Stalingrad. Any good, sir? There's plenty more on him."

"No thanks. That couldn't be my man."

"We could put a trace through CID Records in the morning. Got a picture, sir?"

Bond remembered the Leica film. He hadn't even bothered to have it developed. It would be quicker to mock up the man's face on the Identicast. He said, "Is the Identicast room free?"

"Yes, sir. And I can operate it for you if you like."

"Thanks. I'll come down."

Bond told the switchboard to let heads of sections know where he would be and went out and took the lift down to Records on the first floor.

The big building was extraordinarily quiet at night. Beneath the silence, there was a soft whisper of machinery and hidden life—the muffled clack of a typewriter as Bond passed a door, a quickly suppressed stammer of radio static as he passed another, the soft background whine of the ventilation system. It gave you the impression of being in a battleship in harbour.

The Records duty officer was already at the controls of the Identicast in the projection room. He said to Bond, "Could you give me the main lines of the face, sir? That'll help me leave out the slides that are obviously no good."

Bond did so and sat back and watched the lighted screen.

The Identicast is a machine for building up an approximate picture of a suspect—or of someone who has perhaps only been glimpsed in a street or a train or in a passing car. It works on the magic lantern principle. The operator flashes on the screen various head-shapes and sizes. When one is recognized it stays on the screen. Then various haircuts are shown, and then all the other features follow and are chosen one by one—different shapes of eyes, noses, chins, mouths, eyebrows, cheeks, ears. In the end there is the whole picture of a face, as near as the scanner can remember it, and it is photographed and put on record.

It took some time to put together Goldfinger's extraordinary face, but the final result was an approximate likeness in monochrome. Bond dictated one or two notes about the sunburn, the colour of the hair and the expression of the eyes, and the job was done.

"Wouldn't like to meet that on a dark night," commented the man from Records. "I'll put it through to CID when they come on duty. You should get the answer by lunch time."

Bond went back to the seventh floor. On the other side of the world it was around midnight. Eastern stations were closing down. There was a flurry of signals that had to be dealt with, the night's log to be written up, and then it was eight o'clock. Bond telephoned the canteen for his breakfast. He had just finished it when there came the harsh purr of the red telephone. M! Why the hell had he got in half an hour early?

"Yes, sir."

"Come up to my office, 007. I want to have a word before you go off duty."

"Sir." Bond put the telephone back. He slipped on his coat and ran a hand through his hair, told the switchboard where he would be, took the night log and went up in the lift to the eighth and top floor. Neither the desirable Miss Moneypenny nor the Chief of Staff was on duty. Bond knocked on M's door and went in.

"Sit down, 007." M was going through the pipe-lighting routine. He looked pink and well scrubbed. The lined sailor's face above the stiff white collar and loosely tied spotted bow tie was damnably brisk and cheerful. Bond was conscious of the black stubble on his own chin and of the all-night look of his skin and clothes. He sharpened his mind.

"Quiet night?" M had got his pipe going. His hard, healthy eyes regarded Bond attentively.

"Pretty quiet, sir. Station H—"

M raised his left hand an inch or two. "Never mind. I'll read all about it in the log. Here, I'll take it."

Bond handed over the Top Secret folder. M put it to one side. He smiled one of his rare, rather sardonic, bitten-off smiles. "Things change, 007. I'm taking you off night duty for the present."

Bond's answering smile was taut. He felt the quickening of the pulse he had so often experienced in this room. M had got something for him. He said, "I was just getting into it, sir."

"Quite. Have plenty of opportunity later on. Something's come up. Odd business. Not really your line of country, except for one particular angle which"—M jerked his pipe sideways in a throwaway gesture—"may not be an angle at all."

Bond sat back. He said nothing, waiting.

"Had dinner with the Governor of the Bank last night. One's always hearing something new. At least, all this was new to me. Gold—the seamy side of the stuff. Smuggling, counterfeiting, all that. Hadn't occurred to me that the Bank of England knew so much about crooks. Suppose it's part of the Bank's job to protect our currency." M jerked his eyebrows up. "Know anything about gold?"

"No, sir."

"Well, you will by this afternoon. You've got an appointment with a man called Colonel Smithers at the Bank at four o'clock. That give you enough time to get some sleep?"

"Yes, sir."

"Good. Seems that this man Smithers is head of the Bank's research department. From what the Governor told me, that's nothing more or less than a spy system. First time I knew they had one. Just shows what watertight compartments we all work in. Anyway, Smithers and his chaps keep an eye out for anything fishy in the banking world—particularly any monkeying about with our currency and bullion reserves and what not. There was that business the other day of the Italians who were counterfeiting sovereigns. Making them out of real gold. Right carats and all that. But apparently a sovereign or a French napoleon is worth much more than its melted-down value in gold. Don't ask me why. Smithers can tell you that if you're interested. Anyway, the Bank went after these people with a whole battery of lawyers—it wasn't technically a criminal offence—and, after losing in the Italian courts, they finally nailed them in Switzerland. You probably read about it. Then there was that business of dollar balances in Beirut. Made quite a stir in the papers. Couldn't understand it myself. Some crack in the fence we put round our currency. The wide City boys had found it. Well, it's Smithers's job to smell out that kind of racket. The reason the Governor told me all this is because for years, almost since the war apparently, Smithers has had a bee in his bonnet about some big gold leak out of England. Mostly deduction, plus some kind of instinct. Smithers admits he's got damned little to go on, but he's impressed the Governor enough for him to get permission from the PM to call us in." M broke off. He looked quizzically at Bond. "Ever wondered who are the richest men in England?"

"No, sir."

"Well, have a guess. Or rather, put it like this: Who are the richest Englishmen?"

Bond searched his mind. There were a lot of men who

sounded rich or who were made to sound rich by the newspapers. But who really *had* it, liquid, in the bank? He had to say something. He said hesitatingly, "Well, sir, there's Sassoon. Then that shipping man who keeps to himself—er —Ellerman. They say Lord Cowdray is very rich. There are the bankers—Rothschilds, Barings, Hambros. There was Williamson, the diamond man. Oppenheimer in South Africa. Some of the dukes may still have a lot of money." Bond's voice trailed away.

"Not bad. Not bad at all. But you've missed out the joker in the pack. Man I'd never thought of until the Governor brought up his name. He's the richest of the lot. Man called Goldfinger, Auric Goldfinger."

Bond couldn't help himself. He laughed sharply.

"What's the matter?" M's voice was testy. "What the hell is there to laugh about?"

"I'm sorry, sir." Bond got hold of himself. "The truth is, only last night I was building his face up on the Identicast." He glanced at his watch. In a strangled voice he said, "Be on its way to CID Records. Asked for a Trace on him."

M was getting angry. "What the hell's all this about? Stop behaving like a bloody schoolboy."

Bond said soberly, "Well, sir, it's like this . . ." Bond told the story, leaving nothing out.

M's face cleared. He listened with all his attention, leaning forward across the desk. When Bond had finished, M sat back in his chair. He said "Well, well . . . well" on a diminishing scale. He put his hands behind his head and gazed for minutes at the ceiling.

Bond could feel the laughter coming on again. How would the CID word the resounding snub he would get in the course of the day? He was brought sharply back to earth by M's next words. "By the way, what happened to that ten thousand dollars?"

"Gave it to the girl, sir."

"Really! Why not to the White Cross?"

The White Cross Fund was for the families of Secret Service men and women who were killed on duty.

"Sorry, sir." Bond was not prepared to argue that one.

"Humpf." M had never approved of Bond's womanizing. It was anathema to his Victorian soul. He decided to let it pass. He said, "Well, that's all for now, 007. You'll be hearing all about it this afternoon. Funny about Gold-finger. Odd chap. Seen him once or twice at Blades. He plays bridge there when he's in England. He's the chap the Bank of England's after." M paused. He looked mildly across the table at Bond. "As from this moment, so are you."

CHAPTER 6

TALK OF GOLD

BOND WALKED up the steps and through the fine bronze portals and into the spacious, softly echoing entrance hall of the Bank of England and looked around him. Under his feet glittered the brilliant golden patterns of the Boris Anrep mosaics; beyond, through twenty-feet-high arched windows, green grass and geraniums blazed in the central courtyard. To right and left were spacious vistas of polished Hopton Wood stone. Over all hung the neutral smell of air-conditioned air and the heavy, grave atmosphere of immense riches.

One of the athletic-looking, pink frock-coated com-missionaires came up to him. "Yes, sir?"

"Colonel Smithers?"

"Commander Bond, sir? This way please." The com-missionaire moved off to the right between the pillars. The bronze doors of a discreetly hidden lift stood open. The lift rose a few feet to the first floor. Now there was a long panelled corridor ending in a tall Adam window. The floor was close-carpeted in beige Wilton. The commissionaire knocked at the last of several finely carved oak doors that were just so much taller and more elegant than ordinary doors. A grey-haired woman was sitting at a desk. She looked as if she had once taken a double first. The walls of the room were lined with grey metal filing cabinets. The woman had been writing on a quarto pad of yellow memor-andum paper. She smiled with a hint of conspiracy, picked up a telephone and dialled a number. "Commander Bond is here." She put the telephone back and stood up. "Will you come this way?" She crossed the room to a door covered with green baize and held it open for Bond to go through.

Colonel Smithers had risen from his desk. He said gravely, "Nice of you to have come. Won't you sit down?" Bond took the chair. "Smoke?" Colonel Smithers pushed forward a silver box of Senior Service and himself sat down and began to fill a pipe. Bond took a cigarette and lit it.

Colonel Smithers looked exactly like someone who would be called Colonel Smithers. He had obviously been a colonel, probably on the staff, and he had the smooth, polished, basically serious mien that fitted his name. But for his horn-rimmed glasses, he might have been an efficient, not very well-fed courtier in a royal household.

Bond felt boredom gathering in the corners of the room. He said encouragingly, "It seems that you are to tell me all about gold."

"So I understand. I had a note from the Governor. I gather I need keep nothing from you. Of course you understand"—Colonel Smithers looked over Bond's right shoulder—"that most of what I shall have to say will be confidential." The eyes swept quickly across Bond's face.

Bond's face was stony.

Colonel Smithers felt the silence that Bond had intended he should feel. He looked up, saw that he had put his foot in it, and tried to make amends. "Obviously I needn't have mentioned the point. A man with your training . . ."

Bond said, "We all think our own secrets are the only ones that matter. You're probably right to remind me. Other people's secrets are never quite as important as one's own. But you needn't worry. I shall discuss things with my chief but with no one else."

"Quite, quite. Nice of you to take it that way. In the Bank one gets into the habit of being over-discreet. Now then," Colonel Smithers scurried for cover into his subject. "This business of gold. I take it it's not a matter you've thought about a great deal?"

"I know it when I see it."

"Aha, yes—well now, the great thing to remember about gold is that it's the most valuable and most easily marketable commodity in the world. You can go to any town in the world, almost to any village, and hand over a piece of gold and get goods or services in exchange. Right?" Colonel Smithers's voice had taken on a new briskness. His eyes were alight. He had his lecture pat. Bond sat back. He was prepared to listen to anyone who was master of his subject, any subject. "And the next thing to remember," Colonel Smithers held up his pipe in warning, "is that gold is virtually untraceable. Sovereigns have no serial numbers. If gold bars have Mint marks stamped on them the marks can be shaved off or the bar can be melted down and made into a new bar. That makes it almost impossible to check on the whereabouts of gold, or its origins, or its movements round the world. In England, for instance, we at the Bank can only count the gold in our own vaults, in the vaults of other banks and at the Mint, and make a rough guess at the amounts held by the jewellery trade and the pawnbroking fraternity."

"Why are you so anxious to know how much gold there is in England?"

"Because gold and currencies backed by gold are the foundation of our international credit. We can only tell what the true strength of the pound is, and other countries can only tell it, by knowing the amount of valuta we have behind our currency. And my main job, Mr Bond"—Colonel Smithers's bland eyes had become unexpectedly sharp—"is to watch for any leakage of gold out of England—out of anywhere in the sterling area. And when I spot a leakage, an escape of gold towards some country where it can be exchanged more profitably than at our official buying price, it is my job to put the CID Gold Squad on to the fugitive gold and try to get it back into our vaults, plug the leak and arrest the people responsible. And the trouble is, Mr Bond"—Colonel Smithers gave a forlorn shrug of the shoulders—"that gold attracts the biggest, the most ingenious criminals. They are very hard, very hard indeed, to catch."

"Isn't all this only a temporary phase? Why should this shortage of gold go on? They seem to be digging it out of Africa fast enough. Isn't there enough to go round? Isn't it just like any other black market that disappears when the supplies are stepped up, like the penicillin traffic after the war?"

"I'm afraid not, Mr Bond. It isn't quite as easy as that. The population of the world is increasing at the rate of five thousand four hundred every hour of the day. A small percentage of those people become gold hoarders, people who are frightened of currencies, who like to bury some sovereigns in the garden or under the bed. Another percentage needs gold fillings for their teeth. Others need gold-rimmed spectacles, jewellery, engagement rings. All these new people will be taking tons of gold off the market every year. New industries need gold wire, gold plating, amalgams of gold. Gold has extraordinary properties which are being put to new uses every day. It is brilliant, malleable, ductile, almost unalterable and more dense than any of the common metals except platinum. There's no end to its uses. But it has two defects. It isn't hard enough. It wears out quickly, leaves itself on the linings of our pockets and in the sweat of our skins. Every year, the world's stock is invisibly reduced by friction. I said that gold has two defects." Colonel Smithers looked sad. "The other and by far the major defect is that it is the talisman of fear. Fear, Mr Bond, takes gold out of circulation and hoards it against the evil day. In a period of history when every tomorrow may be the evil day, it is fair enough to say that a fat proportion of the gold that is dug out of one corner of the earth is at once buried again in another corner."

Bond smiled at Colonel Smithers's eloquence. This man lived gold, thought gold, dreamed gold. Well, it was an interesting subject. He might just as well wallow in the stuff. In the days when Bond had been after the diamond smugglers he had had first to educate himself in the fascination, the myth of the stones. He said, "What else ought I to know before we get down to your immediate problem?"

"You're not bored? Well, you were suggesting that gold production was so vast nowadays that it ought to take care of all these various consumers. Unfortunately that is not so. In fact the gold content of the world is being worked out. You may think that large areas of the world have still to be explored for gold. You would be mistaken. Broadly speaking, there only remains the land under the sea and the sea itself, which has a notable gold content. People have been scratching the surface of the world for gold for thousands of years. There were the great gold treasures of Egypt and Mycenae, Montezuma and the Incas. Croesus and Midas emptied the Middle Eastern territories of gold. Europe was worked for it—the valleys of the Rhine and the Po, Malaga and the plains of Granada. Cyprus was emptied, and the Balkans. India got the fever. Ants coming up from under the earth carrying grains of gold led the Indians to their alluvial fields. The Romans worked Wales and Devon and Cornwall. In the Middle Ages there were the finds in Mexico and Peru. These were followed by the opening up of the Gold Coast, then called Negro-land, and after that came the Americas. The famous gold rushes of the Yukon and Eldorado, and the rich strikes at Eureka sounded off the first modern Gold Age. Meanwhile, in Australia, Bendigo and Ballarat had come into production, and the Russian deposits at Lena and in the Urals were making Russia the largest gold producer in the world in the middle of the nineteenth century. Then came the second modern Gold Age—the discoveries on the Witwatersrand. These were helped by the new method of cyaniding instead of separation of the gold from the rock by mercury. Today we are in the third Gold Age with the opening up of the Orange Free State deposits." Colonel Smithers threw up his hands. "Now, gold is pouring out of the earth. Why, the whole production of the Klondike and the Homestake and Eldorado, which were once the wonder of the world, would only add up to two or three years of today's production from Africa! Just to show you, from 1500 to 1900, when approximate figures were kept, the whole world produced about eighteen thousand tons of gold. From 1900 to today we have dug up forty-one thousand tons! At this rate, Mr Bond," Colonel Smithers leaned forward earnestly, "—and please don't quote me—but I wouldn't be surprised if in fifty years' time we have not totally exhausted the gold content of the earth!"

Bond, smothered by this cataract of gold history, found no difficulty in looking as grave as Colonel Smithers. He said, "You certainly make a fascinating story of it. Perhaps the position isn't as bad as you think. They're already mining oil under the sea. Perhaps they'll find a way of mining gold. Now, about this smuggling."

The telephone rang. Colonel Smithers impatiently snatched up the receiver. "Smithers speaking." He listened, irritation growing on his face. "I'm sure I sent you a note about the summer fixtures, Miss Philby. The next match is on Saturday against the Discount Houses." He listened again. "Well, if Mrs Flake won't play goals, I'm afraid she'll have to stand down. It's the only position on the field we've got for her. Everybody can't play centre forward. Yes, please do. Say

I'll be greatly obliged if just this once. I'm sure she'll be very good—right figure and all that. Thank you, Miss Philby."

Colonel Smithers took out a handkerchief and mopped his forehead. "Sorry about that. Sports and welfare are becoming almost too much of a fetish at the Bank. I've just had the women's hockey team thrown into my lap. As if I hadn't got enough to do with the annual gymkhana coming on. However—" Colonel Smithers waved these minor irritations aside—"as you say, time to get on to the smuggling. Well, to begin with, and taking only England and the sterling area, it's a very big business indeed. We employ three thousand staff at the Bank, Mr Bond, and of those no less than one thousand work in the exchange control department. Of those at least five hundred, including my little outfit, are engaged in controlling the illicit movements of valuta, the attempts to smuggle or to evade the Exchange Control Regulations."

"That's a lot." Bond measured it against the Secret Service which had a total force of two thousand. "Can you give me an example of smuggling? In gold. I can't understand these dollar swindles."

"All right." Colonel Smithers now talked in the soft, tired voice of an overworked man in the service of his Government. It was the voice of the specialist in a particular line of law enforcement. It said that he knew most things connected with that line and that he could make a good guess at all the rest. Bond knew the voice well, the voice of the first-class Civil Servant. Despite his prosiness, Bond was beginning to take to Colonel Smithers. "All right. Supposing you have a bar of gold in your pocket about the size of a couple of packets of Players. Weight about five and a quarter pounds. Never mind for the moment where you got it from—stole it or inherited it or something. That'll be twenty-four carat—what we call a thousand fine. Now, the law says you have to sell that to the Bank of England at the controlled price of twelve pounds ten per ounce. That would make it worth around a thousand pounds. But you're greedy. You've got a friend going to India or perhaps you're on good terms with an airline pilot or a steward on the Far East run. All you have to do is cut your bar into thin sheets or plates—you'd soon find someone to do this for you—and sew the plates—they'd be smaller than playing cards—into a cotton belt, and pay your friend a commission to wear it. You could easily afford a hundred pounds for the job. Your friend flies off to Bombay and goes to the first bullion dealer in the bazaar. He will be given one thousand seven hundred pounds for your five-pound bar and you're a richer man than you might have been. Mark you," Colonel Smithers waved his pipe airily, "that's only seventy per cent profit. Just after the war you could have got three hundred per cent. If you'd done only half a dozen little operations like that every year you'd be able to retire by now."

"Why the high price in India?" Bond didn't really want to know. He thought M might ask him.

"It's a long story. Briefly, India is shorter of gold, particularly for her jewellery trade, than any other country."

"What's the size of this traffic?"

"Huge. To give you an idea, the Indian Intelligence Bureau and their Customs *captured* forty-three thousand ounces in 1955. I doubt if that's one per cent of the traffic. Gold's been coming into India from all points of the compass. Latest dodge is to fly it in from Macao and drop it by parachute to a reception committee—a ton at a time—like we used to drop supplies to the Resistance during the war."

"I see. Is there anywhere else I can get a good premium for my gold bar?"

"You could get a small premium in most countries—Switzerland, for instance—but it wouldn't be worth your while. India's still the place."

"All right," said Bond. "I think I've got the picture. Now what's your particular problem?" He sat back and lit a cigarette. He was greatly looking forward to hearing about Mr Auric Goldfinger.

Colonel Smithers's eyes took on their hard, foxy look. He said, "There's a man who came over to England in 1937. He was a refugee from Riga. Name of Auric Goldfinger. He was only twenty when he arrived, but he must have been a bright lad because he smelled that the Russians would be swallowing his country pretty soon. He was a jeweller and goldsmith by trade, like his father and grandfather who had refined gold for Fabergé. He had a little money and probably one of those belts of gold I was telling you about. Stole it from his father, I daresay. Well, soon after he'd been naturalized—he was a harmless sort of chap and in a useful trade and he had no difficulty in getting his papers—he started buying up small pawn-brokers all over the country. He put in his own men, paid them well and changed the name of the shops to 'Goldfinger'. Then he turned the shops over to selling cheap jewellery and buying old gold—you know the sort of place: 'Best Prices for Old Gold. Nothing too Large, Nothing too Small', and he had his own particular slogan: 'Buy Her Engagement Ring With Grannie's Locket.' Goldfinger did very well. Always chose good sites, just on the dividing line between the well-to-do streets and the lower-middle. Never touched stolen goods and got a good name everywhere with the police. He lived in London and toured his shops once a month and collected all the old gold. He wasn't interested in the jewellery side. He let his managers run that as they liked." Colonel Smithers looked quizzically at Bond. "You may think these lockets and gold crosses and things are pretty small beer. So they are, but they mount up if you've got twenty little shops, each one buying perhaps half a dozen bits and pieces every week. Well, the war came and Goldfinger, like all other jewellers, had to declare his stock of gold. I looked up his figure in our old records. It was fifty ounces for the whole chain!—just enough of a working stock to keep his shops supplied with ring setting and so forth, what they call jewellers' findings in the trade. Of course, he was allowed to keep it. He tucked himself away in a machine-tool firm in Wales during the war—well out of the firing line—but kept as many of his shops operating as he could. Must have done well out of the GIs who generally travel with a Gold Eagle or a Mexican fifty-dollar piece as a last reserve. Then, when peace broke out, Goldfinger got moving. He bought himself a house, pretentious sort of place, at Reculver, at the mouth of the Thames. He also invested in a well-found Brixham trawler and an old Silver Ghost Rolls Royce—armoured car, built for some South American president who was killed before he could take delivery. He set up a little factory called 'Thanet Alloy Research' in the grounds of his house and staffed it with a German metallurgist, a prisoner of war who didn't want to go back to Germany, and half a dozen Korean steve-dores he picked up in Liverpool. They didn't know a word of any civilized language so they weren't any security risk. Then, for ten years, all we know is that he made one trip a year to India in his trawler and a few trips in his car every year to Switzerland. Set up a subsidiary of his alloy company near Geneva. He kept his shops going. Gave up collecting the old gold himself—used one of his Koreans whom he had taught to drive a car. All right, perhaps Mr Goldfinger is not a very honest man, but he behaves himself and keeps in well with the police, and with much more blatant fiddling going on all over the country nobody paid him any attention."

Colonel Smithers broke off. He looked apologetically at Bond. "I'm not boring you? I do want you to get the picture of the sort of man this is—quiet, careful, law-abiding and with the sort of drive and single-mindedness we all admire. We didn't even hear of him until he suffered a slight misfortune. In the summer of 1954, his trawler, homeward bound from India, went ashore on the Goodwins and he sold the wreck for a song to the Dover Salvage Company. When this company started breaking the ship up and got as far as the hold they found the timbers impregnated with a sort of brown powder which they couldn't put a name to. They sent a specimen to a local chemist. They were surprised when he said the stuff was gold. I won't bother you with the formula, but you see gold can be made to dissolve in a mixture of hydrochloric and nitric acids, and reducing agents —sulphur dioxide or oxalic acid—precipitate the metal as a brown powder. This powder can be reconstituted into gold ingots by melting at around a thousand degrees Centigrade. Have to watch the chlorine gas, but otherwise it's a simple process.

"The usual nosey parker in the salvage firm gossiped to one of the Dover Customs men and in due course a report filtered up through the police and the CID to me, together with a copy of the cargo clearance papers for each of Goldfinger's trips to India. These gave all the cargoes as mineral dust base for crop fertilizers—all perfectly credible because these modern fertilizers do use traces of various minerals in their make-up. The whole picture was clear as crystal. Goldfinger had been refining down his old gold, precipitating it into this brown powder and shipping it to India as fertilizer. But could we pin it on him? We could not. Had a quiet look at his bank balance and tax returns. Twenty thousand pounds at Barclays in Ramsgate. Income tax and super tax paid promptly each year. Figures showed the natural progress of a well-run jewellery business. We dressed a couple of the Gold Squad up and sent them down to knock on the door of Mr Goldfinger's factory at Reculver. 'Sorry, sir, routine inspection for the Small Engineering Section of the Ministry of Labour. We have to make sure the Factory Acts are being observed for safety and health.' 'Come in. Come in.' Mr Goldfinger positively welcomed them. Mark you, he may have been tipped off by his bank manager or someone, but that factory was entirely devoted to designing a cheap alloy for jewellers' findings—trying out unusual metals like aluminium and tin instead of the usual copper and nickel and palladium that are used in gold alloys. There were traces of gold about, of course, and furnaces to heat up to two thousand degrees and so forth, but after all Goldfinger was a jeweller and a smelter in a small way, and all this was perfectly above-board. The Gold Squad retired discomfited, our legal department decided the brown dust in the trawler's timbers was not enough to prosecute on without supporting evidence, and that was more or less that, except"—Colonel Smithers slowly wagged the stem of his pipe—"that I kept the file open and started sniffing around the banks of the world."

Colonel Smithers paused. The rumble of the City came through the half-open window high up in the wall behind his chair. Bond glanced surreptitiously at his watch. Five o'clock. Colonel Smithers got up from his chair. He placed both hands palm downwards on the desk and leant forward. "It took me five years, Mr Bond, to find out that Mr Goldfinger, in ready money, is the richest man in England. In Zürich, in Nassau, in Panama, in New York, he has twenty million pounds' worth of gold bars on safe deposit. And those bars, Mr Bond, are not Mint bars. They don't carry any official marks of origin whatsoever. They're bars that Mr Goldfinger has melted himself. I flew to Nassau and had a look at the five million pounds' worth or so he holds there in the vaults of the Royal Bank of Canada. Oddly enough, like all artists, he couldn't refrain from signing his handiwork. It needs a microscope to see it, but somewhere, on each Goldfinger bar, a minute letter Z has been scratched in the metal. And that gold, or most of it, belongs to

England. The Bank can do nothing about it, so we are asking you to bring Mr Goldfinger to book, Mr Bond, and get that gold back. You know about the currency crisis and the high bank rate? Of course. Well, England needs that gold, badly—and the quicker the better."

CHAPTER 7

THOUGHTS IN A DB III

BOND followed Colonel Smithers to the lift. While they waited for it, Bond glanced out of the tall window at the end of the passage. He was looking down into the deep well of the back courtyard of the Bank. A trim chocolate-brown lorry with no owner's name had come into the courtyard through the triple steel gates. Square cardboard boxes were being unloaded from it and put on to a short conveyor belt that disappeared into the bowels of the Bank.

Colonel Smithers came over. "Fivers," he commented. "Just come up from our printing works at Loughton."

The lift came and they got in. Bond said, "I'm not very impressed by the new ones. They look like any other country's money. The old ones were the most beautiful money in the world."

They walked across the entrance hall, now dimly lit and deserted. Colonel Smithers said, "As a matter of fact I agree with you. Trouble was that those Reichsbank forgeries during the war were a darn sight too good. When the Russians captured Berlin, amongst the loot they got hold of the plates. We asked the Narodni Bank for them, but they refused to give them up. We and the Treasury decided it was just too dangerous. At any moment, if Moscow had been inclined, they could have started a major raid on our currency. We had to withdraw the old fivers. The new ones aren't much to look at, but at least they'd be hell to forge."

The night guard let them out on to the steps. Threadneedle Street was almost deserted. The long City night was beginning. Bond said goodbye to Colonel Smithers and walked along to the Tube. He had never thought very much about the Bank of England, but now that he had been inside the place he decided that the Old Lady of Threadneedle Street might be old but she still had some teeth left in her head.

Bond had been told to report back to M at six. He did so. M's face was no longer pink and shining. The long day had knocked it about, stressed it, shrunken it. When Bond went in and took the chair across the desk, he noticed the conscious effort M made to clear his mind, cope with the new problem the day was to fling at him. M straightened himself in his chair and reached for his pipe. "Well?"

Bond knew the false belligerence of that particular bark. He told the gist of the story in less than five minutes.

When he had finished, M said thoughtfully, "Suppose we've got to take it on. Don't understand a thing about the pound and bank rate and all that but everyone seems to be taking it damned seriously. Personally I should have thought the strength of the pound depended on how hard we all worked rather than how much gold we'd got. Germans didn't have much gold after the war. Look where they've got in ten years. However, that's probably too easy an answer for the politicians—or more likely too difficult. Got any ideas how to tackle this chap Goldfinger? Any way of getting closer to him, offering to do some dirty work for him or something like that?"

Bond said thoughtfully, "I wouldn't get anywhere sucking up to him, asking him for a job or something of that sort, sir. I should say he's the sort of man who only respects people who are tougher or smarter than he is. I've given him one beating and the only message I got from him was that he'd like me to play golf with him. Perhaps I'd better do just that."

"Fine way for one of my top men to spend his time." The sarcasm in M's voice was weary, resigned. "All right. Go ahead. But if what you say is right, you'd better see that you beat him. What's your cover story?"

Bond shrugged. "I hadn't thought, sir. Perhaps I'd better be thinking of leaving Universal Export. No future in it. Having a holiday while I look round. Thinking of emigrating to Canada. Fed up here. Something like that. But perhaps I'd better play it the way the cards fall. I wouldn't think he's an easy man to fool."

"All right. Report progress. And don't think I'm not interested in this case." M's voice had changed. So had his expression. His eyes had become urgent, commanding. "Now I'll give you one piece of information the Bank didn't give you. It just happens that I also know what Mr Goldfinger's gold bars look like. As a matter of fact I was handling one today—scratched Z and all. It had come in with that haul we made last week when the Redland Resident Director's office 'caught fire' in Tangier. You'll have seen the signals. Well, that's the twentieth of these particular gold bars that have come our way since the war."

Bond interrupted, "But that Tangier bar was out of the SMERSH safe."

"Exactly. I've checked. All the other nineteen bars with the scratched Z have been taken from SMERSH operatives." M paused. He said mildly, "D'you know, 007, I wouldn't be at all surprised if Goldfinger doesn't turn out to be the foreign banker, the treasurer so to speak, of SMERSH."

James Bond flung the DB III through the last mile of straight and did a racing change down into third and then into second for the short hill before the inevitable traffic crawl through Rochester. Leashed in by the velvet claw of the front discs, the engine muttered its protest with a mild back-popple from the twin exhausts. Bond went up into third again, beat the lights at the bottom of the hill and slid resignedly up to the back of the queue that would crawl on for a quarter of an hour—if he was lucky—through the sprawl of Rochester and Chatham.

Bond settled back into second and let the car idle. He reached for the wide gunmetal case of Morland cigarettes on the neighbouring bucket seat, fumbled for one and lit it from the dashboard.

He had chosen the A2 in preference to the A20 to Sandwich because he wanted to take a quick look at Goldfinger-land— Reculver and those melancholy forsaken reaches of the Thames which Goldfinger had chosen for his parish. He would then cross the Isle of Thanet to Ramsgate and leave his bag at the Channel Packet, have an early lunch and be off to Sandwich.

The car was from the pool. Bond had been offered the Aston Martin or a Jaguar 3.4. He had taken the DB III.

Either of the cars would have suited his cover—a well-to-do, rather adventurous young man with a taste for the good, the fast things of life. But the DB III had the advantage of an up-to-date triptyque, an inconspicuous colour—battleship grey—and certain extras which might or might not come in handy. These included switches to alter the type and colour of Bond's front and rear lights if he was following or being followed at night, reinforced steel bumpers, fore and aft, in case he needed to ram, a long-barrelled Colt .45 in a trick compartment under the driver's seat, a radio pick-up tuned to receive an apparatus called the Homer, and plenty of concealed space that would fox most Customs men.

Bond saw a chance and picked up fifty yards, sliding into a ten-yard gap left by a family saloon of slow reactions. The man at the wheel, who wore that infallible badge of the bad driver, a hat clamped firmly on the exact centre of his head, hooted angrily. Bond reached out of the window and raised an enigmatically clenched fist. The hooting stopped.

And now what about this theory of M's? It made sense. The Russians were notoriously incompetent payers of their men. Their centres were always running out of funds—their men complaining to Moscow that they couldn't afford a square meal. Perhaps SMERSH couldn't get the valuta out of the Ministry of Home Security. Or perhaps the Ministry of Home Security couldn't get the money out of the Ministry of Finance. But it had always been the same—endless money troubles that resulted in missed chances, broken promises and waste of dangerous radio time. It would make sense to have a clever financial brain somewhere outside Russia who could not only transmit funds to the centres but also, in this case, make profits large enough to run the SMERSH centres abroad without any financial assistance from Moscow. Not only that. On the side, Goldfinger was appreciably damaging the currency base of an enemy country. If all this was correct, it was typical of SMERSH—a brilliant scheme, faultlessly operated by an outstanding man. And that, reflected Bond as he roared up the hill into Chatham, putting half a dozen cars behind him, would partly explain Goldfinger's greed for more and still more money. Devotion to the cause, to SMERSH, and perhaps the dangled prize of an Order of Lenin, would be the spur to pick up even ten or twenty thousand dollars when the odds were right or could be favourably adjusted. The funds for Red Revolution, for the discipline by fear that was the particular speciality of SMERSH, could never be big enough. Goldfinger was not making the money for himself. He was making it for the conquest of the world! The minor risk of being found out, as he had been by Bond, was nothing. Why? What could the Bank of England get him if every single one of his past operations could be exposed? Two years? Three?

The traffic was thinning through the outskirts of Gillingham. Bond started motoring again, but easily now, not hurrying, following his thoughts as the hands and feet went through their automatic responses.

So, in 'thirty-seven, SMERSH must have sent Goldfinger out with the belt of gold round his young waist. He had shown his special aptitudes, his acquisitive bent, during his training in the spy school in Leningrad. He would have been told there would be a war, that he must dig himself in and start quietly accumulating. Goldfinger must never dirty his hands, never meet an agent, never receive or pass a message. Some routine would have been arranged. 'Second-hand '39 Vauxhall. First offer of £1000 secures', 'Immaculate Rover, £2000', 'Bentley, £5000'. Always an advertisement that would not attract attention or correspondence. The prices would be just too high, the description inadequate. In the Agony column of *The Times*, perhaps. And, obediently, Goldfinger would leave the two thousand pounds or the five thousand pounds gold bar at one of a long, a very long series of post-boxes that had been arranged in Moscow before he left. A particular bridge, a hollow tree, under a rock in a stream somewhere, anywhere in England. And he would never, on any account, visit that postbox again. It was up to Moscow to see that the agent got to the hidden treasure. Later, after the war, when Goldfinger was blossoming out, when he had become a big man, the postboxes would no longer be bridges and trees. Now he would be given dates and safety deposit box numbers, left-luggage lockers at stations. But still there would be the rule that Goldfinger must never revisit the scene, never endanger himself. Perhaps he would only get his instructions once a year, at a casual meeting in some park, in a letter slipped into his pocket on a train journey. But always it would be bars of gold, anonymous, untraceable if captured—except for the tiny Z that his vanity had scratched on his handiwork and that a dull dog at the Bank of England called Colonel Smithers had happened upon in the course of his duties.

Now Bond was running through the endless orchards of the Faversham growers. The sun had come out from behind the smog of London. There was the distant gleam of the Thames on his left. There was traffic on the river—long, glistening tankers, stubby merchantmen, antediluvian Dutch Schuyts. Bond left the Canterbury road and switched on to the incongruously rich highway that runs through the cheap bungaloid world of the holiday lands—Whitstable, Herne Bay, Birchington, Margate. He still idled along at fifty, holding the racing wheel on a light rein, listening to the relaxed purr of the exhausts, fitting the bits of his thoughts into the jigsaw as he had done two nights before with Goldfinger's face on the Identicast.

And, Bond reflected, while Goldfinger was pumping a million, two million pounds a year into the bloody maw of SMERSH, he was pyramiding his reserves, working on them, making them work for him whenever the odds were right, piling up the surplus for the day when the trumpets would sound in the Kremlin and every golden sinew would be mobilized. And no one outside Moscow had been watching the process, no one suspected that Goldfinger—the jeweller, the metallurgist, the resident of Reculver and Nassau, the respected member of Blades, of the Royal St Marks at Sandwich—was one of the greatest conspirators of all time, that he had financed the murder of hundreds, perhaps thousands of victims of SMERSH all over the world. SMERSH, *Smiert Spionam*, Death to Spies—the murder Apparat of the High Praesidium! And only M suspected it, only Bond knew it. And here was Bond, launched against this man by a series of flukes, a train of coincidence that had been started by a plane breaking down on the other side of the world. Bond smiled grimly to himself. How often in his profession had it been the same—the tiny acorn of coincidence that soared into the mighty oak whose branches darkened the sky. And now, once again, he was setting out to bring the dreadful growth down. With what? A bag of golf clubs?

A repainted sky-blue Ford Popular with large yellow ears was scurrying along the crown of the road ahead,

Mechanically Bond gave the horn ring a couple of short, polite jabs. There was no reaction. The Ford Popular was doing its forty. Why should anyone want to go more than that respectable speed? The Ford obstinately hunched its shoulders and kept on its course. Bond gave it a sharp blast, expecting it to swerve. He had to touch his brakes when it didn't. Damn the man! Of course! The usual tense figure, hands held too high up on the wheel, and the inevitable hat, this time a particularly hideous black bowler, square on a large bullet head. Oh well, thought Bond, they weren't *his* stomach ulcers. He changed down and contemptuously slammed the DB III past on the inside. Silly bastard!

Another five miles and Bond was through the dainty teleworld of Herne Bay. The howl of Manston sounded away on his right. A flight of three Super Sabres came in to land. They skimmed below his right-hand horizon as if they were diving into the earth. With half his mind, Bond heard the roar of their jets catch up with them as they landed and taxied in to the hangars. He came up with a crossroads. To the left the signpost said RECULVER. Underneath was the ancient monument sign for Reculver church. Bond slowed, but didn't stop. No hanging about. He motored slowly on, keeping his eyes open. The shoreline was too exposed for a trawler to do anything but beach or anchor. Probably Goldfinger had used Ramsgate. Quiet little port. Customs and police who were probably only on the look-out for brandy coming over from France. There was a thick clump of trees between the road and the shore, a glimpse of roofs and of a medium-sized factory chimney with a thin plume of light smoke or steam. That would be it. Soon there was the gate of a long drive. A discreetly authoritative sign said THANET ALLOYS, and underneath: NO ADMITTANCE EXCEPT ON BUSINESS. All very respectable. Bond drove slowly on. There was nothing more to be seen. He took the next right-hand turn across the Manston plateau to Ramsgate.

It was twelve o'clock. Bond inspected his room, a double with bathroom, on the top floor of the Channel Packet, unpacked his few belongings and went down to the snack bar where he had one vodka and tonic and two rounds of excellent ham sandwiches with plenty of mustard. Then he got back into his car and drove slowly over to the Royal St Marks at Sandwich.

Bond carried his clubs to the professional's shop and through to the workroom. Alfred Blacking was winding a new grip on to a driver.

"Hullo, Alfred."

The professional looked up sharply. His sunburned, leathery face broke into a wide smile. "Why, if it isn't Mr James!" They shook hands. "Must be fifteen, twenty years. What brings you down here, sir? Someone was telling me only the other day that you're in the diplomatic or something. Always abroad. Well, I never! Still the same flat swing, sir?" Alfred Blacking joined his hands and gave a low, flat sweep.

"Afraid so, Alfred. Never had time to get myself out of it. How's Mrs Blacking and Cecil?"

"Can't complain, sir. Cecil was runner-up in the Kent Championship last year. Should win it this year if he can only get out of the shop and on to the course a bit more."

Bond propped his clubs up against the wall. It was good to be back. Everything was just the same. There had been a time in his teens when he had played two rounds a day every day of the week at St Marks. Blacking had always wanted to take him in hand. "A bit of practice, Mr James, and you'd be scratch. No fooling. You really would. What do you want to hang around at six for? It's all there except for that flat swing and wanting to hit the ball out of sight when there's no point in it. And you've got the temperament. A couple of years, perhaps only one, and I'd have you in the Amateur." But something had told Bond that there wasn't going to be a great deal of golf in his life and if he liked the game he'd better forget about lessons and just play as much of it as he could. Yes, it would be about twenty years since he had played his last round on St Marks. He'd never been back—even when there had been that bloody affair of the Moonraker at Kingsdown, ten miles down the coast. Perhaps it had been sentimentality. Since St Marks, Bond had got in a good deal of weekend golf when he was at headquarters. But always on the courses round London—Huntercombe, Swinley, Sunningdale, the Berkshire. Bond's handicap had gone up to nine. But he was a real nine—had to be with the games he chose to play, the ten-pound Nassaus with the tough cheery men who were always so anxious to stand you a couple of double kümmels after lunch.

"Any chance of a game, Alfred?"

The professional glanced through his back window at the parking space round the tall flag-pole. He shook his head. "Doesn't look too good, sir. Don't get many players in the middle of the week at this time of year."

"What about you?"

"Sorry, sir. I'm booked. Playing with a member. It's a regular thing. Every day at two o'clock. And the trouble is that Cecil's gone over to Princes to get in some practice for the championship. What a dashed nuisance!" (Alfred never used a stronger oath.) "It *would* happen like that. How long are you staying, sir?"

"Not long. Never mind. I'll knock a ball round with a caddie. Who's this chap you're playing with?"

"A Mr Goldfinger, sir." Alfred looked discouraging.

"Oh, Goldfinger. I know the chap. Met him the other day in America."

"You did, sir?" Alfred obviously found it difficult to believe that anyone knew Mr Goldfinger. He watched Bond's face carefully for any further reaction.

"Any good?"

"So-so, sir. Pretty useful off nine."

"Must take his game damned seriously if he plays with you every day."

"Well, yes, sir." The professional's face had the expression Bond remembered so well. It meant that Blacking had an unfavourable view of a particular member but that he was too good a servant of the club to pass it on.

Bond smiled. He said, "You haven't changed, Alfred. What you mean is that no one else will play with him. Remember Farquharson? Slowest player in England. I remember you going round and round with him twenty years ago. Come on. What's the matter with Goldfinger?"

The professional laughed. He said, "It's you that hasn't changed, Mr James. You always were dashed inquisitive." He came a step closer and lowered his voice. "The truth is, sir, some members think Mr Goldfinger is just a little bit hot. You know, sir. Improves his lie and so forth." The professional took the driver he was holding, took up a stance, gazed towards an imaginary hole and banged the head of the club up and down on the floor as if addressing an imaginary ball. "Let me see now, is this a brassie lie? What d'you think, caddie?" Alfred Blacking chuckled.

"Well, of course, by the time he's finished hammering the ground behind the ball, the ball's been raised an inch and it *is* a brassie lie." Alfred Blacking's face closed up again. He said non-committally, "But that's only gossip, sir. I've never seen anything. Quiet-spoken gentleman. He's got a place at Reculver. Used to come here a lot. But for the last few years he's only been coming to England for a few weeks at a time. Rings up and asks if anyone's wanting a game and when there isn't anyone he books Cecil or me. Rang up this morning and asked if there was anyone about. There's sometimes a stranger drops in." Alfred Blacking looked quizzically at Bond. "I suppose you wouldn't care to take him on this afternoon? It'll look odd you being here and short of a game. And you knowing him and all. He might think I'd been trying to keep him to myself or something. That wouldn't do."

"Nonsense, Alfred. And you've got your living to make. Why don't we play a three-ball?"

"He won't play them, sir. Says they're too slow. And I agree with him. And don't you worry about my fee. There's a lot of work to do in the shop and I'll be glad of an afternoon to get down to it." Alfred Blacking glanced at his watch. "He'll be along any minute now. I've got a caddie for you. Remember Hawker?" Alfred Blacking laughed indulgently. "Still the same old Hawker. He'll be another that'll be glad to see you down here again."

Bond said, "Well thanks, Alfred. I'd be interested to see how this chap plays. But why not leave it like this? Say I've dropped in to get a club made up. Old member. Used to play here before the war. And I need a new number four wood anyway. Your old one has started to give at the seams a bit. Just be casual. Don't say you've told me he's about. I'll stay in the shop so it'll give him a chance to take his choice without offending me. Perhaps he won't like my face or something. Right?"

"Very good, Mr James. Leave it to me. That's his car coming now, sir." Blacking pointed through the window. Half a mile away, a bright yellow car was turning off the road and coming up the private drive. "Funny looking contraption. Sort of motor car we used to see here when I was a boy."

Bond watched the old Silver Ghost sweep majestically

up the drive towards the club. She was a beauty! The sun glittered off the silver radiator and off the engine-turned aluminium shield below the high perpendicular glass cliff of the windscreen. The luggage rail on the roof of the heavy coach-built limousine body—so ugly twenty years ago, so strangely beautiful today—was polished brass, as were the two Lucas "King of the Road" headlamps that stared so haughtily down the road ahead, and the wide mouth of the old boa-constrictor bulb horn. The whole car, except for a black roof and black carrosserie lines and curved panels below the windows, was primrose yellow. It crossed Bond's mind that the South American president might have had it copied from the famous yellow fleet in which Lord Lonsdale had driven to the Derby and Ascot.

And now? In the driver's seat sat a figure in a café-au-lait dust coat and cap, his big round face obscured by black-rimmed driving goggles. Beside him was a squat figure in black with a bowler hat placed firmly on the middle of his head. The two figures stared straight in front of them with a curious immobility. It was almost as if they were driving a hearse.

The car was coming closer. The six pairs of eyes—the eyes of the two men and the great twin orbs of the car—seemed to be looking straight through the little window and into Bond's eyes.

Instinctively, Bond took a few paces back into the dark recesses of the workroom. He noticed the movement and smiled to himself. He picked up somebody's putter and bent down and thoughtfully addressed a knot in the wooden floor.

PART TWO : COINCIDENCE

CHAPTER 8

ALL TO PLAY FOR

"GOOD AFTERNOON, Blacking. All set?" The voice was casual, authoritative. "I see there's a car outside. Not somebody looking for a game, I suppose?"

"I'm not sure, sir. It's an old member come back to have a club made up. Would you like me to ask him, sir?"

"Who is it? What's his name?"

Bond smiled grimly. He pricked his ears. He wanted to catch every inflection.

"A Mr Bond, sir."

There was a pause. "Bond?" The voice had not changed. It was politely interested. "Met a fellow called Bond the other day. What's his first name?"

"James, sir."

"Oh yes." Now the pause was longer. "Does he know I'm here?" Bond could sense Goldfinger's antennae probing the situation.

"He's in the workshop, sir. May have seen your car drive up." Bond thought: Alfred's never told a lie in his life. He's not going to start now.

"Might be an idea." Now Goldfinger's voice unbent. He wanted something from Alfred Blacking, some information. "What sort of a game does this chap play? What's his handicap?"

"Used to be quite useful when he was a boy, sir. Haven't seen his game since then."

"Hm."

Bond could feel the man weighing it all up. Bond smelled that the bait was going to be taken. He reached into his bag and pulled out his driver and started rubbing down the grip with a block of shellac. Might as well look busy. A board in the shop creaked. Bond honed away industriously, his back to the open door.

"I think we've met before." The voice from the doorway was low, neutral.

Bond looked quickly over his shoulder. "My God, you made me jump. Why—" recognition dawned—"it's Gold, Goldman . . . er—Goldfinger." He hoped he wasn't overplaying it. He said with a hint of dislike, or mistrust, "Where have you sprung from?"

"I told you I played down here. Remember?" Goldfinger was looking at him shrewdly. Now the eyes opened wide. The X-ray gaze pierced through to the back of Bond's skull.

"No."

"Did not Miss Masterton give you my message?"

"No. What was it?"

"I said I would be over here and that I would like a game of golf with you."

"Oh, well," Bond's voice was coldly polite, "we must do that some day."

"I was playing with the professional. I will play with you instead." Goldfinger was stating a fact.

There was no doubt that Goldfinger was hooked. Now Bond must play hard to get.

"Why not some other time? I've come to order a club. Anyway I'm not in practice. There probably isn't a caddie." Bond was being as rude as he could. Obviously the last thing he wanted to do was play with Goldfinger.

"I also haven't played for some time." (Bloody liar, thought Bond.) "Ordering a club will not take a moment." Goldfinger turned back into the shop. "Blacking, have you got a caddie for Mr Bond?"

"Yes, sir."

"Then that is arranged."

Bond wearily thrust his driver back into his bag. "Well, all right then." He thought of a final way of putting Goldfinger off. He said roughly, "But I warn you I like playing for money. I can't be bothered to knock a ball round just for the fun of it." Bond felt pleased with the character he was building up for himself.

Was there a glint of triumph, quickly concealed, in Goldfinger's pale eyes? He said indifferently, "That suits me. Anything you like. Off handicap, of course. I think you said you're nine."

71

"Yes."

Goldfinger said carefully, "Where, may I ask?"

"Huntercombe." Bond was also nine at Sunningdale. Huntercombe was an easier course. Nine at Huntercombe wouldn't frighten Goldfinger.

"And I also am nine. Here. Up on the board. So it's a level game. Right?"

Bond shrugged. "You'll be too good for me."

"I doubt it. However," Goldfinger was offhand, "tell you what I'll do. That bit of money you removed from me in Miami. Remember? The big figure was ten. I like a gamble. It will be good for me to have to try. I will play you double or quits for that."

Bond said indifferently, "That's too much." Then, as if he thought better of it, thought he might win, he said—with just the right amount of craft mixed with reluctance—"Of course you can say that was 'found money'. I won't miss it if it goes again. Oh, well, all right. Easy come easy go. Level match. Ten thousand dollars it is."

Goldfinger turned away. He said, and there was a sudden sweetness in the flat voice, "That's all arranged then, Mr Blacking. Many thanks. Put your fee down on my account. Very sorry we shall be missing our game. Now, let me pay the caddie fees."

Alfred Blacking came into the workroom and picked up Bond's clubs. He looked very directly at Bond. He said, "Remember what I told you, sir." One eye closed and opened again. "I mean about that flat swing of yours. It needs watching—all the time."

Bond smiled at him. Alfred had long ears. He might not have caught the figure, but he knew that somehow this was to be a key game. "Thanks, Alfred. I won't forget. Four Penfolds—with hearts on them. And a dozen tees. I won't be a minute."

Bond walked through the shop and out to his car. The bowler-hatted man was polishing the metal work of the Rolls with a cloth. Bond felt rather than saw him stop and watch Bond take out his zip bag and go into the club house. The man had a square flat yellow face. One of the Koreans.

Bond paid his green-fee to Hampton, the steward, and went into the changing-room. It was just the same—the same tacky smell of old shoes and socks and last summer's sweat. Why was it a tradition of the most famous golf clubs that their standard of hygiene should be that of a Victorian private school? Bond changed his socks and put on the battered old pair of nailed Saxones. He took off the coat of his yellowing black and white hound's tooth suit and pulled on a faded black wind-cheater. Cigarettes? Lighter? He was ready to go.

Bond walked slowly out, preparing his mind for the game. On purpose he had needled this man into a high, tough match so that Goldfinger's respect for him should be increased and Goldfinger's view of Bond—that he was the type of ruthless, hard adventurer who might be very useful to Goldfinger—would be confirmed. Bond had thought that perhaps a hundred-pound Nassau would be the form. But ten thousand dollars! There had probably never been such a high singles game in history—except in the finals of American Championships or in the big amateur Calcutta Sweeps where it was the backers rather than the players who had the money on. Goldfinger's private accounting must have taken a nasty dent. He wouldn't have liked that. He would be aching to get some of his money back. When Bond had talked about playing high, Goldfinger had seen his chance. So be it. But one thing was certain, for a hundred reasons Bond could not afford to lose.

He turned into the shop and picked up the balls and tees from Alfred Blacking.

"Hawker's got the clubs, sir."

Bond strolled out across the five hundred yards of shaven seaside turf that led to the first tee. Goldfinger was practising on the putting green. His caddie stood near by, rolling balls to him. Goldfinger putted in the new fashion—between his legs with a mallet putter. Bond felt encouraged. He didn't believe in the system. He knew it was no good practising himself. His old hickory Calamity Jane had its good days and its bad. There was nothing to do about it. He knew also that the St Marks practice green bore no resemblance, in speed or texture, to the greens on the course.

Bond caught up with the limping, insouciant figure of his caddie who was sauntering along chipping at an imaginary ball with Bond's blaster. "Afternoon, Hawker."

"Afternoon, sir." Hawker handed Bond the blaster and threw down three used balls. His keen sardonic poacher's face split in a wry grin of welcome. "How've you been keepin', sir? Played any golf in the last twenty years? Can you still put them on the roof of the starter's hut?" This referred to the day when Bond, trying to do just that before a match, had put two balls through the starter's window.

"Let's see." Bond took the blaster and hefted it in his hand, gauging the distance. The tap of the balls on the practice green had ceased. Bond addressed the ball, swung quickly, lifted his head and shanked the ball almost at right angles. He tried again. This time it was a dunch. A foot of turf flew up. The ball went ten yards. Bond turned to Hawker, who was looking his most sardonic. "It's all right, Hawker. Those were for show. Now then, one for you." He stepped up to the third ball, took his club back slowly and whipped the club head through. The ball soared a hundred feet, paused elegantly, dropped eighty feet on to the thatched roof of the starter's hut and bounced down.

Bond handed back the club. Hawker's eyes were thoughtful, amused. He said nothing. He pulled out the driver and handed it to Bond. They walked together to the first tee, talking about Hawker's family.

Goldfinger joined them, relaxed, impassive. Bond greeted Goldfinger's caddie, an obsequious, talkative man called Foulks whom Bond had never liked. Bond glanced at Goldfinger's clubs. They were a brand new set of American Ben Hogans with smart St Marks leather covers for the woods. The bag was one of the stitched black leather holdalls favoured by American pros. The clubs were in individual cardboard tubes for easy extraction. It was a pretentious outfit, but the best.

"Toss for honour?" Goldfinger flicked a coin.

"Tails."

It was heads. Goldfinger took out his driver and unpeeled a new ball. He said, "Dunlop 65. Number One. Always use the same ball. What's yours?"

"Penfold. Hearts."

Goldfinger looked keenly at Bond. "Strict Rules of Golf?"

"Naturally."

"Right." Goldfinger walked on to the tee and teed up. He took one or two careful, concentrated practice swings. It was a type of swing Bond knew well—the grooved, mechanical, repeating swing of someone who had studied

74

the game with great care, read all the books and spent five thousand pounds on the finest pro teachers. It would be a good, scoring swing which might not collapse under pressure. Bond envied it.

Goldfinger took up his stance, waggled gracefully, took his club head back in a wide slow arc and, with his eyes glued to the ball, broke his wrists correctly. He brought the club head mechanically, effortlessly, down and through the ball and into a rather artificial, copybook finish. The ball went straight and true about two hundred yards down the fairway.

It was an excellent, uninspiring shot. Bond knew that Goldfinger would be capable of repeating the same swing with different clubs again and again round the eighteen holes.

Bond took his place, gave himself a lowish tee, addressed the ball with careful enmity and, with a flat, racket-player's swing in which there was just too much wrist for safety, lashed the ball away. It was a fine, attacking drive that landed past Goldfinger's ball and rolled on fifty yards. But it had had a shade of draw and ended on the edge of the left-hand rough.

They were two good drives. As Bond handed his club to Hawker and strolled off in the wake of the more impatient Goldfinger, he smelled the sweet smell of the beginning of a knock-down-and-drag-out game of golf on a beautiful day in May with the larks singing over the greatest seaside course in the world.

The first hole of the Royal St Marks is four hundred and fifty yards long—four hundred and fifty yards of undulating fairway with one central bunker to trap a mis-hit second shot and a chain of bunkers guarding three-quarters of the green to trap a well-hit one. You can slip through the unguarded quarter, but the fairway slopes to the right there and you are more likely to end up with a nasty first-chip-of-the-day out of the rough. Goldfinger was well placed to try for this opening. Bond watched him take what was probably a spoon, make his two practice swings and address the ball.

Many unlikely people play golf, including people who are blind, who have only one arm, or even no legs, and people often wear bizarre clothes to the game. Other golfers don't think them odd, for there are no rules of appearance or dress at golf. That is one of its minor pleasures. But Goldfinger had made an attempt to look smart at golf and that is the only way of dressing that is incongruous on a links. Everything matched in a blaze of rust-coloured tweed from the buttoned 'golfer's cap' centred on the huge, flaming red hair, to the brilliantly polished, almost orange shoes. The plus-four suit was too well cut and the plus-fours themselves had been pressed down the sides. The stockings were of a matching heather mixture and had green garter tabs. It was as if Goldfinger had gone to his tailor and said, "Dress me for golf—you know, like they wear in Scotland." Social errors made no impression on Bond, and for the matter of that he rarely noticed them. With Goldfinger it was different. Everything about the man had grated on Bond's teeth from the first moment he had seen him. The assertive blatancy of his clothes was just part of the malevolent animal magnetism that had affected Bond from the beginning.

Goldfinger executed his mechanical, faultless swing. The ball flew true but just failed to make the slope and curled off to the right to finish pinhigh off the green in the short rough. Easy five. A good chip could turn it into a four, but it would have to be a good one.

Bond walked over to his ball. It was lying cocked up, just off the fairway. Bond took his number four wood. Now for the 'all air route'—a soaring shot that would carry the cross-bunkers and give him two putts for a four. Bond remembered the dictum of the pros: "It's never too early to start winning." He took it easy, determined not to press for the long but comfortable carry.

As soon as Bond had hit the shot he knew it wouldn't do. The difference between a good golf shot and a bad one is the same as the difference between a beautiful and a plain woman—a matter of millimetres. In this case, the club face had gone through just that one millimetre too low under the ball. The arc of flight was high and soft—no legs. Why the hell hadn't he taken a spoon or a two iron off that lie? The ball hit the lip of the far bunker and fell back. Now it was the blaster, and fighting for a half.

Bond never worried too long about his bad or stupid shots. He put them behind him and thought of the next. He came up with the bunker, took his blaster and measured the distance to the pin. Twenty yards. The ball was lying well back. Should he splash it out with a wide stance and an outside-in swing, or should he blast it and take plenty of sand? For safety's sake he would blast it out. Bond went down into the bunker. Head down and follow well through. The easiest shot in golf. Try and put it dead. The wish, half way down his back swing, hurried the hands in front of the club head. The loft was killed and there was the ball rolling back off the face. Get it out, you bloody fool, and hole a long putt! Now Bond took too much sand. He was out, but barely on the green. Goldfinger bent to his chip and kept his head down until the ball was half way to the hole. The ball stopped three inches from the pin. Without waiting to be given the putt, Goldfinger turned his back on Bond and walked off towards the second tee. Bond picked up his ball and took his driver from Hawker.

"What does he say his handicap is, sir?"

"Nine. It's a level match. Have to do better than that though. Ought to have taken my spoon for the second."

Hawker said encouragingly, "It's early days yet, sir."

Bond knew it wasn't. It was always too early to start losing.

CHAPTER 9

THE CUP AND THE LIP

GOLDFINGER had already teed up. Bond walked slowly behind him, followed by Hawker. Bond stood and leant on his driver. He said, "I thought you said we would be playing the strict rules of golf. But I'll give you that putt. That makes you one up."

Goldfinger nodded curtly. He went through his practice routine and hit his usual excellent, safe drive.

The second hole is a three hundred and seventy yard dogleg to the left with deep cross-bunkers daring you to take the tiger's line. But there was a light helping breeze. For Goldfinger it would now be a five iron for his second. Bond decided to try and make it easier for himself and only have a wedge for the green. He laid his ears back and hit the ball hard and straight for the bunkers. The breeze got

77

under the slight draw and winged the ball on and over. The ball pitched and disappeared down into the gully just short of the green. A four. Chance of a three.

Goldfinger strode off without comment. Bond lengthened his stride and caught up. "How's the agoraphobia? Doesn't all this wide open space bother it?"

"No."

Goldfinger deviated to the right. He glanced at the distant, half-hidden flag, planning his second shot. He took his five iron and hit a good, careful shot which took a bad kick short of the green and ran down into the thick grass to the left. Bond knew that territory. Goldfinger would be lucky to get down in two.

Bond walked up to his ball, took the wedge and flicked the ball on to the green with plenty of stop. The ball pulled up and lay a yard past the hole. Goldfinger executed a creditable pitch but missed the twelve-foot putt. Bond had two for the hole from a yard. He didn't wait to be given the hole but walked up and putted. The ball stopped an inch short. Goldfinger walked off the green. Bond knocked the ball in. All square.

The third is a blind two hundred and forty yards, all carry, a difficult three. Bond chose his brassie and hit a good one. It would be on or near the green. Goldfinger's routine drive was well hit but would probably not have enough steam to carry the last of the rough and trickle down into the saucer of the green. Sure enough, Goldfinger's ball was on top of the protecting mound of rough. He had a nasty, cuppy lie, with a tuft just behind the ball. Goldfinger stood and looked at the lie. He seemed to make up his mind. He stepped past his ball to take a club from the caddie. His left foot came down just behind the ball, flattening the tuft. Goldfinger could now take his putter. He did so and trickled the ball down the bank towards the hole. It stopped three feet short.

Bond frowned. The only remedy against a cheat at golf is not to play with him again. But that was no good in this match. Bond had no intention of playing with the man again. And it was no good starting a you-did-I-didn't argument unless he caught Goldfinger doing something even more outrageous. Bond would just have to try and beat him, cheating and all.

Now Bond's twenty-foot putt was no joke. There was no question of going for the hole. He would have to concentrate on laying it dead. As usual, when one plays to go dead, the ball stopped short—a good yard short. Bond took a lot of trouble about the putt and holed it, sweating. He knocked Goldfinger's ball away. He would go on giving Goldfinger missable putts until suddenly Bond would ask him to hole one. Then that one might look just a bit more difficult.

Still all square. The fourth is four hundred and sixty yards. You drive over one of the tallest and deepest bunkers in the United Kingdom and then have a long second shot across an undulating hilly fairway to a plateau green guarded by a final steep slope which makes it easier to take three putts than two.

Bond picked up his usual fifty yards on the drive and Goldfinger hit two of his respectable shots to the gully below the green. Bond, determined to get up, took a brassie instead of a spoon and went over the green and almost up against the boundary fence. From there he was glad to get down in three for a half.

The fifth was again a long carry, followed by Bond's favourite second shot on the course—over bunkers and through a valley between high sand-dunes to a distant, taunting flag. It is a testing hole for which the first essential is a well-placed drive. Bond stood on the tee, perched high up in the sand-hills, and paused before the shot while he gazed at the glittering distant sea and at the faraway crescent of white cliffs beyond Pegwell Bay. Then he took up his stance and visualized the tennis court of turf that was his target. He took the club back as slowly as he knew how and started down for the last terrific acceleration before the club head met the ball. There was a dull clang on his right. It was too late to stop. Desperately Bond focused the ball and tried to keep his swing all in one piece. There came the ugly clonk of a mis-hit ball. Bond's head shot up. It was a lofted hook. Would it have the legs? Get on! Get on! The ball hit the top of a mountain of rough and bounced over. Would it reach the beginning of the fairway?

Bond turned towards Goldfinger and the caddies, his eyes fierce. Goldfinger was straightening up. He met Bond's eyes indifferently. "Sorry. Dropped my driver."

"Don't do it again," said Bond curtly. He stood down off the tee and handed his driver to Hawker. Hawker shook his head sympathetically. Bond took out a cigarette and lit it. Goldfinger hit his drive the dead straight regulation two hundred yards.

They walked down the hill in a silence which Goldfinger unexpectedly broke. "What is the firm you work for?"

"Universal Export."

"And where do they hang out?"

"London. Regent's Park."

"What do they export?"

Bond woke up from his angry ruminations. Here, pay attention! This is work, not a game. All right, he put you off your drive, but you've got your cover to think about. Don't let him needle you into making mistakes about it. Build up your story. Bond said casually, "Oh everything from sewing-machines to tanks."

"What's your speciality?"

Bond could feel Goldfinger's eyes on him. He said, "I look after the small arms side. Spend most of my time selling miscellaneous ironmongery to sheiks and rajahs—anyone the Foreign Office decides doesn't want the stuff to shoot at us with."

"Interesting work." Goldfinger's voice was flat, bored.

"Not very. I'm thinking of quitting. Came down here for a week's holiday to think it out. Not much future in England. Rather like the idea of Canada."

"Indeed?"

They were past the rough and Bond was relieved to find that his ball had got a forward kick off the hill on to the fairway. The fairway curved slightly to the left and Bond had even managed to pick up a few feet on Goldfinger. It was Goldfinger to play. Goldfinger took out his spoon. He wasn't going for the green but only to get over the bunkers and through the valley.

Bond waited for the usual safe shot. He looked at his own lie. Yes, he could take his brassie. There came the wooden thud of a mis-hit. Goldfinger's ball, hit off the heel, sped along the ground and into the stony wastes of Hell Bunker—the widest bunker and the only unkempt one, because of the pebbles, on the course.

For once Homer had nodded—or rather, lifted his head.

Perhaps his mind had been half on what Bond had told him. Good show! But Goldfinger might still get down in three more. Bond took out his brassie. He couldn't afford to play safe. He addressed the ball, seeing in his mind's eye its eighty-eight-millimetre trajectory through the valley and then the two or three bounces that would take it on to the green. He laid off a bit to the right to allow for his draw. Now!

There came a soft clinking away to his right. Bond stood away from his ball. Goldfinger had his back to Bond. He was gazing out to sea, rapt in its contemplation, while his right hand played 'unconsciously' with the money in his pocket.

Bond smiled grimly. He said, "Could you stop shifting bullion till after my shot?"

Goldfinger didn't turn round or answer. The noise stopped.

Bond turned back to his shot, desperately trying to clear his mind again. Now the brassie was too much of a risk. It needed too good a shot. He handed it to Hawker and took his spoon and banged the ball safely through the valley. It ran on well and stopped on the apron. A five, perhaps a four.

Goldfinger got well out of the bunker and put his chip dead. Bond putted too hard and missed the one back. Still all square.

The sixth, appropriately called 'The Virgin', is a famous short hole in the world of golf. A narrow green, almost ringed with bunkers, it can need anything from an eight to a two iron according to the wind. Today, for Bond, it was a seven. He played a soaring shot, laid off to the right for the wind to bring it in. It ended twenty feet beyond the pin with a difficult putt over and down a shoulder. Should be a three. Goldfinger took his five and played it straight. The breeze took it and it rolled into the deep bunker on the left. Good news! That would be the hell of a difficult three.

They walked in silence to the green. Bond glanced into the bunker. Goldfinger's ball was in a deep heel-mark. Bond walked over to his ball and listened to the larks. This was going to put him one up. He looked for Hawker to take his putter, but Hawker was the other side of the green, watching with intent concentration Goldfinger play his shot. Goldfinger got down into the bunker with his blaster. He jumped up to get a view of the hole and then settled himself for the shot. As his club went up Bond's heart lifted. He was going to try and flick it out—a hopeless technique from that buried lie. The only hope would have been to explode it. Down came the club, smoothly, without hurry. With hardly a handful of sand the ball curved up out of the deep bunker, bounced once and lay dead!

Bond swallowed. Blast his eyes! How the hell had Goldfinger managed that? Now, out of sour grapes, Bond must try for his two. He went for it, missed the hole by an inch and rolled a good yard past. Hell and damnation! Bond walked slowly up to the putt, knocking Goldfinger's ball away. Come on, you bloody fool! But the spectre of the big swing—from an almost certain one up to a possible one down—made Bond wish the ball into the hole instead of tapping it in. The coaxed ball, lacking decision, slid past the lip. One down!

Now Bond was angry with himself. He, and he alone, had lost that hole. He had taken three putts from twenty feet. He really must pull himself together and get going.

At the seventh, five hundred yards, they both hit good drives and Goldfinger's immaculate second lay fifty yards short of the green. Bond took his brassie. Now for the equalizer! But he hit from the top, his club head came down too far ahead of the hands and the smothered ball shot into one of the right-hand bunkers. Not a good lie, but he must put it on the green. Bond took a dangerous seven and failed to get it out. Goldfinger got his five. Two down. They halved the short eighth in three. At the ninth Bond, determined to turn only one down, again tried to do too much off a poor lie. Goldfinger got his four to Bond's five. Three down at the turn! Not too good. Bond asked Hawker for a new ball. Hawker unwrapped it slowly, waiting for Goldfinger to walk over the hillock to the next tee. Hawker said softly, "You saw what he did at The Virgin, sir?"

"Yes, damn him. It was an amazing shot."

Hawker was surprised. "Oh, you didn't see what he did in the bunker, sir?"

"No, what? I was too far away."

The other two were out of sight over the rise. Hawker silently walked down into one of the bunkers guarding the ninth green, kicked a hole with his toe and dropped the ball in the hole. He then stood just behind the half-buried ball with his feet close together. He looked up at Bond. "Remember he jumped up to look at the line to the hole, sir?"

"Yes."

"Just watch this, sir." Hawker looked towards the ninth pin and jumped, just as Goldfinger had done, as if to get the line. Then he looked up at Bond again and pointed to the ball at his feet. The heavy impact of the two feet just behind the ball had levelled the hole in which it had lain and had squeezed the ball out so that it was now perfectly teed for an easy shot—for just the easy cut-up shot which had seemed utterly impossible from Goldfinger's lie at The Virgin.

Bond looked at his caddie for a moment in silence. Then he said, "Thanks, Hawker. Give me the bat and the ball. Somebody's going to be second in this match, and I'm damned if it's going to be me."

"Yes, sir," said Hawker stolidly. He limped off on the short cut that would take him half way down the tenth fairway.

Bond sauntered slowly over the rise and down to the tenth tee. He hardly looked at Goldfinger who was standing on the tee swishing his driver impatiently. Bond was clearing his mind of everything but cold, offensive resolve. For the first time since the first tee, he felt supremely confident. All he needed was a sign from heaven and his game would catch fire.

The tenth at the Royal St Marks is the most dangerous hole on the course. The second shot, to the skiddy plateau green with cavernous bunkers to right and left and a steep hill beyond, has broken many hearts. Bond remembered that Philip Scrutton, out in four under fours in the Gold Bowl, had taken a fourteen at this hole, seven of them ping-pong shots from one bunker to another, to and fro across the green. Bond knew that Goldfinger would play his second to the apron, or short of it, and be glad to get a five. Bond must go for it and get his four.

Two good drives and, sure enough, Goldfinger well up on the apron with his second. A possible four. Bond took his seven, laid off plenty for the breeze and fired the ball off into the sky. At first he thought he had laid off too much, but then the ball began to float to the left. It pitched and stopped dead in the soft sand blown on to the green from the right-hand bunker. A nasty fifteen-foot putt. Bond would now be glad to get a half. Sure enough, Goldfinger putted up to within a yard. That, thought Bond as he squared up to his putt, he will have to hole. He hit his own putt fairly smartly to get it through the powdering of sand and was horrified to see it going like lightning across the skiddy green. God, he was going to have not a yard, but a two-yard putt back! But suddenly, as if drawn by a magnet, the ball swerved straight for the hole, hit the back of the tin, bounced up and fell into the cup with an audible rattle. The sign from heaven! Bond went up to Hawker, winked at him and took his driver.

They left the caddies and walked down the slope and back to the next tee. Goldfinger said coldly, "That putt ought to have run off the green."

Bond said off-handedly, "Always give the hole a chance!" He teed up his ball and hit his best drive of the day down the breeze. Wedge and one putt? Goldfinger hit his regulation shot and they walked off again. Bond said, "By the way, what happened to that nice Miss Masterton?"

Goldfinger looked straight in front of him. "She left my employ."

Bond thought, good for her! He said, "Oh, I must get in touch with her again. Where did she go to?"

"I couldn't say." Goldfinger walked away from Bond towards his ball. Bond's drive was out of sight, over the ridge that bisected the fairway. It wouldn't be more than fifty yards from the pin. Bond thought he knew what would be in Goldfinger's mind, what is in most golfers' minds when they smell the first scent of a good lead melting away. Bond wouldn't be surprised to see that grooved swing quicken a trifle. It did. Goldfinger hooked into a bunker on the left of the green.

Now was the moment when it would be the end of the game if Bond made a mistake, let his man off the hook. He had a slightly downhill lie, otherwise an easy chip—but to the trickiest green on the course. Bond played it like a man. The ball ended six feet from the pin. Goldfinger played well out of his bunker, but missed the longish putt. Now Bond was only one down.

They halved the dog-leg twelfth in inglorious fives and

the longish thirteenth also in fives, Goldfinger having to hole a good putt to do so.

Now a tiny cleft of concentration had appeared on Goldfinger's massive, unlined forehead. He took a drink of water from the tap beside the fourteenth tee. Bond waited for him. He didn't want a sharp clang from that tin cup when it was out-of-bounds over the fence to the right and the drive into the breeze favouring a slice! Bond brought his left hand over to increase his draw and slowed down his swing. The drive, well to the left, was only just adequate, but at least it had stayed in bounds. Goldfinger, apparently unmoved by the out-of-bounds hazard, hit his standard shot. They both negotiated the transverse canal without damage and it was another half in five. Still one down and now only four to play.

The four hundred and sixty yards fifteenth is perhaps the only hole where the long hitter may hope to gain one clear shot. Two smashing woods will just get you over the line of bunkers that lie right up against the green. Goldfinger had to play short of them with his second. He could hardly improve on a five and it was up to Bond to hit a really godlike second shot from a barely adequate drive.

The sun was on its way down and the shadows of the four men were beginning to lengthen. Bond had taken up his stance. It was a good lie. He had kept his driver. There was dead silence as he gave his two incisive waggles. This was going to be a vital stroke. Remember to pause at the top of the swing, come down slow and whip the club head through at the last second. Bond began to take the club back. Something moved at the corner of his right eye. From nowhere the shadow of Goldfinger's huge head approached the ball on the ground, engulfed it and moved on. Bond let his swing take itself to pieces in sections. Then he stood away from his ball and looked up. Goldfinger's feet were still moving. He was looking carefully up at the sky.

"Shades please, Goldfinger." Bond's voice was furiously controlled.

Goldfinger stopped and looked slowly at Bond. The eyebrows were raised a fraction in inquiry. He moved back and stood still, saying nothing.

Bond went back to his ball. Now then, relax! To hell

with Goldfinger. Slam that ball on to the green. Just stand still and hit it. There was a moment when the world stood still, then . . . then somehow Bond did hit it—on a low trajectory that mounted gracefully to carry the distant surf of the bunkers. The ball hit the bank below the green, bounced high with the impact and rolled out of sight into the saucer round the pin.

Hawker came up and took the driver out of Bond's hand. They walked on together. Hawker said seriously, "That's one of the finest shots I've seen in thirty years." He lowered his voice. "I thought he'd fixed you then, sir."

"He damned nearly did, Hawker. It was Alfred Blacking that hit that ball, not me." Bond took out his cigarettes, gave one to Hawker and lit his own. He said quietly, "All square and three to play. We've got to watch those next three holes. Know what I mean?"

"Don't you worry, sir. I'll keep my eye on him."

They came up with the green. Goldfinger had pitched on and had a long putt for a four, but Bond's ball was only two inches away from the hole. Goldfinger picked up his ball and walked off the green. They halved the short sixteenth in good threes. Now there were the two long holes home. Fours would win them. Bond hit a fine drive down the centre. Goldfinger pushed his far out to the right into deep rough. Bond walked along trying not to be too jubilant, trying not to count his chickens. A win for him at this hole and he would only need a half at the eighteenth for the match. He prayed that Goldfinger's ball would be unplayable or, better still, lost.

Hawker had gone on ahead. He had already laid down his bag and was busily—far too busily to Bond's way of thinking—searching for Goldfinger's ball when they came up.

It was bad stuff—jungle country, deep thick luxuriant grass whose roots still held last night's dew. Unless they were very lucky, they couldn't hope to find the ball. After a few minutes' search Goldfinger and his caddie drifted away still wider to where the rough thinned out into isolated tufts. That's good, thought Bond. That wasn't anything like the line. Suddenly he trod on something. Hell and damnation. Should he stamp it in? He shrugged his shoulders, bent down and gently uncovered the ball so as not to improve the

86

lie. Yes it was a Dunlop 65. "Here you are," he called grudgingly. "Oh no, sorry. You play with a Number One, don't you?"

"Yes," came back Goldfinger's voice impatiently.

"Well, this is a Number Seven." Bond picked it up and walked over to Goldfinger.

Goldfinger gave the ball a cursory glance. He said, "Not mine," and went on poking among the tufts with the head of his driver.

It was a good ball, unmarked and almost new. Bond put it in his pocket and went back to his search. He glanced at his watch. The statutory five minutes was almost up. Another half-minute and by God he was going to claim the hole. Strict rules of golf, Goldfinger had stipulated. All right my friend, you shall have them!

Goldfinger was casting back towards Bond, diligently prodding and shuffling through the grass.

Bond said, "Nearly time, I'm afraid."

Goldfinger grunted. He started to say something when there came a cry from his caddie, "Here you are, sir. Number One Dunlop."

Bond followed Goldfinger over to where the caddie stood on a small plateau of higher ground. He was pointing down. Bond bent and inspected the ball. Yes, an almost new Dunlop One and in an astonishingly good lie. It was miraculous—more than miraculous. Bond stared hard from Goldfinger to his caddie. "Must have had the hell of a lucky kick," he said mildly.

The caddie shrugged his shoulders. Goldfinger's eyes were calm, untroubled. "So it would seem." He turned to his caddie. "I think we can get a spoon to that one, Foulks."

Bond walked thoughtfully away and then turned to watch the shot. It was one of Goldfinger's best. It soared over a far shoulder of rough towards the green. Might just have caught the bunker on the right.

Bond walked on to where Hawker, a long blade of grass dangling from his wry lips, was standing on the fairway watching the shot finish. Bond smiled bitterly at him. He said in a controlled voice, "Is my good friend in the bunker, or is the bastard on the green?"

"Green, sir," said Hawker unemotionally.

Bond went up to his ball. Now things had got tough

again. Once more he was fighting for a half after having a certain win in his pocket. He glanced towards the pin, gauging the distance. This was a tricky one. He said, "Five or six?"

"The six should do it, sir. Nice firm shot." Hawker handed him the club.

Now then, clear your mind. Keep it slow and deliberate. It's an easy shot. Just punch it so that it's got plenty of zip to get up the bank and on to the green. Stand still and head down. Click! The ball, hit with a slightly closed face, went off on just the medium trajectory Bond had wanted. It pitched below the bank. It was perfect! No, damn it. It had hit the bank with its second bounce, stopped dead, hesitated and then rolled back and down again. Hell's bells! Was it Hagen who had said, "You drive for show, but you putt for dough"? Getting dead from below that bank was one of the most difficult putts on the course. Bond reached for his cigarettes and lit one, already preparing his mind for the next crucial shot to save the hole—so long as that bastard Goldfinger didn't hole his from thirty feet!

Hawker walked along by his side. Bond said, "Miracle finding that ball."

"It wasn't his ball, sir." Hawker was stating a fact.

"What do you mean?" Bond's voice was tense.

"Money passed, sir. White, probably a fiver. Foulks must have dropped that ball down his trouser leg."

"Hawker!" Bond stopped in his tracks. He looked round. Goldfinger and his caddie were fifty yards away, walking slowly towards the green. Bond said fiercely, "Do you swear to that? How can you be sure?"

Hawker gave a half-ashamed, lop-sided grin. But there was a crafty belligerence in his eye. "Because his ball was lying under my bag of clubs, sir." When he saw Bond's open-mouthed expression he added apologetically, "Sorry, sir. Had to do it after what he's been doing to you. Wouldn't have mentioned it, but I had to let you know he's fixed you again."

Bond had to laugh. He said admiringly, "Well, you *are* a card, Hawker. So you were going to win the match for me all on your own!" He added bitterly, "But, by God, that man's the flaming limit. I've got to get him. I've simply got to. Now let's think!" They walked slowly on.

Bond's left hand was in his trousers pocket, absent-mindedly fingering the ball he had picked up in the rough. Suddenly the message went to his brain. Got it! He came close to Hawker. He glanced across at the others. Goldfinger had stopped. His back was to Bond and he was taking the putter out of his bag. Bond nudged Hawker. "Here, take this." He slipped the ball into the gnarled hand. Bond said softly, urgently, "Be certain you take the flag. When you pick up the balls from the green, whichever way the hole has gone, give Goldfinger this one. Right?"

Hawker walked stolidly forward. His face was expressionless. "Got it, sir," he said in his normal voice. "Will you take the putter for this one?"

"Yes." Bond walked up to his ball. "Give me a line, would you?"

Hawker walked up on to the green. He stood sideways to the line of the putt and then stalked round to behind the flag and crouched. He got up. "Inch outside the right lip, sir. Firm putt. Flag, sir?"

"No. Leave it in, would you."

Hawker stood away. Goldfinger was standing by his ball on the right of the green. His caddie had stopped at the bottom of the slope. Bond bent to the putt. Come on, Calamity Jane! This one has got to go dead or I'll put you across my knee. Stand still. Club head straight back on the line and follow through towards the hole. Give it a chance. Now! The ball, hit firmly in the middle of the club, had run up the bank and was on its way to the hole. But too hard, damn it! Hit the stick! Obediently the ball curved in, rapped the stick hard and bounced back three inches—dead as a doornail!

Bond let out a deep sigh and picked up his discarded cigarette. He looked over at Goldfinger. Now then, you bastard. Sweat that one out. And by God if you hole it! But Goldfinger couldn't afford to try. He stopped two feet short. "All right, all right," said Bond generously. "All square and one to go." It was vital that Hawker should pick up the balls. If he had made Goldfinger hole the short putt it would have been Goldfinger who would have picked the ball out of the hole. Anyway, Bond didn't want Goldfinger to miss that putt. That wasn't part of the plan.

Hawker bent down and picked up the balls. He rolled

one towards Bond and handed the other to Goldfinger. They walked off the green, Goldfinger leading as usual. Bond noticed Hawker's hand go to his pocket. Now, so long as Goldfinger didn't notice anything on the tee!

But, with all square and one to go, you don't scrutinize your ball. Your motions are more or less automatic. You are thinking of how to place your drive, of whether to go for the green with the second or play to the apron, of the strength of the wind—of the vital figure four that must somehow be achieved to win or at least to halve.

Considering that Bond could hardly wait for Goldfinger to follow him and hit, just once, that treacherous Dunlop Number Seven that looked so very like a Number One, Bond's own drive down the four hundred and fifty yard eighteenth was praiseworthy. If he wanted to, he could now reach the green—if he wanted to!

Now Goldfinger was on the tee. Now he had bent down. The ball was on the peg, its lying face turned up at him. But Goldfinger had straightened, had stood back, was taking his two deliberate practice swings. He stepped up to the ball, cautiously, deliberately. Stood over it, waggled, focusing the ball minutely. Surely he would see! Surely he would stop and bend down at the last minute to inspect the ball! Would the waggle never end? But now the club head was going back, coming down, the left knee bent correctly in towards the ball, the left arm straight as a ramrod. Crack! The ball sailed off, a beautiful drive, as good as Goldfinger had hit, straight down the fairway.

Bond's heart sang. Got you, you bastard! Got you! Blithely Bond stepped down from the tee and strolled off down the fairway planning the next steps which could now be as eccentric, as fiendish as he wished. Goldfinger was beaten already—hoist with his own petard! Now to roast him, slowly, exquisitely.

Bond had no compunction. Goldfinger had cheated him twice and got away with it. But for his cheats at the Virgin and the seventeenth, not to mention his improved lie at the third and the various times he had tried to put Bond off, Goldfinger would have been beaten by now. If it needed one cheat by Bond to rectify the score-sheet that was only poetic justice. And besides, there was more to this than a game of golf. It was Bond's duty to win. By his reading of

Goldfinger he *had* to win. If he was beaten, the score between the two men would have been equalized. If he won the match, as he now had, he would be two up on Goldfinger—an intolerable state of affairs, Bond guessed, to a man who saw himself as all powerful. This man Bond, Goldfinger would say to himself, *has* something. He has qualities I can use. He is a tough adventurer with plenty of tricks up his sleeve. This is the sort of man I need for—for what? Bond didn't know. Perhaps there would be nothing for him. Perhaps his reading of Goldfinger was wrong, but there was certainly no other way of creeping up on the man.

Goldfinger cautiously took out his spoon for the longish second over cross-bunkers to the narrow entrance to the green. He made one more practice swing than usual and then hit exactly the right, controlled shot up to the apron. A certain five, probably a four. Much good would it do him!

Bond, after a great show of taking pains, brought his hands down well ahead of the club and smothered his number three iron so that the topped ball barely scrambled over the cross-bunkers. He then wedged the ball on to the green twenty feet past the pin. He was where he wanted to be—enough of a threat to make Goldfinger savour the sweet smell of victory, enough to make Goldfinger really sweat to get his four.

And now Goldfinger really was sweating. There was a savage grin of concentration and greed as he bent to the long putt up the bank and down to the hole. Not too hard, not too soft. Bond could read every anxious thought that would be running through the man's mind. Goldfinger straightened up again, walked deliberately across the green to behind the flag to verify his line. He walked slowly back beside his line, brushing away—carefully, with the back of his hand—a wisp or two of grass, a speck of top-dressing. He bent again and made one or two practice swings and then stood to the putt, the veins standing out on his temples, the cleft of concentration deep between his eyes.

Goldfinger hit the putt and followed through on the line. It was a beautiful putt that stopped six inches past the pin. Now Goldfinger would be sure that unless Bond sank his difficult twenty-footer, the match was his!

Bond went through a long rigmarole of sizing up his putt. He took his time, letting the suspense gather like a thunder cloud round the long shadows on the livid, fateful green.

"Flag out, please. I'm going to sink this one." Bond charged the words with a deadly certitude, while debating whether to miss the hole to the right or the left or leave it short. He bent to the putt and missed the hole well on the right.

"Missed it, by God!" Bond put bitterness and rage into his voice. He walked over to the hole and picked up the two balls, keeping them in full view.

Goldfinger came up. His face was glistening with triumph. "Well, thanks for the game. Seems I was just too good for you after all."

"You're a good nine handicap," said Bond with just sufficient sourness. He glanced at the balls in his hand to pick out Goldfinger's and hand it to him. He gave a start of surprise. "Hullo!" He looked sharply at Goldfinger. "You play a Number One Dunlop, don't you?"

"Yes, of course." A sixth sense of disaster wiped the triumph off Goldfinger's face. "What is it? What's the matter?"

"Well," said Bond apologetically. "'Fraid you've been playing with the wrong ball. Here's my Penfold Hearts and this is a Number Seven Dunlop." He handed both balls to Goldfinger. Goldfinger tore them off his palm and examined them feverishly.

Slowly the colour flooded over Goldfinger's face. He stood, his mouth working, looking from the balls to Bond and back to the balls.

Bond said softly, "Too bad we were playing to the rules. Afraid that means you lose the hole. And, of course, the match." Bond's eyes observed Goldfinger impassively.

"But, but . . ."

This was what Bond had been looking forward to—the cup dashed from the lips. He stood and waited, saying nothing.

Rage suddenly burst Goldfinger's usually relaxed face like a bomb. "It was a Dunlop Seven you found in the rough. It was your caddie that gave me this ball. On the seventeenth green. He gave me the wrong ball on purpose, the damned che—"

"Here, steady on," said Bond mildly. "You'll get a slander

action on your hands if you aren't careful. Hawker, did you give Mr Goldfinger the wrong ball by mistake or anything?"

"No, sir." Hawker's face was stolid. He said indifferently, "If you want my opinion, sir, the mistake may have been made at the seventeenth when the gentleman found his ball pretty far off the line we'd all marked it on. A Seven looks very much like a One. I'd say that's what happened, sir. It would have been a miracle for the gentleman's ball to have ended up as wide as where it was found."

"Tommy rot!" Goldfinger gave a snort of disgust. He turned angrily on Bond. "You saw that was a Number One my caddie found."

Bond shook his head doubtfully. "I didn't really look closely, I'm afraid. However," Bond's voice became brisk, businesslike, "it's really the job of the player to make certain he's using the right ball, isn't it? I can't see that anyone else can be blamed if you tee the wrong ball up and play three shots with it. Anyway," he started walking off the green, "many thanks for the match. We must have it again one day."

Goldfinger, lit with glory by the setting sun, but with a long black shadow tied to his heels, followed Bond slowly, his eyes fixed thoughtfully on Bond's back.

CHAPTER 10

UP AT THE GRANGE

THERE are some rich men who use their riches like a club. Bond, luxuriating in his bath, thought that Goldfinger was one of them. He was the kind of man who thought he could flatten the world with his money, bludgeoning aside annoyances and opposition with his heavy wad. He had thought to break Bond's nerve by playing him for ten thousand dollars—a flea-bite to him but obviously a small fortune to Bond. In most circumstances he might have succeeded. It needs an iron nerve to 'wait for it' on your swing, to keep your head down on the short putts, when big money hangs on every shot, over eighteen long holes. The pros, playing for their own bread and butter and for their families', know the cold breath of the poor-house on the back of their necks as they come to the eighteenth tee all square. That is why they lead careful lives, not smoking or drinking, and why the one that wins is usually the one with the least imagination.

But, in Bond's case, Goldfinger could not have known that high tension was Bond's natural way of life and that pressure and danger relaxed him. And he could not have known that Bond wanted to play Goldfinger for the highest possible stakes and that he would have the funds of the Secret Service behind him if he lost. Goldfinger, so used to manipulating others, had been blind to the manipulation for once being practised upon himself.

Or had he been? Thoughtfully Bond got out of the bath and dried himself. That powerful dynamo inside the big round head would be humming at this very moment, wondering about Bond, knowing he had been out-cheated, asking itself how it came about that twice Bond had appeared out of the blue and twice queered his pitch. Had Bond played his cards right? Had he made himself appear an interesting challenge, or would Goldfinger's sensitive nose smell a threat? In the latter case there would be no follow-up by Goldfinger and Bond would have to bow out of the case and leave it to M to devise a new approach. How soon would he know if the big fish was hooked? This one would take plenty of time sniffing the bait. It would be good to have just one small bite to tell him he had chosen the right lure.

There was a knock on the door of his bedroom. Bond wrapped the towel round him and walked through. He opened the door. It was the hall porter. "Yes?"

"Telephone message from a Mr Goldfinger, sir. His compliments and would you care to come to his house for dinner tonight. It's the Grange over at Reculver, sir. Six-thirty for drinks beforehand and not to bother to dress."

"Please thank Mr Goldfinger and say I shall be delighted." Bond shut the door and walked across to the open window and stood looking out across the quiet evening sea. "Well, well! Talk of the devil!" Bond smiled to himself, "And then go and sup with him! What was that about a long spoon?"

At six o'clock Bond went down to the bar and had a large vodka and tonic with a slice of lemon peel. The bar was empty save for a group of American Air Force officers from Manston. They were drinking whisky and water and talking baseball. Bond wondered if they had spent the day toting a hydrogen bomb round the skies over Kent, over the four little dots in the dunes that had been his match with Goldfinger. He thought wryly, Not too much of that whisky, cousins, paid for his drink, and left.

He motored slowly over to Reculver, savouring the evening and the drink inside him and the quiet bubble of the twin exhausts. This was going to be an interesting dinner-party. Now was the moment to sell himself to Goldfinger. If he put a foot wrong he was out, and the pitch would have been badly queered for his successor. He was unarmed—it would be fatal for Goldfinger to smell that kind of rat. He felt a moment's qualm. But that was going too fast. No state of war had been declared—the opposite if anything. When they had parted at the golf club, Goldfinger had been cordial in a rather forced, oily fashion. He had inquired where he should send Bond's winnings and Bond had given him the address of Universal Export. He had asked where Bond was staying and Bond had told him and added that he would only be at Ramsgate a few days while he made up his mind about his future. Goldfinger hoped that they would one day have a return match but, alas, he was leaving for France to-morrow and wasn't certain when he would be back. Flying? Yes, taking the Air Ferry from Lydd. Well, thanks for the match. And thank you, Mr Bond. The eyes had given Bond one last X-ray treatment, as if fixing him for a last time in Goldfinger's filing system, and then the big yellow car had sighed away.

Bond had had a good look at the chauffeur. He was a chunky flat-faced Japanese, or more probably Korean, with a wild, almost mad glare in dramatically slanting eyes that belonged in a Japanese film rather than in a Rolls Royce on a sunny afternoon in Kent. He had the snout-like upper lip that sometimes goes with a cleft palate, but he said nothing and Bond had no opportunity of knowing whether his guess was right. In his tight, almost bursting black suit and farcical bowler hat he looked rather like a Japanese wrestler on his day off. But he was not a figure to make one smile. If one had been inclined to smile, a touch of the sinister, the un-explained, in the tight shining patent-leather black shoes that were almost dancing pumps, and in the heavy black leather driving gloves, would have changed one's mind. There was something vaguely familiar to Bond in the man's silhouette. It was when the car drove away and Bond had a glimpse of the head from the rear that he remembered. Those were the head and shoulders and bowler hat of the driver of the sky-blue Ford Popular that had so obstinately hugged the crown of the Herne Bay road at about twelve o'clock that morning. Where had he been coming from? What errand had he been on? Bond remembered something Colonel Smithers had said. Could this have been the Korean who now travelled the country collecting the old gold from the chain of Goldfinger jewellery shops? Had the boot of the innocent, scurrying little saloon been stuffed with the week's takings of presentation watches, signet rings, lockets, gold crosses? As he watched the high, primrose-yellow silhouette of the Silver Ghost disappearing towards Sandwich, Bond thought the answer was yes.

Bond turned off the main road into the drive and followed it down between high Victorian evergreens to the gravel sweep in front of just the sort of house that would be called The Grange—a heavy, ugly, turn-of-the-century mansion with a glass-enclosed portico and sun parlour whose smell of trapped sunshine, rubber plants and dead flies came to Bond in his imagination before he had switched off the engine. Bond got slowly out of the car and stood looking at the house. Its blank, well-washed eyes stared back at him. The house had a background noise, a heavy rhythmic pant like a huge animal with a rather quick pulse. Bond assumed it came from the factory whose plumed chimney reared up like a giant cautionary finger from the high conifers to the right where the stabling and garages would normally be. The quiet watchful façade of the house seemed to be waiting for Bond to do something, make some offensive move to which there would be a quick reply. Bond shrugged his shoulders to lighten his thoughts and went up the steps to the opaque glass-panelled door and pressed the bell. There was no noise of it ringing, but the door slowly opened. The Korean chauffeur still had his bowler hat on. He looked without interest at Bond. He stood motionless, his left hand on the inside doorknob and his outstretched right pointing like a signpost into the dark hall of the house.

Bond walked past him, vanquishing a desire either to stamp on his neat black feet or hit him very hard indeed in the centre of his tightly buttoned black stomach. This Korean matched up with what he had always heard about Koreans, and anyway Bond wanted to do something violent to the heavy, electric atmosphere of the house.

The gloomy hall was also the main living-room. A meagre fire flickered behind the fire-irons in the wide hearth and two club chairs and a Knole sofa stood impassively watching the flames. Between them on a low settee was a well-stocked drink tray. The wide spaces surrounding this spark of life were crowded with massive Rothschildian pieces of furniture of the Second Empire, and ormolu, tortoiseshell, brass and mother-of-pearl winked back richly at the small fire. Behind this orderly museum, dark panelling ran up to a first-floor gallery which was reached by a heavy curved stairway to the left of the hall. The ceiling was laced with the sombre wood-carving of the period.

Bond was standing taking all this in when the Korean came silently up. He flung out his signpost of an arm towards the drink tray and the chairs. Bond nodded and stayed where he was. The Korean walked past him and disappeared through a door into what Bond assumed were the servants' quarters. The silence, helped by the slow iron tick of a massively decorated grandfather clock, gathered and crept nearer.

Bond walked over and stood with his back to the poor fire. He stared offensively back at the room. What a dump! What a bloody awful deathly place to live in. How did one, could one, live in this rich heavy morgue amongst the conifers and evergreens when a hundred yards away there was light and air and wide horizons? Bond took out a cigarette and lit it. What did Goldfinger do for enjoyment, for fun, for sex? Perhaps he didn't need these things. Perhaps the pursuit of gold slaked all his thirsts.

Somewhere in the distance a telephone rang. The bell shrilled twice and stopped. There was the murmur of a voice, then steps echoed down a passage and a door under the stairway opened. Goldfinger came through and quietly closed the door behind him. He was wearing a plum-coloured velvet dinner jacket. He came slowly across the polished wood floor. He didn't hold out his hand. He said, smiling with his mouth, "It was kind of you to come at such short notice, Mr Bond. You were alone and so was I and it occurred to me that we might discuss the price of corn."

It was the sort of remark that rich men make to each other. Bond was amused at being made a temporary member of the club. He said, "I was delighted to get the invitation. I was already bored with worrying over my problems. Ramsgate hasn't much to offer."

"No. And now I have an apology to make. I have had a telephone call. One of my staff—I employ Koreans, by the way—has had some minor trouble with the Margate police and I must go over and straighten it out. Some incident at the fun fair, I understand. These people get easily over-excited. My chauffeur will drive me and we should not be more than half an hour. Meanwhile I fear I must leave you to your own devices. Please help yourself to drinks. There are magazines to read. Will you forgive me? Not more than half an hour I assure you."

"That's quite all right." Bond felt there was something fishy in this. He couldn't put his finger on what it was.

"Well then, au revoir." Goldfinger went to the front door. "But I must give you some light. It's really very dark in here." Goldfinger brushed his hand down a wall-plate of switches and suddenly lights blazed all over the hall—from standard lamps, wall brackets, and four clusters in the ceiling. Now the room was as bright as a film studio. It was an extraordinary transformation. Bond, half dazzled, watched Goldfinger open the front door and stride out. In a minute he heard the sound of a car, but not the Rolls, rev up noisily, change gear and go off fast down the drive.

On an instinct, Bond walked over to the front door and opened it. The drive was empty. In the distance he saw the lights of the car turn left-handed on the main road and make off in the direction of Margate. He turned back into the house and closed the door. He stood still, listening. The silence, except for the heavy clock-tick, was complete. He walked across to the service door and opened it. A long dark passage disappeared towards the back of the house. Bond bent forward, all his senses alert. Silence, dead silence. Bond shut the door and looked thoughtfully round the brilliantly lit hall. He had been left alone in Goldfinger's house, alone with its secrets. Why?

Bond walked over to the drink tray and poured himself a strong gin and tonic. There certainly had been a telephone call, but it could easily have been an arranged call from the factory. The story of the servant was plausible and it was reasonable that Goldfinger should go himself to bail the man out and take his chauffeur with him. Goldfinger had twice mentioned that Bond would be alone for half an hour during which he "would be left to his own devices". This could be innocent, or it could be an invitation for Bond to show his hand, commit some indiscretion. Was somebody watching him? How many of these Koreans were there and what were they doing? Bond glanced at his watch. Five minutes had gone. He made up his mind. Trap or no trap, this was too good a chance to miss. He would have a quick look round—but an innocent one, with some sort of a cover story to explain why he had left the hall. Where should he begin? A look at the factory. His story? That his car had given trouble on the way over—choked petrol feed probably—and that he had gone to see if there was a mechanic who could give him a hand. Flimsy, but it would do. Bond downed his drink and went purposefully to the service door and walked through.

There was a light switch. He turned on the light and walked swiftly down a long passage. It ended with a blank wall and two doors to right and left. He listened for an instant at the left-hand one and heard muffled kitchen noises. He opened the right-hand door and found himself in the paved garage yard he might have expected. The only odd thing about it was that it was brilliantly lit by arc lights. The long wall of the factory occupied the far side and now the rhythmic engine thump was very loud. There was a plain wooden door low down in the wall opposite. Bond walked across the yard to it, looking around him with casual interest. The door was unlocked. He opened it with discretion and walked through, leaving the door ajar. He found himself in a small empty office lit by one naked bulb hanging from the ceiling. There was a desk with papers on it, a time-clock, a couple of filing cabinets and a telephone. Another door led from the office into the main factory space and there was a window beside the door for keeping an eye on the workmen. It would be the foreman's office. Bond walked to the window and looked through.

Bond didn't know what he had expected, but there seemed to be the usual accoutrements of a small metal-working business. Facing him were the open mouths of two blast furnaces, their fires now drawn. Beside these stood a row of kilns for the molten metal, of which sheets of different sizes and colours stood against the wall near by. There was the polished steel table of a circular saw, a diamond saw presumably, for cutting the sheets, and to the left in the shadows a big oil engine connected to a generator pounded away making power. To the right, under arc lights, a group of five men in overalls, four of them Koreans, were at work on —of all things—Goldfinger's Rolls Royce. It stood there gleaming under the lights, immaculate save for the right-hand door which had been taken off its hinges and now lay across two nearby benches minus its door panel. As Bond watched, two men picked up the new door panel, a heavy, discoloured sheet of aluminium-coloured metal, and placed it on the door frame. There were two hand riveters on the floor and soon, Bond thought, the men would rivet the panel into place and paint it to match the rest of the car. All perfectly innocent and above-board. Goldfinger had dented the panel that afternoon and had had a quick repair job done in preparation for his trip tomorrow. Bond gave a quick, sour look round, withdrew from the window and went out by the factory door and closed it softly behind him. Nothing there, damn it. And now what was his story? That he had not wanted to disturb the men at their work— perhaps after dinner, if one of them had a moment.

Bond walked unhurriedly back the way he had come and regained the hall without misadventure.

Bond looked at his watch. Ten minutes to go. Now for the first floor. The secrets of a house are in the bedrooms and bathrooms. Those are the private places where the medicine cabinets, the dressing-table, the bedside drawers, reveal the intimate things, the frailties. Bond had a bad headache. He had gone to look for an aspirin. He acted the part for an invisible audience, massaged his temples, glanced up at the gallery, walked decisively across the floor and climbed the stairs. The gallery gave on to a brightly lit passage. Bond walked down it opening the doors and glancing in. But they were spare bedrooms, the beds not made up. They held a smell of must and shut windows.

A large ginger cat appeared from nowhere and followed him, mewing and rubbing itself against his trouser legs. The end room was the one. Bond went in and closed the door to a crack.

All the lights were on. Perhaps one of the servants was in the bathroom. Bond walked boldly across to the communicating door and opened it. More lights, but no one. It was a big bathroom, probably a spare room converted into a bathroom and, in addition to the bath and lavatory, it held various fitness machines—a rowing machine, a fixed bicycle wheel, Indian clubs and a Ralli Health Belt. The medicine cabinet contained nothing except a great variety of purges—senna pods, cascara, Calsalettes, Enos and various apparatus for the same purpose. There were no other drugs and no aspirin. Bond went back into the bedroom and again drew a blank. It was a typical man's room, comfortable, lived in, with plenty of fitted cupboards. It even smelled neutral. There was a small bookcase beside the bed in which all the books were history or biography, all in English. The drawer of the bedside table yielded a solitary indiscretion, a yellow-backed copy of *The Hidden Sight of Love*, Palladium Publications, Paris.

Bond glanced at his watch. Five more minutes. It was time to go. He took a last look round the room and moved to the door. Suddenly he stopped. What was it he had noticed almost subconsciously ever since he had come into the room? He sharpened his senses. There was an incongruity somewhere. What was it? A colour? An object? A smell? A sound? That was it! From where he stood he could hear the faintest, mosquito-shrill whine. It was almost extra-sensory in its pitch. Where did it come from? What was making it? Now there was something else in the room, something that Bond knew all too well, the smell of danger.

Tensely Bond stepped closer to the fitted cupboard beside the door, softly opened it. Yes, it came from inside the cupboard, from behind a range of sports coats that reached down to the top of three banks of drawers. Sharply Bond swept the coats aside. His jaws clenched at what was behind them.

From three slots near the top of the cupboard, sixteen-millimetre film was inching down in three separate strips into a deep bin behind the false front of the drawers. The bin was almost half full of the slimy snakes of the stuff. Bond's eyes narrowed tensely as he watched the damning evidence coil slowly down on to the pile. So that was it—ciné-cameras, three of them, their lenses concealed God knows where—in the hall, in the garage courtyard, in this room—had been watching his every move from the moment Goldfinger had left the house, switching on the cameras, and, of course, the dazzling lights, as he went out of the door. Why hadn't Bond seen the significance of those lights? Why hadn't he had the elementary imagination to see the trap as well as smell it? Cover stories, indeed! What use were they now when he had spent half an hour snooping round and finding nothing for his pains? That too! He had discovered nothing—unearthed no secret. It had all been an idiotic waste of time. And now Goldfinger had him. Now he was finished, hopelessly blown. Was there any way of saving something from the wreckage? Bond stood riveted, staring at the slow cataracts of film.

Let's see now! Bond's mind raced, thinking of ways out, excuses, discarding them all. Well, at least by opening the cupboard door he had exposed some of the film. Then why not expose it all? Why not, but how? How could the open cupboard door be explained except by his doing? There came a miaow from the open slit of the bedroom door. The cat! Why shouldn't the cat have done it? Pretty thin, but at least it was the shadow of an alibi. Bond opened the door. He picked the cat up in his arms. He went back with it to the cupboard, stroking it brusquely. It purred. Bond leant over the bin of film, picking it up in handfuls so that it would all get the light. Then, when he was satisfied that it must be ruined, he tossed it back and dropped the cat in on top of it. The cat would not be able to get out easily. With any luck it would settle down and go to sleep. Bond left the cupboard door three inches ajar to spoil the continuing film and the bedroom door the same amount and ran down the passage. At the top of the stairs he slowed and sauntered down. The empty hall yawned at his play-acting. He walked across to the fireplace, dashed more drink into his glass and picked up *The Field*. He turned to the golf commentary by Bernard Darwin, ran his eye down it to see what it was about, and then settled into one of the club chairs and lit a cigarette.

What had he found out? What was there on the plus side? Precious little except that Goldfinger suffered from constipation and a dirty mind and that he had wanted to put Bond through an elementary test. He had certainly done it expertly. This was no amateur. The technique was fully up to SMERSH standards, and it was surely the technique of somebody with a very great deal to hide. And now what would happen? For the cat alibi to stand up, Goldfinger would have to have left two doors, one of them vital, ajar, and the cat had got into the room and been intrigued by the whine of the cameras. Most unlikely, almost incredible. Goldfinger would be ninety per cent certain it was Bond—but only ninety. There would still be that ten per cent of uncertainty. Would Goldfinger have learnt much more than he knew before—that Bond was a tricky, resourceful customer and that Bond had been inquisitive, might be a thief? He would guess Bond had been to the bedroom, but Bond's other movements, for whatever they were worth, would remain a secret on the exposed film.

Bond got up and took a handful of other magazines and threw them down beside his chair. The only thing for him to do was brazen it out and make a note for the future, if there was to be a future, that he had better wake his ideas up and not make any more mistakes. There wouldn't be enough ginger cats in the world to help him out of one more tight spot like the one he was in.

There had been no noise of a car coming down the drive, not a sound from the door, but Bond felt the evening breeze on his neck and he knew that Goldfinger had come back into the room.

THE ODD-JOB MAN

BOND THREW down *The Field* and stood up. The front door closed noisily. Bond turned. "Hullo." His face registered polite surprise. "Didn't hear you arrive. How did it go?"

Goldfinger's expression was equally bland. They might have been old friends, neighbours in the country who were accustomed to drop in on each other for a drink. "Oh, it sorted itself out. My chap had had a row in a pub with some American Air Force men who had called him a bloody Jap. I explained to the police that Koreans don't like being called Japs. They let him off with a caution. Terribly sorry to have been so long. Hope you weren't bored. Do have another drink."

"Thanks. But it's hardly seemed five minutes since you left. Been reading what Darwin has to say about the fourteen club rule. Interesting point of view . . ." Bond launched into a detailed review of the article, adding his own comments on the rule.

Goldfinger stood patiently until it was over. He said, "Yes, it's a complicated business. Of course you play rather a different game from me, more workmanlike. With my kind of swing, I find I need all the clubs I'm allowed. Well, I'll just go up and wash and then we'll have dinner. Shan't be a moment."

Bond busied himself noisily with pouring another drink, sat down and picked up *Country Life*. He watched Goldfinger climb the stairs and disappear down the corridor. He could visualize every step. He found he was reading the periodical upside down. He turned it round and stared blindly at a fine photograph of Blenheim Palace.

There was dead silence upstairs. Then a distant lavatory chain was pulled and a door clicked shut. Bond reached for his drink, took a deep swallow and put the glass down beside his chair. Goldfinger was coming down the stairs. Bond turned the pages of *Country Life* and flicked ash off his cigarette into the grate.

Now Goldfinger was crossing the floor towards him. Bond lowered his paper and looked up. Goldfinger was carrying the ginger cat tucked carelessly under one arm. He reached the fireplace, bent forward and pressed the bell.

He turned towards Bond. "Do you like cats?" His gaze was flat, incurious.

"Sufficiently."

The service door opened. The chauffeur stood in the frame. He still wore his bowler hat and his shiny black gloves. He gazed impassively at Goldfinger. Goldfinger crooked a finger. The chauffeur approached and stood within the circle by the fire.

Goldfinger turned to Bond. He said conversationally, "This is my handy man." He smiled thinly. "That is something of a joke. Oddjob, show Mr Bond your hands." He smiled again at Bond. "I call him Oddjob because that describes his functions on my staff."

The Korean slowly pulled off his gloves and came and stood at arm's length from Bond and held out his hands palm upwards. Bond got up and looked at them. They were big and fat with muscle. The fingers all seemed to be the same length. They were very blunt at the tips and the tips glinted as if they were made of yellow bone.

"Turn them over and show Mr Bond the sides."

There were no fingernails. Instead there was this same, yellowish carapace. The man turned the hands sideways. Down each edge of the hands was a hard ridge of the same bony substance.

Bond raised his eyebrows at Goldfinger.

Goldfinger said, "We will have a demonstration." He pointed at the thick oak banisters that ran up the stairs. The rail was a massive six inches by four thick. The Korean obediently walked over to the stairs and climbed a few steps. He stood with his hands at his sides, gazing across at Goldfinger like a good retriever. Goldfinger gave a quick nod. Impassively the Korean lifted his right hand high and straight above his head and brought the side of it down like an axe across the heavy polished rail. There was a splintering crash and the rail sagged, broken through the centre. Again the hand went up and flashed down. This time it swept right through the rail leaving a jagged gap. Splinters clattered down on to the floor of the hall. The Korean straightened himself and stood to attention, waiting for further orders. There was no flush of effort in his face and no hint of pride in his achievement.

Goldfinger beckoned. The man came back across the floor. Goldfinger said, "His feet are the same, the outside edges of them. Oddjob, the mantelpiece." Goldfinger pointed at the heavy shelf of carved wood above the fireplace. It was about seven feet off the ground—six inches higher than the top of the Korean's bowler hat.

"Garch a har?"

"Yes, take off your coat and hat." Goldfinger turned to Bond. "Poor chap's got a cleft palate. I shouldn't think there are many people who understand him beside me."

Bond reflected how useful that would be, a slave who could only communicate with the world through his interpreter—better even than the deaf mutes of the harems, more tightly bound to his master, more secure.

Oddjob had taken off his coat and hat and placed them neatly on the floor. Now he rolled his trouser legs up to the knee and stood back in the wide well-planted stance of the judo expert. He looked as if a charging elephant wouldn't put him off balance.

"Better stand back, Mr Bond." The teeth glittered in the wide mouth. "This blow snaps a man's neck like a daffodil." Goldfinger drew aside the low settee with the drink tray. Now the Korean had a clear run. But he was only three long steps away. How could he possibly reach the high mantelpiece?

Bond watched, fascinated. Now the slanting eyes in the flat yellow mask were glinting with a fierce intentness. Faced by such a man, thought Bond, one could only go down on one's knees and wait for death.

Goldfinger lifted his hand. The bunched toes in the polished soft leather shoes seemed to grip the ground. The Korean took one long crouching stride with knees well bent and then whirled off the ground. In mid-air his feet slapped together like a ballet dancer's, but higher than a ballet dancer's have ever reached, and then the body bent sideways and downwards and the right foot shot out like a piston. There came a crashing thud. Gracefully the body settled back down on the hands, now splayed on the floor, the elbows bent to take the weight and then straightened sharply to throw the man up and back on his feet.

Oddjob stood to attention. This time there was a gleam of triumph in his flat eyes as he looked at the three-inch jagged bite the edge of his foot had taken out of the mantelpiece.

Bond looked at the man in deep awe. And only two nights ago, he, Bond, had been working on his manual of unarmed combat! There was nothing, absolutely nothing, in all his reading, all his experience, to approach what he had just witnessed. This was not a man of flesh and blood.

This was a living club, perhaps the most dangerous animal on the face of the earth. Bond had to do it, had to give homage to this uniquely dreadful person. He held out his hand.

"Softly, Oddjob." Goldfinger's voice was the crack of a whip.

The Korean bowed his head and took Bond's hand in his. He kept his fingers straight and merely bent his thumb in a light clasp. It was like holding a piece of board. He released Bond's hand and went to his neat pile of clothes.

"Forgive me, Mr Bond, and I appreciate your gesture." Goldfinger's face showed his approval. "But Oddjob doesn't know his own strength—particularly when he is keyed up. And those hands are like machine-tools. He could have crushed your hand to pulp without meaning to. Now then," Oddjob had dressed and was standing respectfully at attention, "you did well, Oddjob. I'm glad to see you are in training. Here—" Goldfinger took the cat from under his arm and tossed it to the Korean who caught it eagerly—"I am tired of seeing this animal around. You may have it for dinner." The Korean's eyes gleamed. "And tell them in the kitchen that we will have our own dinner at once."

The Korean inclined his head sharply and turned away.

Bond hid his disgust. He realized that all this exhibition was simply a message to him, a warning, a light rap on the knuckles. It said, "You see my power, Mr Bond. I could easily have killed you or maimed you. Oddjob was giving an exhibition and you got in the way. I would certainly be innocent, and Oddjob would get off with a light sentence. Instead, the cat will be punished in your place. Bad luck on the cat, of course."

Bond said casually, "Why does the man always wear that bowler hat?"

"Oddjob!" The Korean had reached the service door. "The hat." Goldfinger pointed at a panel in the woodwork near the fireplace.

Still holding the cat under his left arm, Oddjob turned and walked stolidly back towards them. When he was half way across the floor, and without pausing or taking aim, he reached up to his hat, took it by the rim and flung it sideways with all his force. There was a loud clang. For an instant the rim of the bowler hat stuck an inch deep in the panel Goldfinger had indicated, then it fell and clattered on the floor.

Goldfinger smiled politely at Bond. "A light but very strong alloy, Mr Bond. I fear that will have damaged the felt covering, but Oddjob will put on another. He's surprisingly quick with a needle and thread. As you can imagine, that blow would have smashed a man's skull or half severed his neck. A homely and a most ingeniously concealed weapon, I'm sure you'll agree."

"Yes, indeed." Bond smiled with equal politeness. "Useful chap to have around."

Oddjob had picked up his hat and disappeared. There came the boom of a gong. "Ah, dinner! Shall we go in?" Goldfinger led the way to a door concealed in the panelling to the right of the fireplace. He pressed a hidden latch and they walked through.

The small dining-room matched the heavy wealth of the hall. It was brilliantly lit from a central chandelier and by candles on a round table that glittered with silver and glass. They sat down opposite each other. Two yellow-faced servants in white mess-jackets brought dishes from a loaded serving-table. The first course was some curried mess with rice. Goldfinger noticed Bond's hesitation. He gave a dry chuckle. "It's all right, Mr Bond. Shrimp, not the cat."

"Ah." Bond's expression was non-committal.

"Please try the Moselle. I hope it will be to your taste. It is a Piesporter Goldtröpfchen '53. Help yourself. These people are as likely to pour it into your plate as your glass."

There was a slim bottle in an ice bucket in front of Bond. He poured some of the wine and tasted it. It was nectar and ice cold. Bond congratulated his host. Goldfinger gave a curt nod.

"I don't myself drink or smoke, Mr Bond. Smoking, I find the most ridiculous of all the varieties of human behaviour and practically the only one that is entirely against nature. Can you imagine a cow or any animal taking a mouthful of smouldering straw then breathing in the smoke and blowing it out through its nostrils? Pah!" Goldfinger showed a rare trace of emotion. "It is a vile practice. As for drinking, I am something of a chemist and I have yet to find a liquor that is free from traces of a number of poisons, some of them deadly, such as fusel oil, acetic acid, ethyl-acetate, acetaldehyde and furfurol. A quantity of some of these poisons taken neat would kill you. In the small amounts you find in a bottle of liquor they produce various ill effects most of which are lightly written off as 'a hangover'." Goldfinger paused with a forkful of curried shrimp half way to his mouth. "Since you are a drinker, Mr Bond, I will give you one word of good advice. Never drink so-called Napoleon brandy, particularly when it is described as 'aged in the wood'. That particular potion contains more of the poisons I have mentioned than any other liquor I have analysed. Old bourbon comes next." Goldfinger closed his animadversions with a mouthful of shrimp.

"Thank you. I'll remember. Perhaps for those reasons I have recently taken to vodka. They tell me its filtration through activated charcoal is a help." Bond, dredging this piece of expertise out of dim recollections of something he had read, was rather proud of having been able to return Goldfinger's powerful serve.

Goldfinger glanced at him sharply. "You seem to understand something of these matters. Have you studied chemistry?"

"Only dabbled in it." It was time to move on. "I was very impressed by that chauffeur of yours. Where did he learn that fantastic combat stuff? Where did it come from? Is that what the Koreans use?"

Goldfinger patted his mouth with his napkin. He snapped his fingers. The two men cleared away the plates and brought roast duckling and a bottle of Mouton Rothschild 1947 for Bond. When they had withdrawn into immobility at each end of the serving-table, Goldfinger said, "Have you ever heard of Karate? No? Well that man is one of the three in the world who have achieved the Black Belt in Karate. Karate is a branch of judo, but it is to judo what a Spandau is to a catapult."

"I could see that."

"The demonstration was an elementary one. Mr Bond—" Goldfinger held up the drumstick he had been gnawing— "I can tell you that if Oddjob had used the appropriate single blow on any one of seven spots on your body, you would now be dead." Goldfinger bit at the side of the drumstick with relish.

Bond said seriously, "That's interesting. I only know five ways of killing Oddjob with one blow."

Goldfinger seemed not to hear the comment. He put down his drumstick and took a deep draught of water. He sat back and spoke while Bond went on eating the excellent food. "Karate, Mr Bond, is based on the theory that the human body possesses five striking surfaces and thirty-seven vulnerable spots—vulnerable, that is, to an expert in Karate whose finger-tips, the side of the hands and the feet are hardened into layers of corn, which is far stronger and more flexible than bone. Every day of his life, Mr Bond, Oddjob spends one hour hitting either sacks of unpolished rice or a strong post whose top is wound many times round with thick rope. He then spends another hour at physical training which is more that of a ballet school than of a gymnasium."

"When does he practise tossing the bowler hat?" Bond had no intention of succumbing to this psychological warfare.

Goldfinger frowned at the interruption. "I have never inquired," he said without humour. "But I think you can take it that Oddjob keeps his eye in at all his skills. However, you were asking where Karate originated. It originated in China where wandering Buddhist priests became an easy prey for footpads and bandits. Their religion did not allow them to carry weapons, so they developed their own form of unarmed combat. The inhabitants of Okinawa refined the art to its present form when the Japanese forbade them to carry weapons. They developed the five striking surfaces of the human body—the fist, the edge of the hand, the fingertips, the ball of the foot and the elbows—and toughened them until they were enveloped in layers of corn. There is no follow-through in a Karate blow. The entire body is stiffened at the moment of impact, with the emphasis on the hips, and then instantly relaxed so that balance is never lost. It is astonishing what Oddjob can do. I have seen him hit a brick wall with his entire force and not hurt his hand. He can split three half-inch thick boards, piled one upon the other, with one blow of his hand. You have seen what he can do with his foot."

Bond took a deep draught of the delicious claret. "All this must be rather hard on your furniture."

Goldfinger shrugged. "I have no more use for this house. I thought a demonstration would amuse you. I hope you agree that Oddjob earned his cat." The X-ray eyes blazed briefly across the table.

"Does he train on cats?"

"He regards them as a great delicacy. He acquired the taste during a famine in his country when he was young."

Bond thought it was time to delve rather more deeply. "Why do you need such a man? He can't be very good company."

"Mr Bond—" Goldfinger snapped his fingers for the two servants—"it happens that I am a rich man, a very rich man, and the richer the man the more he needs protection. The ordinary bodyguard or detective is usually a retired policeman. Such men are valueless. Their reactions are slow, their methods old-fashioned, and they are open to bribery. Moreover, they have a respect for human life. That is no good if I wish to stay alive. The Koreans have no such feelings. That is why the Japanese employed them as guards for their prison camps during the war. They are the cruellest, most ruthless people in the world. My own staff are hand picked for these qualities. They have served me well. I have no complaints. Nor have they. They are well paid and well fed and housed. When they want women, street women are brought down from London, well remunerated for their services and sent back. The women are not much to look at, but they are white and that is all the Koreans ask—to submit the white race to the grossest indignities. There are sometimes accidents but—" the pale eyes gazed blankly down the table—"money is an effective winding-sheet."

Bond smiled.

"You like the aphorism? It is my own."

An excellent cheese soufflé came and was followed by coffee. They ate in silence, both apparently comfortable and relaxed by these confidences. Bond certainly was. Goldfinger, obviously by design, was letting his hair down—not far, not farther than his shoulders, but he was showing Bond one of his private faces, presumably the one to which he thought Bond would respond—the ruthlessly efficient, cold-blooded tycoon. Perhaps, after all, Bond's spying in the house, which Goldfinger must at least presume, had revealed something about Bond that Goldfinger was pleased to know—that Bond had a crooked side to him, that he wasn't 'a gentleman' in more than appearance. Now there should be more probing and then, with luck, the proposition would follow.

Bond sat back and lit a cigarette. He said, "That's a beautiful car you've got. Must be about the last of the series. About 1925, wasn't it—two blocks of three cylinders with two plugs for each cylinder, one set fired from the mag. and the other from the coil?"

"You are correct. But in other respects I have had to introduce some modifications. I have added five leaves to the springs and fitted disc brakes to the rear wheels to increase the braking power. The Servo-operated front-wheel brakes were not sufficient."

"Oh. Why not? The top speed wouldn't be more than fifty. The body can't be all that heavy."

Goldfinger raised his eyebrows. "You think not? One ton of armour plating and armour-plated glass make a big difference."

Bond smiled. "Ah! I see. You certainly do take good care of yourself. But how does that work flying the Channel? Doesn't the car go through the floor of the plane?"

"I take a plane to myself. The Silver City company knows the car. It is a regular routine, twice a year."

"Just touring round Europe?"

"A golfing holiday."

"Great fun. Always wanted to do it myself."

Goldfinger didn't take the bait. "You can afford to now."

Bond smiled. "Oh, that extra ten thousand dollars. But I may need that if I decide to move to Canada."

"You think you could make money there? Do you want to make a lot of money?"

Bond's voice was eager. "Very much. There's no other point in working."

"Unfortunately most ways of making big money take a long time. By the time one has made the money one is too old to enjoy it."

"That's the trouble. I'm always on the lookout for shortcuts. You won't find them here. Taxation's too heavy."

"Quite. And the laws are strict."

"Yes. I found that out."

"Indeed?"

"Got on the fringe of the heroin racket. Only just got out

without burning my fingers. Of course this'll go no further?"

Goldfinger shrugged his shoulders. "Mr Bond, someone said that 'law is the crystallized prejudices of the community'. I agree with that definition. It happens to apply most strongly to the traffic in drugs. Even if it didn't, I am not concerned with assisting the police."

"Well, it was like this . . ." Bond launched into the story of the Mexican traffic, swapping roles with Blackwell. He ended up, "I was lucky to get away with it, but it didn't make me particularly popular with Universal Export."

"I daresay not. An interesting story. You seem to have shown resource. You are not tempted to continue in the same line of business?"

Bond shrugged his shoulders. "A bit too tricky. To judge by this Mexican, the big men in the business aren't quite big enough when it comes to the pinch. When things got tough he didn't fight back—except with his mouth."

"Well, Mr Bond," Goldfinger got up from the table and Bond followed suit. "It's been an interesting evening. I don't know that I would go back into heroin. There are safer ways of making big money. You want to be certain that the odds are right and then you should hazard everything. Doubling one's money isn't easy and the chances don't occur frequently. You would like to hear another of my aphorisms?"

"Yes."

"Well, Mr Bond," Goldfinger gave the rich man's thin smile. "The safest way to double your money is fold it twice and put it in your pocket."

Bond, the bank clerk harkening to the bank manager, smiled dutifully but made no comment. This just wasn't good enough. He was getting nowhere. But instinct told him not to put his foot down on the accelerator.

They went back into the hall. Bond held out his hand. "Well, many thanks for the excellent dinner. Time I went and got some sleep. Perhaps we shall run into each other again some day."

Goldfinger pressed Bond's hand briefly and pushed it away from him. It was another mannerism of the millionaire subconsciously afraid of 'the touch'. He looked hard at Bond. He said enigmatically, "I shouldn't be at all surprised, Mr Bond."

On his way across the Isle of Thanet in the moonlight, Bond turned the phrase over and over in his mind. He undressed and got into bed thinking of it, unable to guess its significance. It could mean that Goldfinger intended to get in touch with Bond, or it could mean that Bond must try and keep in touch with Goldfinger. Heads the former, tails the latter. Bond got out of bed and took a coin from the dressing-table and tossed it. It came down tails. So it was up to him to keep close to Goldfinger!

So be it. But his cover would have to be pretty darn good the next time they 'ran into' each other. Bond got back into bed and was instantly asleep.

CHAPTER 12

LONG TAIL ON A GHOST

Punctually at nine the next morning Bond got on to the Chief of Staff: "James here. I've had a look at the property. Been all over it. Had dinner last night with the owner. I can say pretty well for certain that the managing director's view is right. Something definitely wrong about the property. Not enough facts to send you a surveyor's report. Owner's going abroad tomorrow, flying from Ferryfield. Wish I knew his departure time. Like to have another sight of his Rolls. Thought I'd make him a present of a portable wireless set. I'll be going over a bit later in the day. Could you get Miss Ponsonby to book me? Destination unknown for the present. I'll be keeping in touch. Anything your end?"

"How did the game of golf go?"

"I won."

There was a chuckle at the other end. "Thought you had. Pretty big stakes, weren't they?"

"How did you know?"

"Had Mr Scotland on last night. Said he'd had a tip on the telephone that someone of your name was in possession of a large amount of undeclared dollars. Had we got such a person and was it true? Chap wasn't very senior and didn't know about Universal. Told him to have a word with the Commissioner and we got an apology this morning about the same time as your secretary found an envelope containing ten thousand dollars in your mail! Pretty sly of your man, wasn't it?"

Bond smiled. Typical of Goldfinger to have thought of a way of getting him into trouble over the dollars. Probably made the call to Scotland Yard directly after the game. He had wanted to show Bond that if you gave Goldfinger a knock you'd get at least a thorn in your hand. But the Universal Export cover seemed to have stuck. Bond said, "That's pretty hot! The twister! You might tell the managing director that this time it goes to the White Cross. Can you fix the other things?"

"Of course. Call you back in a few minutes. But watch your step abroad and call us at once if you get bored and need company. So long."

"'Bye." Bond put down the receiver. He got up and set about packing his bag. He could see the scene in the Chief of Staff's office as the conversation was played back off the tape while the Chief of Staff translated the call to Miss Moneypenny. "Says he agrees that Goldfinger is up to something big but he can't make out what. G. is flying this morning with his Rolls from Ferryfield. 007 wants to follow. (Let's say two hours later to let G. get well away on the other side. Fix the reservation, would you?) He wants us to have a word with Customs so that he can take a good look at the Rolls and plant a Homer in the boot. (Fix that too, please.) He'll keep in touch through stations in case he needs help . . ."

And so forth. It was an efficient machine. Bond finished packing and, when the London call came giving him his various clearances, he went downstairs, paid his bill and got quickly out of Ramsgate on to the Canterbury road.

London had said that Goldfinger was booked on a special flight leaving at twelve. Bond got to Ferryfield by eleven, made himself known to the Chief Passport Control and the Customs officers who were expecting him, had his car taken out of sight into an empty hangar and sat and smoked and talked minor shop with the passport men. They thought he was from Scotland Yard. He let them go on thinking it. No, he said, Goldfinger was all right. It was possible that one of his servants was trying to smuggle something out of the country. Rather confidential. If Bond could just be left alone with the car for ten minutes? He wanted to have a look at the tool kit. Would the Customs give the rest of the Rolls their Grade A going over for hidden compartments? They'd be glad to do so.

At eleven-forty-five one of the Customs men put his head round the door. He winked at Bond. "Coming in now. Chauffeur on board. Going to ask both to board the plane before the car. Tell them it's something to do with the weight distribution. Not so phoney as it sounds. We know this old crate. She's armour-plated. Weighs about three tons. Call you when we're ready."

"Thanks." The room emptied. Bond took the fragile little parcel out of his pocket. It contained a dry-cell battery wired to a small vacuum tube. He ran his eye over the wiring and put the apparatus back in his coat pocket and waited.

At eleven-fifty-five the door opened. The officer beckoned. "No trouble. They're on the plane." ·

The huge gleaming Silver Ghost stood in the Customs bay out of sight of the plane. The only other car was a dove-grey Triumph TR3 convertible with its hood down. Bond went to the back of the Rolls. The Customs men had unscrewed the plate of the spare tool compartment. Bond pulled out the tray of tools and made a show of minutely examining them and the tray. He knelt down. Under cover of rummaging at the sides of the compartment, he slipped the battery and tube into the back of it. He replaced the tool tray. It fitted all right. He stood up and brushed his hands together. "Negative," he said to the Customs officer.

The officer fitted the plate on and screwed it down with the square key. He stood up. "Nothing funny about the chassis or the bodywork. Plenty of room in the frame and upholstery but we couldn't get at them without doing a major job. All right to go?"

"Yes, and thanks." Bond walked back into the office. He heard the quick solid whine of the old self-starter. A minute later, the car came out of the bay and idled superbly over to the loading ramp. Bond stood at the back of the office and watched it being eased up the ramp. The big jaws of the Bristol Freighter clanged shut. The chocks were jerked away and the dispatcher raised a thumb. The two engines coughed heavily and fired and the great silver dragonfly trundled off towards the runway.

When the plane was on the runway, Bond walked round to his car and climbed into the driver's seat. He pressed a switch under the dash. There was a moment's silence, then a loud harsh howl came from the hidden loud-speaker. Bond turned a knob. The howl diminished to a deep drone. Bond waited until he heard the Bristol take off. As the plane rose and made for the coast the drone diminished. In five minutes it had gone. Bond tuned the set and picked it up again. He followed it for five minutes as the plane made off across the Channel and then switched the set off. He motored round to the Customs bay, told the AA that he would be back at one-thirty for the two o'clock flight, and drove slowly off towards a pub he knew in Rye. From now on, so long as he kept within about a hundred miles of the Rolls, the Homer, the rough radio transmitter he had slipped into its tool compartment, would keep contact with Bond's receiver. All he had to do was watch the decibels and not allow the noise to fade. It was a simple form of direction finding which allowed one car to put a 'long tail' on another and keep in touch without any danger of being spotted. On the other side of the Channel, Bond would have to discover the road Goldfinger had taken out of Le Touquet, get well within range and close up near big towns or wherever there was a major fork or crossroads. Sometimes Bond would make a wrong decision and have to do some fast motoring to catch up again. The DB III would look after that. It was going to be fun playing hare and hounds across Europe. The sun was shining out of a clear sky. Bond felt a moment's sharp thrill down his spine. He smiled to himself, a hard, cold, cruel smile. Goldfinger, he thought, for the first time in your life you're in trouble—bad trouble.

There is always an *agent cycliste* at the dangerous crossroads where Le Touquet's quiet N38 meets the oily turbulence of the major N1. Yes, certainly he had seen the Rolls. One could not fail to remark it. A real aristocrat of a car. To the right, monsieur, towards Abbeville. He will be an hour ahead, but with that *bolide* of yours . . .!

As soon as Bond had cleared his papers at the airport,

the Homer had picked up the drone of the Rolls. But it was impossible to tell if Goldfinger was heading north—for the Low Countries or Austria or Germany—or if he was off to the south. For that sort of fix you needed two radio cars to get a bearing. Bond raised a hand to the agent and gave his engine the gun. He would have to close up fast. Goldfinger would be through Abbeville and would already have taken the major fork on to N1 for Paris or N28 for Rouen. A lot of time and distance would be wasted if Bond made the wrong guess.

Bond swept along the badly cambered road. He took no chances but covered the forty-three kilometres to Abbeville in a quarter of an hour. The drone of the Homer was loud. Goldfinger couldn't be more than twenty miles ahead. But which way at the fork? On a guess Bond took the Paris road. He beat the car along. For a time there was little change in the voice of the Homer. Bond could be right or wrong. Then, imperceptibly, the drone began to fade. Blast! Turn back or press on fast and take one of the secondary roads across to Rouen and catch up with him there? Bond hated turning back. Ten kilometres short of Beauvais he turned right. For a time it was bad going but then he was on to the fast N30 and could afford to drift into Rouen, led on by the beckoning voice of his pick-up. He stopped on the outskirts of the town and listened with one ear while consulting his Michelin. By the waxing drone he could tell that he had got ahead of Goldfinger. But now there was another vital fork, not quite so easy to retrieve if Bond guessed wrong again. Either Goldfinger would take the Alençon-Le Mans-Tours route to the south, or he meant to move southeast, missing Paris, by way of Evreux, Chartres and Orleans. Bond couldn't afford to get closer to the centre of Rouen and perhaps catch a glimpse of the Rolls and of the way it would take. He would have to wait until the Homer went on the wane and then make his own guess.

It was a quarter of an hour later before Bond could be sure that the Rolls was well past. This time he again took the left leg of the fork. He thrust the pedal into the floor and hurried. Yes. This time the drone was merging into a howl. Bond was on the track. He slowed to forty, tuned down his receiver to a whisper and idled along, wondering where Goldfinger was heading for.

Five o'clock, six, seven. The sun set in Bond's driving mirror and still the Rolls sped on. They were through Dreux and Chartres and on to the long straight fifty-mile stretch into Orleans. If that was to be the night stop the Rolls wouldn't have done badly at all—over two hundred and fifty miles in something over six hours. Goldfinger was certainly no slouch when it came to motoring. He must be keeping the old Silver Ghost at maximum outside the towns. Bond began to close up.

There were rear-lights ahead—dim ones. Bond had his fog lights on. He switched on the Marchals. It was some little sports car. Bond closed up. MG? Triumph? Austin Healey? It was a pale grey Triumph two-seater with the hood up. Bond blinked his lights and swept past. Now there was the glare of another car ahead. Bond dowsed his headlamps and drove on the fogs. The other car was a mile down the road. Bond crept up on it. At a quarter of a mile, he flashed the Marchals on and off for a quick look. Yes, it was the Rolls. Bond dropped back to a mile and stayed there, vaguely noticing the dim lights of the TR3 in his mirror. On the outskirts of Orleans, Bond pulled into the side of the road. The Triumph growled casually past.

Bond had never cared for Orleans. It was a priest and myth ridden town without charm or gaiety. It was content to live off Joan of Arc and give the visitor a hard, holy glare while it took his money. Bond consulted his Michelin. Goldfinger would stop at five-star hotels and eat fillets of sole and roast chicken. It would be the Arcades for him —perhaps the Moderne. Bond would have liked to stay outside the town and sleep on the banks of the Loire in the excellent Auberge de la Montespan, his belly full of *quenelles de brochet*. He would have to stick closer to his fox. He decided on the Hôtel de la Gare and dinner at the station buffet.

When in doubt, Bond always chose the station hotels. They were adequate, there was plenty of room to park the car and it was better than even chances that the Buffet de la Gare would be excellent. And at the station one could hear the heartbeat of the town. The night-sounds of the trains were full of its tragedy and romance.

The drone on the receiver had stayed constant for ten minutes. Bond noted his way to the three hotels and cautiously crept into the town. He went down to the river and along the lighted *quais*. He had been right. The Rolls was outside the Arcades. Bond turned back into the town and made for the station.

The Hôtel de la Gare was all he had expected—cheap, old-fashioned, solidly comfortable. Bond had a hot bath, went back to his car to make sure the Rolls hadn't moved, and walked into the station restaurant and ate one of his favourite meals—two *œufs cocotte à la crème*, a large *sole meunière* (Orleans was close enough to the sea. The fish of the Loire are inclined to be muddy) and an adequate Camembert. He drank a well-iced pint of Rosé d'Anjou and had a Hennessy's Three Star with his coffee. At ten-thirty he left the restaurant, checked on the Rolls and walked the virtuous streets for an hour. One more check on the Rolls and bed.

At six o'clock the next morning the Rolls hadn't moved. Bond paid his bill, had a *café complet*—with a double ration of coffee—at the station, motored down to the *quais* and backed his car up a side street. This time he could not afford to make a mistake. Goldfinger would either cross the river and head south to join N7 for the Riviera, or he would follow the north bank of the Loire, also perhaps for the Riviera, but also on the route for Switzerland and Italy. Bond got out of the car and lounged against the parapet of the river wall, watching between the trunks of the plane trees. At eight-thirty, two small figures came out of the Arcades. The Rolls moved off. Bond watched it follow the *quais* until it was out of sight, then he got behind the wheel of the Aston Martin and set off in pursuit.

Bond motored comfortably along the Loire in the early summer sunshine. This was one of his favourite corners of the world. In May, with the fruit trees burning white and the soft wide river still big with the winter rains, the valley was green and young and dressed for love. He was thinking this when, before Châteauneuf, there was a shrill scream from twin Bosch horns and the little Triumph tore past. The hood was down. There was the blur of a pretty face hidden by white motoring goggles with dark blue lenses. Although Bond only saw the edge of a profile—a slash of red mouth and the fluttering edge of black hair under a pink handkerchief with white spots, he knew she was pretty from the way she held her head. There was the authority of someone who is used to being admired, combined with the self-consciousness of a girl driving alone and passing a man in a smart car.

Bond thought: That *would* happen today! The Loire is dressed for just that—chasing that girl until you run her to ground at lunch-time, the contact at the empty restaurant by the river, out in the garden under the vine trellis. The *friture* and the ice-cold Vouvray, the cautious sniffing at each other and then the two cars motoring on in convoy until that evening, well down to the south, there would be the place they had agreed on at lunch—olive trees, crickets singing in the indigo dusk, the discovery that they liked each other and that their destinations could wait. Then, next day ("No, not tonight. I don't know you well enough, and besides I'm tired") they would leave her car in the hotel garage and go off in his at a tangent, slowly, knowing there was no hurry for anything, driving to the west, away from the big roads. What was that place he had always wanted to go to, simply because of the name? Yes, Entre Deux Seins, a village near Les Baux. Perhaps there wasn't even an inn there. Well, then they would go on to Les Baux itself, at the Bouches du Rhône on the edge of the Camargue. There they would take adjoining rooms (not a double room, it would be too early for that) in the fabulous Baumanière, the only hotel-restaurant in France with Michelin's supreme accolade. They would eat the *gratin de langouste* and perhaps, because it was traditional on such a night, drink champagne. And then ...

Bond smiled at his story and at the dots that ended it. Not today. Today you're working. Today is for Goldfinger, not for love. Today the only scent you may smell is Goldfinger's expensive after-shave lotion, not ... what would she use? English girls made mistakes about scent. He hoped it would be something slight and clean. Balmain's Vent Vert perhaps, or Caron's Muguet. Bond tuned up his receiver for reassurance, then hushed it and motored on, relaxed, playing with his thoughts of the girl, filling in the details. Of course he might meet up with her again. They seemed to be keeping pretty close company. She must have spent the night in Orleans. Where? What a waste. But wait a minute! Suddenly Bond woke up from his daydreaming. The open hood reminded him. He'd seen that Triumph before. It had been at Ferryfield, must have taken the flight after Goldfinger. It was true he hadn't seen the girl or noted the registration number, but surely it was the same. If so, for her to be still on Goldfinger's tail after three hundred miles was more than coincidence. And she had been driving with dimmed lights the night before! Here, what's going on?

Bond stepped on the accelerator. He was approaching Nevers. He'd anyway have to close up for the next big turning. He would kill two birds with one stone and also see what the girl was up to. If she was keeping station somewhere between him and Goldfinger there would have to be some furious thinking. And it would be a blasted nuisance. It was hard enough keeping up with Goldfinger. With another tail sandwiched between them, it would become hellish difficult.

She was still there, perhaps two miles behind the Rolls, keeping well back. As soon as he caught sight of her little glittering rump (as he described it to himself) Bond slowed. Well, well! Who *was* she? What the hell was all this about? Bond motored on, his face morose and thoughtful.

The little convoy kept on, still following the wide black sheen of N7 that runs like a thick, dangerous nerve down through the heart of France. But at Moulins Bond nearly lost the scent. He had to double back quickly and get on to N73. Goldfinger had turned at right angles and was now making for Lyons and Italy, or for Mâcon and Geneva. Bond had to do some fast motoring, and then was only just in time to avoid running into trouble. He had not worried much about the pitch of the Homer. He had counted on a sight of the Triumph to slow him down. Suddenly he realized that the drone was becoming a howl. If he hadn't braked hard down from the ninety he was doing, he would have been on top of the Rolls. As it was, he was barely creeping along when he came over a rise and saw the big yellow car stopped by the wayside a mile ahead. There was a blessed cart-track. Bond swerved into it and stopped under cover of a low hedge. He took a small pair of binoculars out of the glove compartment, got out of the car and walked back. Yes, damn it! Goldfinger was sitting below a small bridge on the bank of a stream. He was wearing a white dust coat and white linen driving helmet in the style of German tourists.

He was eating, having a picnic. The sight made Bond hungry. What about his own lunch? He examined the Rolls. Through the rear window he could see part of the Korean's black shape in the front seat. There was no sign of the Triumph. If the girl had still been on Goldfinger's tail she would have had no warning. She would have just kept her head down and stepped on the gas. Now she would be somewhere ahead, waiting in ambush for the Rolls to come by. Or would she? Perhaps Bond's imagination had run away with him. She was probably on her way to the Italian lakes to join an aunt, some friends, a lover.

Now Goldfinger was on his feet. Tidy man. That's right, pick up the scraps of paper and tuck them away carefully under the bridge. Why not throw them in the stream? Suddenly Bond's jaws tightened. What did those actions of Goldfinger remind him of? Was Bond romancing again, or was the bridge a post box? Had Goldfinger been instructed to leave something, one of his bars of gold, under this particular bridge? France, Switzerland, Italy. It was convenient for all of them—the Communist cell in Lyons for instance, one of the strongest in France. And this was a good place to use with a clear field of view up and down the road.

Goldfinger scrambled up the bank. Bond drew back under cover. He heard the distant grind of the old self-starter. He cautiously watched the Rolls until it had disappeared.

It was a pretty bridge over a pretty stream. It had a survey number set in the arch—79/6—the sixth bridge from some town on N79. Easy to find. Bond got quickly out of the car and slid down the shallow bank. It was dark and cool under the arch. There were the shadows of fish in the slow, clear, pebbled water. Bond searched the edge of the masonry near the grass verge. Exactly in the centre, below the road, there was a patch of thick grass against the wall. Bond parted the grass. There was a sprinkling of freshly turned earth. Bond dug with his fingers.

There was only one. It was smooth to the touch and brick-shaped. It needed some strength to lift it. Bond brushed the earth off the dull yellow metal and wrapped the heavy bar in his handkerchief. He held the bar under his coat and climbed back up the bank on to the empty road.

CHAPTER 13

"IF YOU TOUCH ME THERE . . ."

BOND FELT pleased with himself. A whole lot of people were going to get very angry with Goldfinger. You can do a lot of dirty work with twenty thousand pounds. Now plans would have to be altered, conspiracies postponed, perhaps even lives saved. And, if it ever got to an inquiry by SMERSH, which was unlikely as they were the sort of realistic people who cut their losses, it could only be assumed that some sheltering tramp had found the gold bar.

Bond lifted the secret flap under the passenger seat and slipped the bar inside. Dangerous stuff. He would have to contact the next station of the Service and hand it over to them. They would get it back to London in the Embassy bag. Bond would have to report this quickly. It confirmed a lot. M might even want to warn the Deuxième and have the bridge watched to see who came. But Bond hoped that would not happen. He didn't want a scare started just when he was getting close to Goldfinger. He wanted the skies over Goldfinger to be blue and clear.

Bond got moving. Now there were other things to think about. He must catch up with the Rolls before Mâcon and get the next fork, to Geneva or Lyons, right. He must solve the problem of the girl and if possible get her off the road. Pretty or not, she was confusing the issue. And he must stop and buy himself something to eat and drink. It was one o'clock and the sight of Goldfinger eating had made him hungry. And it was time to fill up and check the water and oil.

The drone of the Homer grew louder. He was in the outskirts of Mâcon. He must close up and take the risk of being spotted. The busy traffic would hide his low-slung car. It was vital to know if the Rolls crossed the Saône for the Bourg road or if it turned right at the bridge and joined the N6 for Lyons. Far down the Rue Rambuteau there was a glimpse of yellow. Over the railway bridge and through the little square. The high yellow box kept on towards the river. Bond watched the passers-by turn their heads to follow the gleaming Rolls. The river. Would

Goldfinger turn right or keep on across the bridge? The Rolls kept straight on. So it was Switzerland! Bond followed over into the suburb of St Laurent. Now for a butcher and a baker and a wine shop. A hundred yards ahead the golden head of a calf hung over the pavement. Bond glanced in his driving mirror. Well, well! The little Triumph was only feet away from his tail. How long had she been there? Bond had been so intent on following the Rolls that he hadn't glanced back since entering the town. She must have been hiding up a side street. So! Now coincidence was certainly out. Something must be done. Sorry, sweetheart. I've got to mess you up. I'll be as gentle as I can. Hold tight. Bond stopped abruptly in front of the butcher's shop. He banged the gears into reverse. There was a sickening scrunch and tinkle. Bond switched off his engine and got out.

He walked round to the back of the car. The girl, her face tense with anger, had one beautiful silken leg on the road. There was an indiscreet glimpse of white thigh. The girl stripped off her goggles and stood, legs braced and arms akimbo. The beautiful mouth was taut with anger.

The Aston Martin's rear bumper was locked into the wreckage of the Triumph's lamps and radiator grille. Bond said amiably, "If you touch me there again you'll have to marry me."

The words were hardly out of his mouth before the open palm cracked across his face. Bond put up a hand and rubbed his cheek. Now there was quite a crowd. There was a murmur of approval and ribaldry. "Allez y la gosse! Maintenant le knock-out!"

The girl's rage had not dissipated with the blow. "You bloody fool! What the hell do you think you're doing?"

Bond thought: If only pretty girls were always angry they would be beautiful. He said, "Your brakes can't be up to much."

"*My* brakes! What the hell do you mean? You reversed into me."

"Gears slipped. I didn't know you were so close." It was time to calm her down. "I'm most frightfully sorry. I'll pay for all the repairs and everything. It really is bad luck. Let's see what the damage is. Try and back away. Doesn't look as if our bumpers have over-ridden." Bond put a foot on the Triumph's bumpers and rocked.

"Don't you dare touch my car! Leave it alone." Angrily the girl climbed back into the driver's seat. She pressed the self-starter. The engine fired. Metal clanged under the bonnet. She switched off and leant out. "There you are, you idiot! You've smashed the fan."

Bond had hoped he had. He got into his own car and eased it away from the Triumph. Bits of the Triumph, released by Bond's bumper, tinkled on to the road. He got out again. The crowd had thinned. There was a man in a mechanic's overalls. He volunteered to call a breakdown van and went off to do so. Bond walked over to the Triumph. The girl had got out and was waiting for him. Her expression had changed. Now she was more composed. Bond noticed that her eyes, which were dark blue, watched his face carefully.

Bond said, "It really won't be too bad. Probably knocked the fan out of alignment. They'll put temporary headlamps in the sockets and straighten up the chrome. You'll be off again by tomorrow morning. Now," Bond reached into his pocket for his notecase, "this is maddening for you and I'll certainly take all the blame. Here's a hundred thousand francs to cover the damage and your expenses for the night and telephoning your friends and so on. Please take it and call it quits. I'd love to stay here and see you get on the road all right tomorrow morning. But I've got an appointment this evening and I've simply got to make it."

"No." The one word was cool, definite. The girl put her hands behind her back and waited.

"But . . ." What was it she wanted, the police? Have him charged with dangerous driving?

"I've got an appointment this evening too. I've got to make it. I've got to get to Geneva. Will you please take me there? It's not far. Only about a hundred miles. We could do it in two hours in that." She gestured at the DB III. "Will you? Please?"

There was a desperate urgency in the voice. No cajolery, no threats, only a blazing need.

For the first time Bond examined her as more than a pretty girl who perhaps—they were the only explanations Bond had found to fit the facts—wanted to be picked up by Goldfinger or had a blackmail on him. But she didn't look capable of either of these things. There was too much character in the face, too much candour. And she wasn't wearing the uniform of a seductress. She wore a white, rather masculine cut, heavy silk shirt. It was open at the neck, but it would button up to a narrow military collar. The shirt had long wide sleeves gathered at the wrists. The girl's nails were unpainted and her only piece of jewellery was a gold ring on her engagement finger (true or false?). She wore a very wide black stitched leather belt with double brass buckles. It rose at the back to give some of the support of a racing driver's corset belt. Her short skirt was charcoal-grey and pleated. Her shoes were expensive-looking black sandals which would be comfortable and cool for driving. The only touch of colour was the pink handkerchief which she had taken off her head and now held by her side with the white goggles. It all looked very attractive. But the get-up reminded Bond more of an equipment than a young girl's dress. There was something faintly mannish and open-air about the whole of her behaviour and appearance. She might, thought Bond, be a member of the English women's ski team, or spend a lot of her time in England hunting or show-jumping.

Although she was a very beautiful girl she was the kind who leaves her beauty alone. She had made no attempt to pat her hair into place. As a result, it looked as a girl's hair should look—untidy, with bits that strayed and a rather crooked parting. It provided the contrast of an uneven, jagged dark frame for the pale symmetry of the face, the main features of which were blue eyes under dark brows, a desirable mouth, and an air of determination and independence that came from the high cheek-bones and the fine line of the jaw. There was the same air of self-reliance in her figure. She held her body proudly—her fine breasts out-thrown and unashamed under the taut silk. Her stance, with feet slightly parted and hands behind her back, was a mixture of provocation and challenge.

The whole picture seemed to say, "Now then, you handsome bastard, don't think you can 'little woman' me. You've got me into this mess and, by God, you're going to get me out! You may be attractive, but I've got my life to run, and I know where I'm going."

Bond weighed her request. How much of a nuisance would she be? How soon could he get rid of her and get on with his business? Was there any security risk? Against the disadvantages, there was his curiosity about her and what she was up to, the memory of the fable he had spun round her and which had now taken its first step towards realization, and, finally, the damsel-in-distress business—any woman's appeal for help.

Bond said curtly, "I'll be glad to take you to Geneva. Now then," he opened up the back of the Aston Martin, "let's get your things in. While I fix up about the garage here's some money. Please buy us lunch—anything you like for yourself. For me, six inches of Lyon sausage, a loaf of bread, butter, and half a litre of Mâcon with the cork pulled."

Their eyes met and exchanged a flurry of masculine/ feminine master/slave signals. The girl took the money. "Thank you. I'll get the same things for myself." She went to the boot of the Triumph and unlocked it. "No, don't bother. I can manage these." She hauled out a bag of golf clubs with the cover zipped shut and a small, expensive looking suitcase. She brought them over to the Aston Martin and, rejecting Bond's offer of help, fitted them in alongside Bond's suitcase. She watched him lock the back of the car and went back to the Triumph. She took out a wide, black-stitched leather shoulder bag.

Bond said, "What name and address shall I give?"

"What?"

Bond repeated his question, wondering if she would lie about the name or the address, or both.

She said, "I shall be moving about. Better say the Bergues at Geneva. The name's Soames. Miss Tilly Soames." There was no hesitation. She went into the butcher's shop.

A quarter of an hour later they were on their way.

The girl sat upright and kept her eyes on the road. The drone on the Homer was faint. The Rolls must have gained fifty miles. Bond hurried. They flashed through Bourg and over the river at Pont d'Ain. Now they were in the foothills of the Jura and there were the S-bends of N84. Bond went at them as if he was competing in the Alpine Trials. After the girl had swayed against him twice she kept her hand on the handle on the dash and rode with the car as if she were his spare driver. Once, after a particularly sharp dry skid that almost took them over the side, Bond glanced at her profile. Her lips were parted and her nostrils slightly flared. The eyes were alight. She was enjoying herself.

They came to the top of the pass and there was the run down towards the Swiss frontier. Now the Homer was sending out a steady howl. Bond thought, I must take it easy or we shall be running into them at the Customs. He put his hand under the dash and tuned the noise down. He pulled in to the side of the road. They sat in the car and ate a polite but almost silent picnic, neither making any attempt at conversation, both, it seemed, with other things on their minds. After ten minutes, Bond got going again. He sat relaxed, motoring easily down the curving road through the young whispering pines.

The girl said, "What's that noise?"

"Magneto whine. Gets worse when I hurry. Started at Orleans. Have to get it fixed tonight."

She seemed satisfied with this mumbo-jumbo. She said diffidently, "Where are you heading for? I hope I haven't taken you very far out of your way."

Bond said in a friendly voice, "Not at all. As a matter of fact, I'm going to Geneva too. But I may not stop there tonight. May have to get on. Depends on my meeting. How long will you be there?"

"I don't know. I'm playing golf. There's the Swiss Women's Open Championship at Divonne. I'm not really that class, but I thought it would be good for me to try. Then I was going to play on some of the other courses."

Fair enough. No reason why it shouldn't be true. But Bond was certain it wasn't the whole truth. He said, "Do you play a lot of golf? What's your home course?"

"Quite a lot. Temple."

It had been an obvious question. Was the answer true, or just the first golf course she had thought of? "Do you live near there?"

"I've got an aunt who lives at Henley. What are you doing in Switzerland. Holiday?"

"Business. Import and Export."

"Oh."

Bond smiled to himself. It was a stage conversation. The voices were polite stage voices. He could see the scene, beloved of the English theatre—the drawing-room, sunshine on hollyhocks outside french windows, the couple sitting on the sofa, on the edge of it, she pouring out the tea. "Do you take sugar?"

They came out into the foothills. There was a long straight stretch of road and in the distance the small group of buildings of the French Customs.

The girl gave him no chance to get a glimpse of her passport. As soon as the car stopped she said something about tidying up and disappeared into the 'Dames'. Bond had gone through the Controle and was dealing with the triptyque when she reappeared, her passport stamped. At the Swiss Customs she chose the excuse of getting something out of her suitcase. Bond hadn't got time to hang about and call her bluff.

Bond hurried on into Geneva and pulled up at the imposing entrance of the Bergues. The *baggagiste* took her suitcase and golf clubs. They stood together on the steps. She held out her hand. "Goodbye." There was no melting of the candid blue eyes. "And thank you. You drive beautifully." Her mouth smiled. "I'm surprised you got into the wrong gear at Mâcon."

Bond shrugged. "It doesn't often happen. I'm glad I did. If I can get my business finished, perhaps we could meet again."

"That would be nice." The tone of voice said it wouldn't be. The girl turned and went in through the swingdoors.

Bond ran down to his car. To hell with her! Now to pick up Goldfinger. Then to the little office on the Quai Wilson. He tuned the Homer and waited a couple of minutes. Goldfinger was close, but moving away. He could either be following the right or the left bank of the lake. From the pitch of the Homer, he was at least a mile outside the town. Which way? To the left towards Lausanne? To the right towards Evian? The DB III was already on the left-hand road. Bond decided to follow its nose. He got moving.

Bond caught up with the high yellow silhouette just before Coppet, the tiny lakeside hamlet made famous by Madame de Staël. He hid behind a lorry. At his next reconnaissance the Rolls had disappeared. Bond motored on, watching to the left. At the entrance to the village, big solid iron gates were closing in a high wall. Dust hung in the air. Above the wall was a modest placard. It said, in faded yellow on blue, ENTREPRISES AURIC A.G. The fox had gone to earth!

Bond went on until he found a turning to the left. He followed this until there was a lane which led back through the vineyards to the woods behind Coppet and to the château of Madame de Staël. Bond stopped among the trees. Now he should be directly above the Entreprises Auric. He took his binoculars, got out and followed a foot-path down towards the village. Soon, on his right, was a spiked iron railing. There was rolled barbed wire along its top. A hundred yards lower down the hill the railing merged into a high stone wall. Bond walked slowly back up the path looking for the secret entrance the children of Coppet would have made to get at the chestnut trees. He found it—two bars of the railing widened to allow a small body through. Bond stood on the lower railing with all his weight, widened the gap by another couple of inches and wormed his way through.

Bond walked warily through the trees, watching each step for dead branches. The trees thinned. There were glimpses of a huddle of low buildings behind a small *manoir*. Bond picked the thick trunk of a fir tree and got behind it. Now he was looking down on the buildings. The nearest was about a hundred yards away. There was an open courtyard. In the middle of the courtyard stood the dusty Silver Ghost.

Bond took out the binoculars and examined everything minutely.

The house was a well-proportioned square block of old red brick with a slate roof. It consisted of two storeys and an attic floor. It would probably contain four bedrooms and two principal rooms. The walls were partly covered by a very old wistaria in full bloom. It was an attractive house. In his mind's eye Bond could see the white-painted panelling inside. He smelled the sweet musty sunshiny smell of the rooms. The back door gave on to the wide paved courtyard in which stood the Rolls. The courtyard was open on Bond's side but closed on the other two sides by single-storey corrugated iron workshops. A tall zinc chimney rose from the angle of the two workshops. The chimney was topped by a zinc cowl. On top of the zinc cowl was the revolving square mouth of what looked to Bond like a Decca radar scanner you see on the bridges of most ships. The apparatus whirled steadily round. Bond couldn't imagine what purpose it served on the roof of this little factory among the trees.

Suddenly the silence and immobility of the peaceful scene were broken. It was as if Bond had put a penny in the slot of a diorama on Brighton pier. Somewhere a tinny clock struck five. At the signal, the back door of the house opened and Goldfinger came out, still dressed in his white linen motoring coat, but without the helmet. He was followed by a nondescript, obsequious little man with a toothbrush moustache and horn-rimmed spectacles. Goldfinger looked pleased. He went up to the Rolls and patted its bonnet. The other man laughed politely. He took a whistle out of his waistcoat pocket and blew it. A door in the right-hand workshop opened and four workmen in blue overalls filed out and walked over to the car. From the open door they had left there came a whirring noise and a heavy engine started up and settled into the rhythmic pant Bond remembered from Reculver.

The four men disposed themselves round the car. At a word from the little man, who was presumably the foreman, they began to take the car to pieces.

By the time they had lifted the four doors off their hinges, removed the bonnet cover from the engine and had set about the rivets on one of the mudguards, it was clear that they were methodically stripping the car of its armour plating.

Almost as soon as Bond had come to this conclusion, the black, bowler-hatted figure of Oddjob appeared at the back door of the house and made some sort of a noise at Goldfinger. With a word to the foreman, Goldfinger went indoors and left the workmen to it.

It was time for Bond to get going. He took a last careful look round to fix the geography in his mind and edged back among the trees.

"I am from Universal Export."

"Oh yes?" Behind the desk there was a reproduction of the Annigoni portrait of the Queen. On the other walls were advertisements for Ferguson tractors and other agricultural machinery. From outside the wide window came the hum of traffic along the Quai Wilson. A steamer hooted. Bond glanced out of the window and watched it ride across the middle distance. It left an enchanted wake across the flawless evening mirror of the lake. Bond looked back into the politely inquiring eyes in the bland, neutral, business-man's face.

"We were hoping to do business with you."

"What sort of business?"

"Important business."

The man's face broke into a smile. He said cheerfully, "It's 007, isn't it? Thought I recognized you. Well now, what can I do for you?" The voice became cautious. "Only one thing, better make it quick and get along. There's been the hell of a heat on since the Dumont business. They've got me taped—the locals and Redland. All very peaceful of course, but you won't want them sniffing round you."

"I thought it might be like that. It's only routine. Here." Bond unbuttoned his shirt and took out the heavy chunk of gold. "Get that back, would you? And transmit this when you have a chance." The man pulled a pad towards him and wrote in shorthand to Bond's dictation.

When the man had finished he put the pad in his pocket. "Well, well! Pretty hot stuff. Wilco. My routine's at midnight. This"—he indicated the gold—"can go to Berne for the bag. Anything else?"

"Ever heard of the 'Entreprises Auric' at Coppet? Know what they do?"

"I know what every engineering business in the area does. Have to. Tried to sell them some hand riveters last year. They make metal furniture. Pretty good stuff. The Swiss railways take some of it, and the airlines."

"Know which airlines?"

The man shrugged. "I heard they did all the work for Mecca, the big charter line to India. Their terminus is Geneva. They're quite a big competitor with All-India. Mecca's privately owned. Matter of fact, I did hear that Auric & Co. had some money in it. No wonder they've got the contract for the seating.

A slow, grim smile spread across Bond's face. He got up and held out his hand. "You don't know it, but you've just done a whole jigsaw puzzle in under a minute. Many thanks. Best of luck with the tractor business. Hope we'll meet again one day."

Out in the street, Bond got quickly into his car and drove along the *quai* to the Bergues. So that was the picture! For two days he'd been trailing a Silver Ghost across Europe.

It was an armour-plated Silver Ghost. He'd watched the last bit of plating being riveted on in Kent, and the whole lot being stripped off at Coppet. Those sheets would already be in the furnaces at Coppet, ready to be modelled into seventy chairs for a Mecca Constellation. In a few days' time those chairs would be stripped off the plane in India and replaced with aluminium ones. And Goldfinger would have made what? Half a million pounds? A million?

For the Silver Ghost wasn't silver at all. It was a Golden Ghost—all the two tons of its bodywork. Solid, eighteen-carat, white gold.

CHAPTER 14

THINGS THAT GO THUMP IN THE NIGHT

JAMES BOND booked in at the Hôtel des Bergues, took a bath and shower and changed his clothes. He weighed the Walther PPK in his hand and wondered whether he should take it or leave it behind. He decided to leave it. He had no intention of being seen when he went back to the Entreprises Auric. If, by dreadful luck, he was seen, it would spoil everything to get into a fight. He had his story, a poor one, but at least one that would not break his cover. He would have to rely on that. But Bond did choose a particular pair of shoes that were rather heavier than one could expect from their casual build.

At the desk he asked if Miss Soames was in. He was not surprised when the receptionist said they had no Miss Soames staying in the hotel. The only question was whether she had left the hotel when Bond was out of sight or had registered under another name.

Bond motored across the beautiful Pont du Mont Blanc and along the brightly lit *quai* to the Bavaria, a modest Alsatian brasserie that had been the rendezvous of the great in the days of the League of Nations. He sat by the window and drank Enzian washed down with pale Löwenbräu. He thought first about Goldfinger. There was now no doubt what he was up to. He financed a spy network, probably SMERSH, and he made fortunes smuggling gold to India, the country where he could get the biggest premium. After the loss of his Brixham trawler, he had thought out this new way. He first made it known that he had an armoured car. That would only be considered eccentric. Many English bodybuilders exported them. They used to go to Indian rajahs; now they went to oil sheiks and South American presidents. Goldfinger had chosen a Silver Ghost because, with his modifications, the chassis was strong enough, the riveting was already a feature of the bodywork, and there was the largest possible area of metal sheeting. Perhaps Goldfinger had run it abroad once or twice to get Ferryfield used to it. Then, on the next trip, he took off the armour plating in his works at Reculver. He substituted eighteen-carat white gold. Its alloy of nickel and silver would be strong enough. The colour of the metal would not betray him if he got in a smash or if the bodywork were scratched. Then off to Switzerland and to the little factory. The workmen would have been as carefully picked as the ones at Reculver. They would take off the plates and mould them into aircraft seats which would then be upholstered and installed in Mecca Airlines—run presumably by some stooge of Goldfinger's who got a cut on each 'gold run'. On these runs— once, twice, three times a year?—the plane would accept only light freight and a few passengers. At Bombay or Calcutta the plane would need an overhaul, be re-equipped. It would go to the Mecca hangar and have new seats fitted. The old ones, the gold ones, would go to the bullion brokers. Goldfinger would get his sterling credit in Nassau or wherever he chose. He would have made his hundred, or two hundred, per cent profit and could start the cycle all over again, from the 'We Buy Old Gold' shops in Britain to Reculver—Geneva—Bombay.

Yes, thought Bond, gazing out across the glistening, starlit lake, that's how it would be—a top-notch smuggling circuit with a minimum risk and maximum profit. How Goldfinger must smile as he pressed the bulb of the old boa-constrictor horn and swept past the admiring policemen of three countries! He certainly seemed to have the answer—the philosopher's stone, the finger of gold! If he hadn't been such an unpleasant man, if he wasn't doing all this to sustain the trigger finger of SMERSH, Bond would have felt admiration for this monumental trickster whose operations were so big that they worried even the Bank of England. As it was, Bond only wanted to destroy Goldfinger, seize his gold, get him behind bars. Goldfinger's gold-lust was too strong, too ruthless, too dangerous to be allowed the run of the world.

It was eight o'clock. The Enzian, the firewater distilled from gentian that is responsible for Switzerland's chronic alcoholism, was beginning to warm Bond's stomach and melt his tensions. He ordered another double and with it a choucroute and a carafe of Fondant.

And what about the girl, this pretty, authoritarian joker that had suddenly been faced in the deal? What in hell was she about? What about this golf story? Bond got up and went to the telephone booth at the back of the room. He got on to the *Journal de Genève* and through to the sports editor. The man was helpful, but surprised at Bond's question. No. The various championships were of course played in the summer when the other national programmes were finished and it was possible to lure a good foreign entry to Switzerland. It was the same with all other European countries. They liked to bring in as many British and American players as possible. It increased the gates. "Pas de quoi, monsieur."

Bond went back to his table and ate his dinner. So much for that. Whoever she was, she was an amateur. No professional would use a cover that could be broken down by one telephone call. It had been in the back of Bond's mind—reluctantly, because he liked the girl and was excited by her—that she could, she just could have been an agent of SMERSH sent to keep an eye on Goldfinger, or Bond or both. She had some of the qualities of a secret agent, the independence, the strength of character, the ability to walk alone. But that idea was out. She hadn't got the training.

Bond ordered a slice of gruyère, pumpernickel and coffee. No, she was an enigma. Bond only prayed that she hadn't got some private plot involving either him or Goldfinger that was going to mess up his own operation.

And his own job was so nearly finished! All he needed was the evidence of his own eyes that the story he had woven round Goldfinger and the Rolls was the truth. One look into the works at Coppet—one grain of white gold dust—and he could be off to Berne that very night and be on to the duty officer over the Embassy scrambler. Then, quietly, discreetly, the Bank of England would freeze Goldfinger's accounts all over the world and perhaps, already tomorrow, the Special Branch of the Swiss police would be knocking on the door of Entreprises Auric. Extradition would follow, Goldfinger would go to Brixton, there would be a quiet, rather complicated case in one of the smuggling courts like Maidstone or Lewes. Goldfinger would get a few years, his naturalization would be revoked and his gold hoard, illegally exported, would trickle back into the vaults below the Bank of England. And SMERSH would gnash its blood-stained teeth and add another page to Bond's bulging zapiska.

Time to go for the last lap. Bond paid his bill and went out and got into his car. He crossed the Rhône and motored slowly along the glittering *quai* through the evening traffic. It was an average night for his purpose. There was a blazing three-quarter moon to see by, but not a breath of wind to hide his approach through the woods to the factory. Well, there was no hurry. They would probably be working through the night. He would have to take it very easily and carefully. The geography of the place and the route he had plotted for himself ran before Bond's eyes like a film while the automatic pilot that is in all good drivers took the car along the wide white highway beside the sleeping lake.

Bond followed his route of the afternoon. When he had turned off the main road he drove on his sidelights. He nosed the car off the lane into a clearing in the woods and switched off the engine. He sat and listened. In the heavy silence there was only a soft ticking from the hot metal under the bonnet and the hasty trip of the dashboard clock. Bond got out, eased the door shut and walked softly down the little path through the trees.

Now he could hear the soft heavy pant of the generator engine . . . thumpah . . . thumpah . . . thumpah. It seemed a watchful, rather threatening noise. Bond reached the gap in the iron bars, slipped through and stood, straining his senses forward through the moon-dappled trees.

THUMPAH . . . THUMPAH . . . THUMPAH. The great iron puffs were on top of him, inside his brain. Bond felt the skin-crawling tickle at the groin that dates from one's first game of hide and seek in the dark. He smiled to himself at the animal danger signal. What primeval chord had been struck by this innocent engine noise coming out of the tall zinc chimney? The breath of a dinosaur in its cave? Bond tightened his muscles and crept forward foot by foot, moving small branches carefully out of his way, placing each step as cautiously as if he was going through a minefield.

The trees were thinning. Soon he would be up with the big sheltering trunk he had used before. He looked for it and then stood frozen, his pulse racing. Below the trunk of his tree, spreadeagled on the ground, was a body.

Bond opened his mouth wide and breathed slowly in and out to release the tension. Softly he wiped his sweating palms down his trousers. He dropped slowly to his hands and knees and stared forward, his eyes widened like camera lenses.

The body under the tree moved, shifted cautiously to a new position. A breath of wind whispered in the tops of the trees. The moonbeams danced quickly across the body and then were still. There was a glimpse of thick black hair, black sweater, narrow black slacks. And something else—a straight gleam of metal along the ground. It began beneath the clump of black hair and ran past the trunk of the trees into the grass.

Bond slowly, wearily bent his head and looked at the ground between his spread hands. It was the girl, Tilly. She was watching the buildings below. She had a rifle—a rifle that must have been among the innocent golf clubs—ready to fire on them. Damn and blast the silly bitch!

Bond slowly relaxed. It didn't matter who she was or what she was up to. He measured the distance, planned each stride—the trajectory of the final spring, left hand to her neck, right to the gun. Now!

Bond's chest skidded over the hump of the buttocks and thudded into the small of the girl's back. The impact emptied the breath out of her with a soft grunt. The fingers of Bond's left hand flew to the throat and found the carotid artery. His right hand was on the waist of the rifle's stock. He prised the fingers away, felt that the safety catch was on and reached the rifle far to one side.

Bond eased the weight of his chest off the girl's back and moved his fingers away from her neck. He closed them softly over her mouth. Beneath him, he felt the body heave, the lungs labouring for breath. She was still out. Carefully Bond gathered the two hands behind the girl's back and held them with his right. Beneath him the buttocks began to squirm. The legs jerked. Bond pinned the legs to the ground with his stomach and thighs, noting the strong muscles bunched under him. Now the breath was rasping through his fingers. Teeth gnawed at his hand. Bond inched carefully forwards along the girl. He got his mouth through her hair to her ear. He whispered urgently, "Tilly, for Christ's sake. Stay still! This is me, Bond. I'm a friend. This is vital. Something you don't know about. Will you stay still and listen?"

The teeth stopped reaching for his fingers. The body relaxed and lay soft under his. After a time, the head nodded once.

Bond slid off her. He lay beside her, still holding her hands prisoned behind her back. He whispered, "Get your breath. But tell me, were you after Goldfinger?"

The pale face glanced sideways and away. The girl whispered fiercely into the ground, "I was going to kill him."

Some girl Goldfinger had put in the family way. Bond let go her hands. She brought them up and rested her head on them. Her whole body shuddered with exhaustion and released nerves. The shoulders began to shake softly. Bond reached out a hand and smoothed her hair, quietly, rhythmically. His eyes carefully went over the peaceful, unchanged scene below. Unchanged? There was something. The radar thing on the cowl of the chimney. It wasn't going round any more. It had stopped with its oblong mouth pointing in their direction. The fact had no significance for Bond. Now the girl wasn't crying any more. Bond nuzzled his mouth close to her ear. Her hair smelled of jasmine. He whispered, "Don't worry. I'm after him too. And I'm going to damage him far worse than you could have done. I've been sent after him by London. They want him. What did he do to you?"

She whispered, almost to herself, "He killed my sister. You knew her—Jill Masterton."

Bond said fiercely, "What happened?"

"He has a woman once a month. Jill told me this when she first took the job. He hypnotizes them. Then he—he paints them gold."

"Christ! Why?"

139

"I don't know. Jill told me he's mad about gold. I suppose he sort of thinks he's—that he's sort of possessing gold. You know—marrying it. He gets some Korean servant to paint them. The man has to leave their backbones unpainted. Jill couldn't explain that. I found out it's so they wouldn't die. If their bodies were completely covered with gold paint, the pores of the skin wouldn't be able to breathe. Then they'd die. Afterwards, they're washed down by the Korean with resin or something. Goldfinger gives them a thousand dollars and sends them away."

Bond saw the dreadful Oddjob with his pot of gold paint, Goldfinger's eyes gloating over the glistening statue, the fierce possession. "What happened to Jill?"

"She cabled me to come. She was in an emergency ward in a hospital in Miami. Goldfinger had thrown her out. She was dying. The doctors didn't know what was the matter. She told me what had happened to her—what he had done to her. She died the same night." The girl's voice was dry—matter of fact. "When I got back to England I went to Train, the skin specialist. He told me this business about the pores of the skin. It had happened to some cabaret girl who had to pose as a silver statue. He showed me details of the case and the autopsy. Then I knew what had happened to Jill. Goldfinger had had her painted all over. He had murdered her. It must have been out of revenge for—for going with you." There was a pause. The girl said dully, "She told me about you. She—she liked you. She told me if ever I met you I was to give you this ring."

Bond closed his eyes tight, fighting with a wave of mental nausea. More death! More blood on his hands. This time, as the result of a careless gesture, a piece of bravado that had led to twenty-four hours of ecstasy with a beautiful girl who had taken his fancy and, in the end, rather more than his fancy. And this petty sideswipe at Goldfinger's ego had been returned by Goldfinger a thousand, a millionfold. "She left my employ"—the flat words in the sunshine at Sandwich two days before. How Goldfinger must have enjoyed saying that! Bond's fingernails dug into the palms of his hands. By God, he'd pin this murder on Goldfinger if it was the last act of his life. As for himself . . .? Bond knew the answer. This death he would not be able to excuse as being part of his job. This death he would have to live with.

The girl was pulling at her finger—at the Claddagh ring, the entwined hands round the gold heart. She put her knuckle to her mouth. The ring came off. She held it up for Bond to take. The tiny gold circle, silhouetted against the trunk of the tree, glittered in the moonlight.

The noise in Bond's ear was something between a hiss and a shrill whistle. There was a dry, twanging thud. The aluminium feathers of the steel arrow trembled like a humming bird's wings in front of Bond's eyes. The shaft of the arrow straightened. The gold ring tinkled down the shaft until it reached the bark of the tree.

Slowly, almost incuriously, Bond turned his head.

Ten yards away—half in moonlight, half in shadow—the black melon-headed figure crouched, its legs widely straddled in the judo stance. The left arm, thrust forward against the glinting semicircle of the bow, was straight as a duellist's. The right hand, holding the feathers of the second arrow, was rigid against the right cheek. Behind the head, the taut right elbow lanced back in frozen suspense. The silver tip of the second arrow pointed exactly between the two pale raised profiles.

Bond breathed the words, "Don't move an inch." Aloud he said, "Hullo, Oddjob. Damned good shot."

Oddjob jerked the tip of the arrow upwards.

Bond got to his feet, shielding the girl. He said softly out of the corner of his mouth, "He mustn't see the rifle." He said to Oddjob, speaking casually, peaceably, "Nice place Mr Goldfinger has here. Want to have a word with him sometime. Perhaps it's a bit late tonight. You might tell him I'll be along tomorrow." Bond said to the girl, "Come on, darling. We've had our walk in the woods. Time to get back to the hotel." He took a step away from Oddjob towards the fence.

Oddjob stamped his forward foot. The point of the second arrow swung to the centre of Bond's stomach.

"Oargn." Oddjob jerked his head sideways and downwards towards the house.

"Oh, you think he'd like to see us now? All right. You don't think we'll be disturbing him? Come on, darling." Bond led the way to the left of the tree, away from the rifle that lay in the shadowed grass.

As they went slowly down the hill, Bond talked softly

to the girl, briefing her. "You're my girl friend. I brought you out from England. Seem surprised and interested by our little adventure. We're in a tough spot. Don't try any tricks." Bond jerked back his head. "This man's a killer."

The girl said angrily, "If only you hadn't interfered."

"Same to you," said Bond shortly. He took it back. "I'm sorry, Tilly. Didn't mean that. But I don't think you could have got away with it."

"I had my plans. I'd have been over the frontier by midnight."

Bond didn't answer. Something had caught his eye. On top of the tall chimney, the oblong mouth of the radarthing was revolving again. It was that that had spotted them—heard them. It must be some kind of sonic detector. What a bag of tricks this man was! Bond hadn't meant to underestimate Goldfinger. Had he managed to do so—decisively? Perhaps, if he had had his gun . . .? No. Bond knew that even his split-second draw wouldn't have beaten the Korean—wouldn't do so now. There was a total deadliness about this man. Whether Bond had been armed or unarmed, it would have been a man fighting a tank.

They reached the courtyard. As they did so, the back door of the house opened. Two more Koreans, who might have been the servants from Reculver, ran out towards them through the warm splash of electric light. They carried ugly-looking polished sticks. "Stop!" Both men wore the savage, empty grin that men from Station J, who had been in Japanese prison camps, had described to Bond. "We search. No trouble or . . ." The man who had spoken, cut the air with a whistling lash of his stick. "Hands up!"

Bond put his hands slowly up. He said to the girl, "Don't react . . . whatever they do."

Oddjob came forward and stood, menacingly, watching the search. The search was expert. Bond coldly watched the hands on the girl, the grinning faces.

"Okay. Come!"

They were herded through the open door and along a stone-flagged passage to the narrow entrance hall at the front of the house. The house smelled as Bond had imagined it would—musty and fragrant and summery. There were white-panelled doors. Oddjob knocked on one of them.

"Yes?"

Oddjob opened the door. They were prodded through.

Goldfinger sat at a big desk. It was neatly encumbered with important-looking papers. The desk was flanked by grey metal filing cabinets. Beside the desk, within reach of Goldfinger's hand, stood a short-wave wireless set on a low table. There was an operator's keyboard and a machine that ticked busily and looked like a barograph. Bond guessed that this had something to do with the detector that had intercepted them.

Goldfinger wore his purple velvet smoking-jacket over an open-necked white silk shirt. The open neck showed a tuft of orange chest-hair. He sat very erect in a high-backed chair. He hardly glanced at the girl. The big china-blue eyes were fixed on Bond. They showed no surprise. They held no expression except a piercing hardness.

Bond blustered, "Look here, Goldfinger. What the hell's all this about? You put the police on to me over that ten thousand dollars and I got on your tracks with my girl friend here, Miss Soames. I've come to find out what the hell you mean by it. We climbed the fence—I know it's trespassing, but I wanted to catch you before you moved on somewhere else. Then this ape of yours came along and damned near killed one of us with his bow and arrow. Two more of your bloody Koreans held us up and searched us. What the hell's going on? If you can't give me a civil answer and full apologies I'll put the police on you."

Goldfinger's flat, hard stare didn't flicker. He might not have heard Bond's angry-gentleman's outburst. The finely chiselled lips parted. He said, "Mr Bond, they have a saying in Chicago: 'Once is happenstance. Twice is coincidence. The third time it's enemy action.' Miami, Sandwich and now Geneva. I propose to wring the truth out of you." Goldfinger's eyes slid slowly past Bond's head. "Oddjob. The Pressure Room."

PART THREE : ENEMY ACTION

CHAPTER 15

THE PRESSURE ROOM

BOND'S REACTION was automatic. There was no reason behind it. He took one quick step forward and hurled himself across the desk at Goldfinger. His body, launched in a shallow dive, hit the top of the desk and ploughed through the litter of papers. There was a heavy thud as the top of his head crashed into Goldfinger's breastbone. The momentum of the blow rocked Goldfinger in his chair. Bond kicked back at the edge of the desk, got a purchase and rammed forward again. As the chair toppled backwards and the two bodies went down in the splintering woodwork, Bond's fingers got to the throat and his thumbs went into its base and downwards with every ounce of his force.

Then the whole house fell on Bond, a baulk of timber hit him at the base of the neck and he rolled sluggishly off Goldfinger on to the floor and lay still.

The vortex of light through which Bond was whirling slowly flattened into a disc, a yellow moon, and then into a burning Cyclops eye. Something was written round the fiery eyeball. It was a message, an important message for him. He must read it. Carefully, one by one, Bond spelled out the tiny letters. The message said: SOCIÉTÉ ANONYME MAZDA. What was its significance? A hard bolt of water hit Bond in the face. The water stung his eyes and filled his mouth. He retched desperately and tried to move. He couldn't. His eyes cleared, and his brain. There was a throbbing pain at the back of his neck. He was staring up into a big enamelled light bowl with one powerful bulb. He was on some sort of a table and his wrists and ankles were bound to its edges. He felt with his fingers. He felt polished metal.

A voice, Goldfinger's voice, flat, uninterested, said, "Now we can begin."

Bond turned his head towards the voice. His eyes were dazzled by the light. He squeezed them hard and opened them. Goldfinger was sitting in a canvas chair. He had taken off his jacket and was in his shirt sleeves. There were red marks round the base of his throat. On a folding table beside him were various tools and metal instruments and a control panel. On the other side of the table Tilly Masterton sat in another chair. She was strapped to it by her wrists and ankles. She sat bolt upright as if she was in school. She looked incredibly beautiful, but shocked, remote. Her eyes gazed vacantly at Bond. She was either drugged or hypnotized.

Bond turned his head to the right. A few feet away stood the Korean. He still wore his bowler hat but now he was stripped to the waist. The yellow skin of his huge torso glinted with sweat. There was no hair on it. The flat pectoral muscles were as broad as dinner plates and the stomach was concave below the great arch of the ribs. The biceps and forearms, also hairless, were as thick as thighs. The ten-minutes-to-two oil slicks of the eyes looked pleased, greedy. The mouthful of blackish teeth formed an oblong grin of anticipation.

Bond raised his head. The quick look round hurt. They were in one of the factory workrooms. White light blazed round the iron doors of two electric furnaces. There were bluish sheets of metal stacked in wooden frames. From somewhere came the whir of a generator. There was a distant, muffled sound of hammering, and, behind the sound, the faraway iron pant of the power plant.

Bond glanced down the table on which he lay spread-eagled. He let his head fall back with a sigh. There was a narrow slit down the centre of the polished steel table. At the far end of the slit, like a foresight framed in the vee of his parted feet, were the glinting teeth of a circular saw.

Bond lay and stared up at the little message on the lamp bulb. Goldfinger began to speak in a relaxed conversational voice. Bond pulled the curtains tight across the ghastly peep-show of his imagination and listened.

"Mr Bond, the word 'pain' comes from the Latin *poena* meaning 'penalty'—that which must be paid. You must now pay for the inquisitiveness which your attack upon me proves, as I suspected, to be inimical. Curiosity, as they say, killed the cat. This time it will have to kill two cats, for I fear I must also count this girl an enemy. She tells me she is staying at the Bergues. One telephone call proved that to be false. Oddjob was sent to where you were both hidden and recovered her rifle and also a ring which it happens that I recognize. Under hypnotism the rest came out. This girl came here to kill me. Perhaps you did too. You have both failed. Now must come the *poena*. Mr Bond—" the voice was weary, bored—"I have had many enemies in my time. I am very successful and immensely rich, and riches, if I may inflict another of my aphorisms upon you, may not make you friends but they greatly increase the class and variety of your enemies."

"That's very neatly put."

Goldfinger ignored the interruption. "If you were a free man, with your talent for inquiry, you would be able to find round the world the relics of those who have wished me ill, or who have tried to thwart me. There have, as I said, been many of these people and you would find, Mr Bond, that their remains resemble those of hedgehogs squashed upon the roads in summertime."

"Very poetic simile."

"By chance, Mr Bond. I am a poet in deeds—not often in words. I am concerned to arrange my actions in appropriate and effective patterns. But that is by the way. I wish to convey to you that it was a most evil day for you when you first crossed my path and, admittedly in a very minor fashion, thwarted a minuscule project upon which I was engaged. On that occasion it was someone else who suffered the *poena* that should have been meted out to you. An eye was taken for the eye, but it was not yours. You were lucky and, if you had then found an oracle to consult, the oracle would have said to you, 'Mr Bond, you have been fortunate. Keep away from Mr Auric Goldfinger. He is a most powerful man. If Mr Goldfinger wanted to crush you, he would only have to turn over in his sleep to do so.'"

"You express yourself most vividly." Bond turned his head. The great brown and orange football of a head was bent slightly forward. The round moon-face was bland, indifferent. Casually, one hand reached out to the control panel and pressed down a switch. There came a slow metallic growl from the end of the table on which Bond lay. It curved quickly up to a harsh whine and then to a shrill high whistle that was barely audible. Bond turned his head wearily away. How soon could he manage to die? Was there any way he could hasten death? A friend of his had survived the Gestapo. He had described to Bond how he had tried to commit suicide by holding his breath. By superhuman will-power, after a few minutes without breathing, unconsciousness had come. But, with the blackout of the senses, will and intention had also left the body. At once reason was forgotten. The body's instinct to live manned the pumps and got breath back into the body again. But Bond could try it. There was nothing else to help him through the pain barrier before the blessing of death. For death was the only exit. He knew he could never squeal to Goldfinger and live with himself again—even in the unlikely event that Goldfinger could be bought off with the truth. No, he must stick to his thin story and hope that the others who would now follow him on Goldfinger's trail would have better luck. Who would M choose? Probably 008, the second killer in the small section of three. He was a good man, more careful than Bond. M would know that Goldfinger had killed Bond and he would give 008 licence to kill in return. 258 in Geneva would put him on to the scent that would end with Bond's inquiry about the Entreprises Auric. Yes, fate would catch up with Goldfinger if Bond could only keep his mouth shut. If he gave the least clue away, Goldfinger would escape. That was unthinkable.

"Now then, Mr Bond," Goldfinger's voice was brisk. "Enough of these amiabilities. Sing, as my Chicago friends put it, and you will die quickly and painlessly. The girl also. Sing not, and your death will be one long scream. The girl I shall then give to Oddjob, as I did that cat, for supper. Which is it to be?"

Bond said, "Don't be a fool, Goldfinger. I told my friends at Universal where I was going and why. The girl's parents know that she went with me. I made inquiries about this factory of yours before we came here. We shall be traced here very easily. Universal is powerful. You will have the police after you within days of our disappearance. I will make a deal with you. Let us go and nothing more will be heard of the matter. I will vouch for the girl. You are making a stupid mistake. We are two perfectly innocent people."

Goldfinger said in a bored voice, "I'm afraid you don't understand, Mr Bond. Whatever you have managed to find out about me, which I suspect is very little, can only be a grain of the truth. I am engaged upon gigantic enterprises. To take the gamble of letting either of you leave here alive would be quite ludicrous. It is out of the question. As for my being bothered by the police, I shall be delighted to receive them if they come. Those of my Koreans who can speak won't do so—nor will the mouths of my electric furnaces which will have vaporized you both and all your belongings at two thousand degrees Centigrade. No, Mr Bond, make your choice. Perhaps I can encourage you"—there came the noise of a lever moving across iron teeth. "The saw is now approaching your body at about one inch every minute. Meanwhile," he glanced at Oddjob and held up one finger, "a little massage from Oddjob. To begin with, only grade one. Grades two and three are still more persuasive."

Bond closed his eyes. The sickly zoo-smell of Oddjob enveloped him. Big, rasping fingers set to work on him carefully, delicately. A pressure here, combined with a pressure there, a sudden squeeze, a pause, and then a quick, sharp blow. Always the hard hands were surgically accurate. Bond ground his teeth until he thought they would break. The sweat of pain began to form pools in the sockets of his closed eyes. The shrill whine of the saw was getting louder. It reminded Bond of the sawdust-scented sounds of long ago summer evenings at home in England. Home? This was his home, this cocoon of danger he had chosen to live in. And here he would be buried 'in some corner of a foreign blast furnace that is for ever two thousand degrees Centigrade'. God rest ye merry gentlemen of the Secret Service! What should he give himself as an epitaph? What should be his 'famous last words'? That you have no choice about your birth, but you can choose the way you die? Yes, it would look well on a tombstone—not *Savoir vivre* but *Savoir mourir*.

"Mr Bond." Goldfinger's voice held an ounce of urgency. "Is this really necessary? Just tell me the truth. Who are you? Who sent you here? What do you know? Then it will be so easy. You shall both have a pill. There will be no pain. It will be like taking a sleeping draught. Otherwise it will be so messy—so messy and distressing. And are you being fair to the girl? Is this the behaviour of an English gentleman?"

Oddjob's torment had stopped. Bond turned his head slowly towards the voice and opened his eyes. He said, "Goldfinger, there is nothing more to tell because there is nothing. If you will not accept my first bargain I will make you another. The girl and I will work for you. How about that? We are capable people. You could put us to good use."

"And get a knife, two knives in my back? Thank you no, Mr Bond."

Bond decided it was time to stop talking. It was time to start winding up the mainspring of will-power that must not run down again until he was dead. Bond said politely, "Then you can go and —— yourself." He expelled all the breath from his lungs and closed his eyes.

"Even I am not capable of that, Mr Bond," said Goldfinger with good humour. "And now, since you have chosen the stony path instead of the smooth, I must extract what interest I can from your predicament by making the path as stony as possible. Oddjob, grade two."

The lever on the table moved across iron teeth. Now Bond could feel the wind of the saw between his knees. The hands came back.

Bond counted the slowly pounding pulse that utterly possessed his body. It was like the huge panting power plant in the other part of the factory but, in his case, it was slowly decelerating. If only it would slow down quicker. What was this ridiculous will to live that refused to listen to the brain? Who was making the engine run on although the tank was dry of fuel? But he must empty his mind of thought, as well as his body of oxygen. He must become a vacuum, a deep hole of unconsciousness.

Still the light burned red through his eyelids. Still he could feel the bursting pressure in his temples. Still the slow drum of life beat in his ears.

A scream tried to force its way through the clamped teeth.

Die damn you die die damn you die damn you die damn you die damn you die . . .

CHAPTER 16

THE LAST AND THE BIGGEST

THE wings of a dove, the heavenly choir, Hark the Herald Angels Sing—what else ought he to remember about Paradise? It was all so exactly like what he had been told in the nursery—this sensation of flying, the darkness, the drone of a million harps. He really must try and remember the dope about the place. Let's see now, one got to the Pearly Gates ...

A deep fatherly voice said, almost in his ear, "This is your captain speaking." (Well, well. Who was this. Saint Peter?) "We are coming in to land now. Will you please fasten your seat belts and extinguish your cigarettes. Thank you."

There must be a whole lot of them, going up together. Would Tilly be on the same trip? Bond squirmed with embarrassment. How would he introduce her to the others, to Vesper for instance? And when it came to the point, which would he like the best? But perhaps it would be a big place with countries and towns. There was probably no more reason why he should run into one of his former girl friends here than there had been on earth. But still there were a lot of people he'd better avoid until he got settled in and found out the form. Perhaps, with so much love about, these things wouldn't matter. Perhaps one just loved all the girls one met. Hm. Tricky business!

With these unworthy thoughts in his mind, Bond relapsed into unconsciousness.

The next thing he knew was a gentle sensation of swaying. He opened his eyes. The sun blinded them. He closed them again. A voice above and behind his head said, "Watch it, bud. That ramp's steeper than it looks." Almost immediately there was a heavy jolt. A surly voice in front said, "Cheesus, you're telling me. Why in hell can't they put down rubber."

Bond thought angrily, that's a fine way to talk up here. Just because I'm new and they think no one's listening.

There was the bang of a swing door. Something hit Bond sharply on a protruding elbow. He shouted "Hey!" and tried to reach his elbow and rub it, but his hands wouldn't move.

"Whaddya know. Hey, Sam, better call the doc. This one's come round."

"Sure! Here, put him alongside the other." Bond felt himself being lowered. It was cooler now. He opened his eyes. A big round Brooklyn face was bent over his. The eyes met his and smiled. The metal supports of the stretcher touched the ground. The man said, "How ya feelin', mister?"

"Where am I?" Now there was panic in Bond's voice. He tried to rise but couldn't. He felt the sweat break out on his body. God! Was this still part of the old life? At the thought of it, a wave of grief poured through his body. Tears burned his eyes and trickled down his cheeks.

"Hey, hey! Take it easy, mister. You're okay. This is Idlewild, New York. You're in America now. No more troubles, see." The man straightened up. He thought Bond was a refugee from somewhere. "Sam, get movin'. This guy's in shock."

"Okay, okay." The two voices receded, mumbling anxiously.

Bond found he could move his head. He looked round. He was in a white-painted ward—presumably something to do with the health department of the airport. There was a row of tidy beds. Sun poured down from high windows, but it was cool, air-conditioned. He was on a stretcher on the floor. There was another one next to it. He strained his head sideways. It was Tilly. She was unconscious. Her pale face, framed in the black hair, pointed at the ceiling.

The door at the end of the ward sighed open. A doctor in a white coat stood and held it. Goldfinger, looking brisk, cheerful, walked swiftly down between the beds. He was followed by Oddjob. Bond wearily closed his eyes. Christ! So that was the score.

Feet gathered round his stretcher. Goldfinger said breezily, "Well, they certainly look in good shape, eh, Doctor? That's one of the blessings of having enough money. When one's friends or one's staff are ill one can get them the very best medical attention. Nervous breakdowns, both of them.

And in the same week! Would you believe it? But I blame myself for working them both too hard. Now it's my duty to get them back on their feet again. Dr Foch—he's the best man in Geneva, by the way—was quite definite. He said, 'They need rest, Mr Goldfinger. Rest, rest and again rest.' He gave them sedatives and now they're on their way to the Harkness Pavilion at the Presbyterian." Goldfinger chuckled fatly. "Sow and you shall reap, eh, Doctor? When I gave the Harkness a million dollars' worth of X-ray equipment, I certainly never expected anything back. But now? I only had to put through a call and they've got two fine rooms waiting for them. Now then—" there was a rustle of notes —"thank you for all your help with Immigration. Fortunately they both had valid visas and I think Immigration was satisfied that Mr Auric Goldfinger was a sufficient guarantee that neither of them wants to overthrow the United States Government by force, what?"

"Yes indeed, and thank you Mr Goldfinger. Anything I can do . . . I understand you have a private ambulance waiting outside."

Bond opened his eyes and looked at where the doctor's voice came from. He saw a pleasant, serious young man with rimless glasses and a crew-cut. Bond said quietly and with desperate sincerity, "Doctor, there is absolutely nothing wrong with me or this girl. We have been drugged and brought here against our will. Neither of us works or has ever worked for Goldfinger. I am warning you that we have been kidnapped. I demand to see the Chief of Immigration. I have friends in Washington and New York. They will vouch for me. I beg of you to believe me." Bond held the man's eyes in his, willing him to believe.

The doctor looked worried. He turned to Goldfinger. Goldfinger shook his head—discreetly so that Bond would not be insulted. A surreptitious hand went up and tapped the side of his head away from Bond. Goldfinger raised helpless eyebrows. "You see what I mean, Doctor? It's been like this for days. Total nervous prostration combined with persecution mania. Dr Foch said they often go together. It may need weeks at the Harkness. But I'm going to pull him round if it's the last thing I do. It's the shock of these unfamiliar surroundings. Perhaps a shot of intraval sodium. . ."

The doctor bent to his black bag. "I guess you're right,

Mr Goldfinger. So long as Harkness is looking after the case."
There came the tinkle of instruments.

Goldfinger said, "It's terribly sad to see a man break
down so utterly, a man who has been one of my best assis-
ants." He bent a sweet, fatherly smile on Bond. There
was a catch in his voice. "You'll be all right, James. Just
relax and have a nice sleep. I was afraid the flight might be
too much for you. Just relax and leave everything to me."

Bond felt the swab on his arm. He heaved. Against his
will, a shower of curses poured from his lips. Then he felt
the needle and opened his mouth and screamed and screamed
while the doctor knelt beside him and delicately, patiently,
wiped away the sweat from his forehead.

Now it was a grey painted box of a room. There were no
windows. Light came from a single bowl lamp inset in the
centre of the ceiling. Round the lamp were concentric
slits in the plaster and there was the neutral smell and faint
hum of air-conditioning. Bond found he could sit up.
He did so. He felt drowsy but well. He suddenly realized
that he was ravenously hungry and thirsty. When had he
last had a meal? Two, three days ago? He put his feet down
on the floor. He was naked. He examined his body. Oddjob
had been careful. There was no sign of damage save for the
group of needle-marks on his right forearm. He got up,
conquering dizziness, and took a few steps in the room. He
had been lying on a ship's type bunk with drawers under it.
The only other furniture in the room was a plain deal table
and an upright wooden chair. Everything was clean, func-
tional, Spartan. Bond knelt to the drawers under the bunk
and opened them. They contained all the contents of his
suitcase except his watch and the gun. Even the rather heavy
shoes he had been wearing on his expedition to Entreprises
Auric were there. He twisted one of the heels and pulled.
The broad double-sided knife slid smoothly out of its scab-
bard in the sole. With the fingers wrapped round the locked
heel it made a workmanlike stabbing dagger. Bond verified
that the other shoe held its knife and clicked the heels back
into position. He pulled out some clothes and put them on.
He found his cigarette case and lighter and lit a cigarette.
There were two doors of which one had a handle. He opened
this one. It led into a small, well-appointed bathroom and

lavatory. His washing and shaving things were neatly laid out. There were a girl's things beside them. Bond softly opened the other door into the bathroom. It was a similar room to his own. Tilly Masterton's black hair showed on the pillow of the bunk. Bond tiptoed over and looked down. She was sleeping peacefully, a half-smile on the beautiful mouth. Bond went back into the bathroom, softly closed the door and went to the mirror over the basin and looked at himself. The black stubble looked more like three days than two. He set to work to clean himself up.

Half an hour later, Bond was sitting on the edge of his bunk thinking, when the door without a handle opened abruptly. Oddjob stood in the entrance. He looked incuriously at Bond. His eyes flickered carefully round the room. Bond said sharply, "Oddjob, I want a lot of food, quickly. And a bottle of bourbon, soda and ice. Also a carton of Chesterfields, king-size, and either my own watch or another one as good as mine. Quick march! Chop-chop! And tell Goldfinger I want to see him, but not until I've had something to eat. Come on! Jump to it! Don't stand there looking inscrutable. I'm hungry."

Oddjob looked redly at Bond as if wondering which piece to break. He opened his mouth, uttered a noise between an angry bark and a belch, spat drily on the floor at his feet and stepped back, whirling the door shut. When the slam should have come, the door decelerated abruptly and closed with a soft, decisive, double click.

The encounter put Bond in good humour. For some reason Goldfinger had decided against killing them. He wanted them alive. Soon Bond would know why he wanted them alive but, so long as he did, Bond intended to stay alive on his own terms. Those terms included putting Oddjob and any other Korean firmly in his place, which, in Bond's estimation, was rather lower than apes in the mammalian hierarchy.

By the time an excellent meal together with everything else, including his watch, Bond had asked for, had been brought by one of the Korean servants, Bond had learned nothing more about his circumstances except that his room was close to water and not far from a railway bridge. Assuming his room was in New York, it was either on the Hudson or the East River. The railway was electric and sounded like a subway, but Bond's New York geography was not good enough to place it. His watch had stopped. When he asked the time he got no answer.

Bond had eaten all the food on the tray and was smoking and sipping a solid bourbon and soda when the door opened. Goldfinger came in alone. He was wearing a regulation businessman's clothes and looked relaxed and cheerful. He closed the door behind him and stood with his back to it. He looked searchingly at Bond. Bond smoked and looked politely back.

Goldfinger said, "Good morning, Mr Bond. I see you are yourself again. I hope you prefer being here to being dead. So as to save you the trouble of asking a lot of conventional questions, I will tell you where you are and what has happened to you. I will then put to you a proposition to which I require an unequivocal reply. You are a more reasonable man than most, so I need only give you one brief warning. Do not attempt any dramatics. Do not attack me with a knife or a fork or that bottle. If you do, I shall shoot you with this." A small-calibre pistol grew like a black thumb out of Goldfinger's right fist. He put the hand with the gun back in his pocket. "I very seldom use these things. When I have had to, I have never needed more than one ·25-calibre bullet to kill. I shoot at the right eye, Mr Bond. And I never miss."

Bond said, "Don't worry, I'm not as accurate as that with a bourbon bottle." He hitched up the knee of his trousers and put one leg across the other. He sat relaxed. "Go ahead."

"Mr Bond," Goldfinger's voice was amiable. "I am an expert in many other materials beside metals and I have a keen appreciation of everything that is one thousand fine, as we say of the purest gold. In comparison with that degree of purity, of value, human material is of a very low grade indeed. But occasionally one comes across a piece of this stuff that can at least be put to the lower forms of use. Oddjob is an example of what I mean—simple, unrefined clay, capable of limited exploitation. At the last moment my hand hesitated to destroy a utensil with the durability I observed in yourself. I may have made a mistake in staying my hand. In any case I shall take the fullest steps to protect myself from the consequences of my impulse. It was something you said that saved your life. You suggested that you and Miss Masterton would work for me. Normally I would have no use for either of you, but it just happens that I am on the brink of a certain enterprise in which the services of both of you could be of a certain minimal assistance. So I took the gamble. I gave you both the necessary sedatives. Your bills were paid and your things fetched from the Bergues where Miss Masterton turned out to be registered under her real name. I sent a cable in your name to Universal Export. You had been offered employment in Canada. You were flying over to explore the prospects. You were taking Miss Masterton as your secretary. You would write further details. A clumsy cable, but it will serve for the short period I require your services. (It won't, thought Bond, unless you included in the text one of the innocent phrases that would tell M that the cable was authentic. By now, the Service would know he was working under enemy control. Wheels would be turning very fast indeed.) And in case you think, Mr Bond, that my precautions were inadequate, that you will be traced, let me tell you that I am no longer in the least interested about your true identity nor the strength and resources of your employers. You and Miss Masterton have utterly disappeared, Mr Bond. So have I, so have all my staff. The airport will refer inquiries to the Harkness Pavilion at the Presbyterian Hospital. The hospital will never have heard of Mr Goldfinger nor of his patients. The FBI and the CIA have no record of me, for I have no criminal history. No doubt the immigration authorities will have details of my comings and goings over the years, but these will not be helpful. As for my present whereabouts, and yours, Mr Bond, we are now in the warehouse of the Hi-speed Trucking Corporation, a formerly respectable concern which I own through nominees and which has been equipped, most thoroughly, as the secret headquarters for the enterprise of which I spoke. You and Miss Masterton will be confined to these quarters. Here you will live and work and possibly, though personally I have doubts about Miss Masterton's inclinations in that respect, make love."

"And what will our work consist of?"

"Mr Bond—" For the first time since Bond had known Goldfinger, the big, bland face, always empty of expression, showed a trace of life. A look almost of rapture illuminated the eyes. The finely chiselled lips pursed into a thin, beatic curve. "Mr Bond, all my life I have been in love. I have been in love with gold. I love its colour, its brilliance, its divine heaviness. I love the texture of gold, that soft sliminess that I have learnt to gauge so accurately by touch that I can estimate the fineness of a bar to within one carat. And I love the warm tang it exudes when I melt it down into a true golden syrup. But, above all, Mr Bond, I love the power that gold alone gives to its owner—the magic of controlling energy, exacting labour, fulfilling one's every wish and whim and, when need be, purchasing bodies, minds, even souls. Yes, Mr Bond, I have worked all my life for gold and, in return, gold has worked for me and for those enterprises that I have espoused. I ask you," Goldfinger gazed earnestly at Bond, "is there any other substance on earth that so rewards its owner?"

"Many people have become rich and powerful without possessing an ounce of the stuff. But I see your point. How much have you managed to collect and what do you do with it?"

"I own about twenty million pounds' worth, about as much as a small country. It is now all in New York. I keep it where I need it. My treasure of gold is like a compost heap. I move it here and there over the face of the earth and, wherever I choose to spread it, that corner blossoms and blooms. I reap the harvest and move on. At this moment I am proposing to encourage, to force, a certain American enterprise with my golden compost. Therefore the gold bars are in New York."

"How do you choose these enterprises? What attracts you to them?"

"I espouse any enterprise that will increase my stock of gold. I invest, I smuggle, I steal." Goldfinger made a small gesture of the hands, opening the palms persuasively. "If you will follow the simile, regard history as a train speeding along through time. Birds and animals are disturbed by the noise and tumult of the train's passage, they fly away from it or run fearfully or cower, thinking they hide. I am like the hawk that follows the train—you have no doubt seen them doing this, in Greece for instance—ready to pounce on anything that may be flushed by the train's passage, by the passage of history. To give you a simple example: the progress of history produces a man who invents penicillin. At the same time, history creates a world war. Many people are dying or afraid of dying. Penicillin will save them. Through bribery at certain military establishments on the Continent, I obtain stocks of penicillin. I water these down with some harmless powder or liquid and sell them at immense profit to those who crave the stuff. You see what I mean, Mr Bond? You have to wait for the prey, watch it carefully and then pounce. But, as I say, I do not search out such enterprises. I allow the train of history to flush them towards me."

"What's the latest one? What have Miss Masterton and I got to do with it?"

"The latest one, Mr Bond, is the last one. It is also the biggest." Goldfinger's eyes were now blank, focused inwards. His voice became low, almost reverential at what he saw. "Man has climbed Everest and he has scraped the depths of the ocean. He has fired rockets into outer space and split the atom. He has invented, devised, created in every realm of human endeavour, and everywhere he has triumphed, broken records, achieved miracles. I said in every realm, but there is one that has been neglected, Mr Bond. That one is the human activity loosely known as crime. The so-called criminal exploits committed by individual humans—I do not of course refer to their idiotic wars, their clumsy destruction of each other—are of miserable dimensions: little bank robberies, tiny swindles, picayune forgeries. And yet, ready to hand, a few hundred miles from here, opportunity for the greatest crime in history stands waiting. The stage is set, the gigantic prize is offered. Only the actors are missing. But the producer is at last here, Mr Bond"—Goldfinger raised a finger and tapped his chest—"and he has chosen his cast. This very afternoon the script will be read to the leading actors. Then rehearsals will begin and, in one week, the curtain will go up for the single, the unique performance. And then will come the applause, the applause for the greatest extra-legal coup of all time. And, Mr Bond, the world will rock with that applause for centuries."

Now a dull fire burned in Goldfinger's big pale eyes and there was a touch of extra colour in his red-brown cheeks. But he was still calm, relaxed, profoundly convinced. There's no trace here, reflected Bond, of the madman, the visionary. Goldfinger had some fantastic exploit in mind, but he had gauged the odds and knew they were right. Bond said, "Well, come on. What is it, and what do we have to do about it?"

"It is a robbery, Mr Bond. A robbery against no opposition, but one that will need detailed execution. There will be much paper-work, many administrative details to supervise. I was going to do this myself until you offered your services. Now you will do it, with Miss Masterton as your secretary. You have already been partly remunerated for this work with your life. When the operation is successfully completed you will receive one million pounds in gold. Miss Masterton will receive half a million."

Bond said enthusiastically, "Now you're talking. What are we going to do? Rob the end of the rainbow?"

"Yes," Goldfinger nodded. "That is exactly what we are going to do. We are going to burgle fifteen billion dollars' worth of gold bullion, approximately half the supply of mined gold in the world. We are going, Mr Bond, to take Fort Knox."

CHAPTER 17

HOODS' CONGRESS

"FORT KNOX." Bond shook his head seriously. "Isn't that rather a tall order for two men and a girl?"

Goldfinger shrugged impatiently. "Please put away your sense of humour for one week, Mr Bond. Then laugh as much as you please. I shall have under my command approximately one hundred men and women. These people will be hand picked from the six most powerful gangster groups in the United States. This force will amount to the toughest and most compact fighting unit that has ever been assembled in peace time."

"All right. How many men guard the vault at Fort Knox?"

Goldfinger slowly shook his head. He knocked once on the door behind him. The door flicked open. Oddjob stood on the threshold, crouching, alert. When he saw that the meeting was still peaceful he straightened himself and waited. Goldfinger said, "You will have many questions to ask, Mr Bond. They will all be answered this afternoon. Beginning at two-thirty. It is now exactly twelve o'clock." Bond glanced at his watch and adjusted it. "You and Miss Masterton will attend the meeting at which the proposition will be put to the heads of the six organizations I have mentioned. No doubt these people will ask the same questions as occur to you. Everything will be explained. Afterwards you will settle down to detailed work with Miss Masterton. Ask for what you want. Oddjob will see to your welfare and also be on permanent guard. Do not be obstreperous or you will instantly be killed. And do not waste time trying to escape or to contact the outside world. I have hired your services and I shall require every ounce of them. Is that a bargain?"

Bond said drily, "I've always wanted to be a millionaire."

Goldfinger didn't look at him. He looked at his fingernails. Then he gave Bond one last hard glance and went out and shut the door behind him.

Bond sat and gazed at the closed door. He brusquely ran both hands through his hair and down over his face. He said "Well, well" aloud to the empty room, got up and walked through the bathroom to the girl's bedroom. He knocked on the door.

"Who is it?"

"Me. Are you visible?"

"Yes." The voice was unenthusiastic. "Come in."

She was sitting on the edge of the bed, pulling on a shoe. She was wearing the things Bond had first seen her in. She looked cool and collected and unsurprised by her surroundings. She looked up at Bond. Her eyes were aloof, disdainful. She said coldly, precisely, "You've got us into this. Get us out."

Bond said amiably, "I may be able to. I got us out of our graves."

"After getting us into them."

Bond looked thoughtfully at the girl. He decided it would be ungallant to spank her, so to speak, on an empty stomach. He said, "This won't get us anywhere. We're in this together, whether we like it or not. What do you want for breakfast or lunch? It's a quarter past twelve. I've eaten. I'll order yours and then come back and tell you the score. There's only one way out of here and Oddjob, that Korean ape, is guarding it. Now then, breakfast or lunch?"

She unbent an inch. "Thank you. Scrambled eggs and coffee, please. And toast and marmalade."

"Cigarettes?"

"No, thank you. I don't smoke."

Bond went back to his room and knocked on the door. It opened an inch.

Bond said, "All right, Oddjob. I'm not going to kill you yet."

The door opened farther. Oddjob's face was impassive. Bond gave the order. The door closed. Bond poured himself a bourbon and soda. He sat on the edge of the bed and wondered how he was going to get the girl on his side. From the beginning she had resented him. Was that only because of her sister? Why had Goldfinger made that cryptic remark about her 'inclinations'? What was there about her that he himself felt—something withdrawn, inimical. She was beautiful—physically desirable. But there was a cold, hard centre to her that Bond couldn't understand or define. Oh well, the main thing was to get her to go along. Otherwise life in prison would be intolerable.

Bond went back into her room. He left both doors open so that he could hear. She was still sitting on the bed wrapped in a coiled immobility. She watched Bond carefully. Bond leaned against the jamb of the door. He took a long pull at his whisky. He said, looking her in the eye, "You'd better know that I'm from Scotland Yard"—the euphemism would serve. "We're after this man Goldfinger. He doesn't mind. He thinks no one can find us for at least a week. He's probably right. He saved our lives because he wants us to work for him on a crime. It's big business. Pretty scatter-brained. But there's a lot of planning and paperwork. We've got to look after that side. Can you do shorthand and typing?"

"Yes." Her eyes were alight. "What's the crime?"

Bond told her. He said, "Of course it all sounds ridiculous and I daresay a few questions and answers will show these gangsters, if they don't show Goldfinger, that the whole thing's impossible. But I don't know. Goldfinger's an extraordinary man. From what I know about him, he never moves unless the odds are right. And I don't think he's mad—at least not madder than other kinds of geniuses —scientists and so on. And there's no doubt he's a genius in his particular field."

"So what are you going to do about it?"

Bond lowered his voice. He said, "What are *we* going to do about it, you mean. *We* are going to play along. And to the hilt. No shirking and no funny business. We're going to be greedy for the money and we're going to give him absolutely top-notch service. Apart from saving our lives, which mean less than nothing to him, it's the only hope we, or rather I because that's my line of country, can have of a chance to queer his pitch."

"How are you going to do that?"

"I haven't the faintest idea. Something may turn up."

"And you expect me to go along with you?"

"Why not? Any other suggestions?"

She pursed her lips obstinately. "Why should I do what you say?"

Bond sighed. "There's no point in being a suffragette about this. It's either that or get yourself killed after breakfast. It's up to you."

The mouth turned down with distaste. She shrugged her shoulders. She said ungraciously, "Oh, all right then." Suddenly her eyes flared. "Only don't ever touch me or I shall kill you."

There came the click of Bond's bedroom door. Bond looked mildly down at Tilly Masterton. "The challenge is attractive. But don't worry. I won't take it up." He turned and strolled out of the room.

One of the Koreans passed him carrying the girl's breakfast. In his room another Korean had brought in a typist's desk and chair and a Remington portable. He arranged them in the corner away from the bed. Oddjob was standing in the doorway. He held out a sheet of paper. Bond went up to him and took it.

It was a foolscap memo sheet. The writing, with a ball point, was neat, careful, legible, undistinguished. It said:

Prepare ten copies of this agenda.
Meeting held under the chairmanship of Mr Gold

Secretaries: J. Bond
Miss Tilly Masterton

	Present
Helmut M. Springer	The Purple Gang. Detroit
Jed Midnight	Shadow Syndicate. Miami and Havana
Billy (The Grinner) Ring	The Machine. Chicago
Jack Strap	The Spangled Mob. Las Vegas
Mr Solo	Unione Siciliano
Miss Pussy Galore	The Cement Mixers. Harlem. New York City

Agenda

A project with the code name OPERATION GRAND SLAM.
(Refreshments.)

At the end of this was written, 'You and Miss Masterton will be fetched at 2.20. Both will be prepared to take notes. Formal dress, please.'

Bond smiled. The Koreans left the room. He sat down at the desk, slipped paper and carbons into the typewriter and set to. At least he would show the girl that he was prepared to do his stint. Gosh, what a crew! Even the Mafia had come in. How had Goldfinger persuaded them all to come? And who in heaven's name was Miss Pussy Galore?

Bond had the copies finished by two o'clock. He went into the girl's room and gave them to her together with a shorthand notebook and pencils. He also read her Goldfinger's note. He said, "You'd better get these names in your head. They probably won't be hard to identify. We can ask if we get stuck. I'll go and get into my formal dress." He smiled at her. "Twenty minutes to go."

She nodded.

Walking down the corridor behind Oddjob, Bond could hear the sounds of the river—the slapping of water on the piles below the warehouse, the long mournful hoot of a ferry clearing her way, the distant thump of diesels. Somewhere beneath his feet a truck started up, revved and then growled away presumably towards the West Side Highway. They must be on the top tier of the long two-tiered building. The grey paint in the corridor smelled new. There were no side doors. Light came from bowls in the ceiling. They reached the end. Oddjob knocked. There was the sound of a Yale key being turned and two lots of bolts being pulled and they walked through and into a large bright sunlit room. The room was over the end of the warehouse and a wide picture window, filling most of the facing wall, framed the river and the distant, brown muddle of Jersey City. The room had been dressed for the conference. Goldfinger sat with his back to the window at a large round table with a green baize cloth, carafes of water, yellow scratch-pads and pencils. There were nine comfortable armchairs and on the scratch-pads in front of six of them were small oblong white parcels sealed with red wax. To the right, against the wall, was a long buffet table gleaming with silver and cut glass. Champagne stood in silver coolers and there was a row of other bottles. Among the various foods Bond noticed two round five-pound tins of Beluga caviar and several terrines of foie gras. On the wall opposite the buffet hung a blackboard above a table on which there were papers and one large oblong carton.

Goldfinger watched them come towards him across the thick wine-red carpet. He gestured to the chair on his left for Tilly Masterton and to the one on the right for Bond. They sat down.

"The agenda?" Goldfinger took the copies, read the top one and handed them back to the girl. He gave a circular wave of the hand and she got up and distributed the copies round the table. He put his hand beneath the table and pressed a hidden bell. The door at the back of the room opened. One of the Koreans came in and stood waiting. "Is everything ready?" The man nodded. "You understand that no one is to come into this room but the people on your list? Good. Some of them, perhaps all, will bring a companion. The companions will remain in the anteroom. See that they have everything they wish. The cards are there and the dice? Oddjob." Goldfinger glanced up at the Korean who had remained behind Bond's chair. "Go and take up your position. What is the signal?" Oddjob held up two fingers. "Right. Two rings on the bell. You may go. See that all the staff carry out their duties to perfection."

Bond said casually, "How many staff have you got?"

"Twenty. Ten Koreans and ten Germans. They are all excellent men, hand picked. Much goes on in this building. It is like below-decks in a man-of-war." Goldfinger laid his hands flat on the table in front of him. "And now, your duties. Miss Masterton, you will take notes of any practical points that arise, anything that is likely to require action by me. Do not bother with the argument and chatter. Right?"

Bond was glad to see that Tilly Masterton now looked bright and businesslike. She nodded briskly, "Certainly."

"And, Mr Bond, I shall be interested in any reactions you may have to the speakers. I know a great deal about all these people. In their own territories they are paramount chiefs. They are only here because I have bribed them to come. They know nothing of me and I need to persuade them that I know what I am talking about and will lead them to success. Greed will do the rest. But there may be one or more who wish to back out. They will probably reveal themselves. In their cases I have made special arrangements. But there may be doubtful ones. During the talk, you will scribble with your pencil on this agenda. Casually you will note with a plus or a minus sign opposite the names whether you consider each one for or against the project. I shall be able to see what sign you have made. Your views may be useful. And do not forget, Mr Bond, that one traitor among them, one backslider, and we could quickly find ourselves either dead or in prison for life."

"Who is this Pussy Galore from Harlem?"

"She is the only woman who runs a gang in America. It is a gang of women. I shall need some women for this operation. She is entirely reliable. She was a trapeze artiste. She had a team. It was called 'Pussy Galore and her Abrocats'." Goldfinger did not smile. "The team was unsuccessful, so she trained them as burglars, cat burglars. It grew into a gang of outstanding ruthlessness. It is a Lesbian organization which now calls itself 'The Cement Mixers'. Even the big American gangs respect them. She is a remarkable woman."

A buzzer sounded very softly beneath the table. Goldfinger straightened himself. The door at the end of the room opened briskly and five men came in. Goldfinger rose in his chair and ducked his head in welcome. He said, "My name is Gold. Will you please be seated."

There was a careful murmur. Silently the men closed round the table, pulled out chairs and sat down. Five pairs of eyes looked coldly, warily at Goldfinger. Goldfinger sat down. He said quietly, "Gentlemen, in the parcels before you you will find one twenty-four-carat gold bar, value fifteen thousand dollars. I thank you for the courtesy of your attendance. The agenda is self-explanatory. Perhaps, while we wait for Miss Galore, I could run through your names for the information of my secretaries, Mr Bond here, and Miss Masterton. No notes will be made of this meeting, except on action you may wish me to take, and I can assure you there are no microphones. Now then, Mr Bond, on your right is Mr Jed Midnight of the Shadow Syndicate operating out of Miami and Havana."

Mr Midnight was a big, good-living man with a jovial face but slow careful eyes. He wore a light blue tropical suit over a white silk shirt ornamented with small green palm trees. The complicated gold watch on his wrist must have weighed nearly half a pound. He smiled tautly at Bond and said, "Howdo."

"Then we have Mr Billy Ring who controls the famous Chicago 'Machine'."

Bond thought he had never seen anyone who was less of a 'Billy'. It was a face out of a nightmare and, as the face turned towards Bond, it knew it was, and watched Bond for his reactions. It was a pale, pear-shaped, baby face with downy skin and a soft thatch of straw-coloured hair, but the eyes, which should have been pale blue, were a tawny brown. The whites showed all round the pupils and gave a mesmeric quality to the hard thoughtful stare, unsoftened by a tic in the right eyelid which made the right eye wink with the heart-beat. At some early stage in Mr Ring's career someone had cut off Mr Ring's lower lip—perhaps he had talked too much—and this had given him a permanent false smile like the grin of a Hallowe'en pumpkin. He was about forty years old. Bond summed him up as a merciless killer. Bond smiled cheerfully into the hard stare of Mr Ring's left eye and looked past him at the man Goldfinger introduced as Mr Helmut Springer of the Detroit Purple Gang.

Mr Springer had the glazed eyes of someone who is either very rich or very dead. The eyes were pale blue opaque glass marbles which briefly recognized Bond and then turned inwards again in complete absorption with self. The rest of Mr Springer was a 'man of distinction'—casually pin-striped, Hathaway-shirted, Aqua-Velva'd. He gave the impression of someone who found himself in the wrong company—a first-class ticket holder in a third-class compartment, a man from the stalls who has been shown by mistake to a seat in the pit.

Mr Midnight put his hand up to his mouth and said softly for Bond's benefit, "Don't be taken in by the Duke. My friend Helmut was the man who put the piquéd shirt on the hood. Daughter goes to Vassar, but it's protection money that pays for her hockey-sticks." Bond nodded his thanks.

"And Mr Solo of the Unione Siciliano."

Mr Solo had a dark heavy face, gloomy with the knowledge of much guilt and many sins. His thick horn-rimmed spectacles helioed briefly in Bond's direction and then bent again to the business of cleaning Mr Solo's nails with a pocket knife. He was a big, chunky man, half boxer, half head waiter, and it was quite impossible to tell what was on his mind or where his strength lay. But there is only one head of the Mafia in America and, if Mr Solo had the job, thought Bond, he had got it by strength out of terror. It would be by the exercise of both that he kept it.

"Howdy." Mr Jack Strap of the Spangled Mob had the synthetic charm of a front man for the Las Vegas casinos, but Bond guessed he had inherited from the late lamented brothers Spang thanks to other qualities. He was an expansive, showily dressed man of about fifty. He was coming to the end of a cigar. He smoked it as if he was eating it, munching hungrily. From time to time he turned his head sideways and discreetly spat a scrap of it out on to the carpet behind him. Behind this compulsive smoking there would be a lot of tension. Mr Strap had quick conjuror's eyes. He seemed to know that his eyes frightened people because now, presumably not wanting to frighten Bond, he gave them charm by crinkling them at the corners.

The door at the back of the room opened. A woman in a black masculine-cut suit with a high coffee-coloured lace jabot stood in the doorway. She walked slowly, unselfconsciously down the room and stood behind the empty chair. Goldfinger had got to his feet. She examined him carefully and then ran her eyes round the table. She said a collective, bored "Hi" and sat down. Mr Strap said "Hi Pussy," and the others, except Mr Springer who merely bowed, made careful sounds of welcome.

Goldfinger said, "Good afternoon, Miss Galore. We have just been through the formality of introductions. The agenda is before you, together with the fifteen-thousand-dollar gold bar I asked you to accept to meet the expense and inconvenience of attending this meeting."

Miss Galore reached for her parcel and opened it. She weighed the gleaming yellow brick in her hand. She gave Goldfinger a direct, suspicious look. "All the way through?"

"All the way through."

Miss Galore held his eyes. She said "Pardon my asking" with the curt tone of a hard woman shopper at the sales.

Bond liked the look of her. He felt the sexual challenge all beautiful Lesbians have for men. He was amused by the uncompromising attitude that said to Goldfinger and to the room, "All men are bastards and cheats. Don't try any masculine hocus on me. I don't go for it. I'm in a separate league." Bond thought she would be in her early thirties. She had pale, Rupert Brooke good looks with high cheekbones and a beautiful jawline. She had the only violet eyes Bond had ever seen. They were the true deep violet of a pansy and they looked candidly out at the world from beneath straight black brows. Her hair, which was as black as Tilly Masterton's, was worn in an untidy urchin cut. The mouth was a decisive slash of deep vermilion. Bond thought she was superb and so, he noticed, did Tilly Masterton who was gazing at Miss Galore with worshipping eyes and lips that yearned. Bond decided that all was now clear to him about Tilly Masterton.

Goldfinger said, "And now I must introduce myself. My name is not Gold. My credentials are as follows. By various operations, most of them illegitimate, I have made a large sum of money in twenty years. That sum now stands at sixty million dollars." (A respectful hm-ing went round the table.) "My operations have, for the most part, been confined to Europe, but you may be interested to know that I founded and subsequently disposed of the 'Golden Poppy Distributors' who operated out of Hongkong." (Mr Jack Strap whistled softly.) "The 'Happy Landings Travel Agency', which some of you may have employed in emergency, was organized and owned by me until I disbanded it." (Mr Helmut Springer screwed a rimless monocle into one glazed eye so that he could examine Goldfinger more closely.)

"I mention these minor concerns to show you that, although you may not know me, I have, in the past, acted at many removes on, I believe, all your behalfs." ("Well, whaddya know!" muttered Mr Jed Midnight with something like awe in his voice.) "That, gentlemen and—er—madam, is how I knew of you and how I came to invite here tonight what I have learned through my own experience to be the aristocracy, if I may so describe it, of American crime."

Bond was impressed. Goldfinger had, in three minutes flat, got the meeting on his side. Now everyone was looking towards Goldfinger with profound attention. Even Miss Pussy Galore's eyes were rapt. Bond knew nothing about the Golden Poppy Distributors or the Happy Landings Agency, but they must have run like clockwork from the expressions on their former customers' faces. Now everyone was hanging on Goldfinger's words as if he was Einstein.

Goldfinger's face showed no emotion. He made a throw-away gesture of his right hand. He said flatly, "I have mentioned two projects of mine that were successful. They were small. There have been many others of a higher calibre. Not one of them has failed, and, so far as I know, my name is on the police files of no country. I say this to show you that I thoroughly understand my—our—profession. And now, gentlemen and madam, I propose to offer you partnership in an undertaking that will assuredly place in each of your treasuries, within one week, the sum of one billion dollars." Mr Goldfinger held up his hand. "We have different views in Europe and America as to what constitutes the arithmetical expression 'a billion'. I use the word in the sense of one thousand million. Do I make myself clear?"

CHAPTER 18

CRIME DE LA CRIME

A TUG hooted on the river. Another answered. A flurry of engine noises receded.

Mr Jed Midnight, on Bond's right, cleared his throat. He said emphatically, "Mister Gold, or whatever your name is, don't you worry about definitions. A billion dollars is a lot of money whichever way you say it. Keep talking."

Mr Solo raised slow black eyes and looked across the table at Goldfinger. He said, "Is very moch money, yess. But how moch your cut, mister?"

"Five billion."

Jack Strap from Las Vegas gave a short boisterous laugh. "Listen fellers, what's a few billion between friends. If Mister—er—Whoosis can lead me to a billion dollars I'll be glad to slip him a fin or even maybe a mega-fin for his trouble. Don't let's be small-minded about this, huh?"

Mr Helmut Springer tapped his monocle on the gold brick in front of him. Everyone looked towards him. "Mister —ah—Gold." It was the grave voice of the family lawyer. "These are big figures you mention. As I understand it, a total of some eleven billion dollars is involved."

Mr Goldfinger said with precision, "The exact figure will be nearer fifteen billion. For convenience I referred only to the amounts I thought it would be possible for us to carry away."

A sharp excited giggle came from Mr Billy Ring.

"Quite, quite, Mr Gold." Mr Springer screwed his monocle back into his eye to observe Goldfinger's reactions. "But quantities of bullion or currency to that amount are to be found gathered together in only three depositories in the United States. They are the Federal Mint in Washington, the Federal Reserve Bank in New York City, and Fort Knox in Kentucky. Do you intend that we should—er—'knock off' one of these? And if so which?"

"Fort Knox."

Amidst the chorus of groans, Mr Midnight said resignedly, "Mister, I never met any guy outside Hollywood that had what you've got. There it's called 'vision'. And vision, mister, is a talent for mistaking spots before the eyes for fabulous projects. You should have a talk with your head-shrinker or get yourself Miltownized." Mr Midnight shook his head sorrowfully. "Too bad. That billion sure felt good while I had it."

Miss Pussy Galore said in a deep, bored voice, "Sorry mister, none of my set of bent pins could take that kind of piggy-bank." She made to get up.

Goldfinger said amiably, "Now hear me through, gentlemen and—er—madam. Your reaction was not unexpected. Let me put it this way: Fort Knox is a bank like any other bank. But it is a much bigger bank and its protective devices are correspondingly stronger and more ingenious. To penetrate them will require corresponding strength and ingenuity. That is the only novelty in my project—that it is a big one. Nothing else. Fort Knox is no more impregnable than other fortresses. No doubt we all thought the Brink organization was unbeatable until half a dozen determined men robbed a Brink-armoured car of a million dollars back in 1950. It is impossible to escape from Sing Sing and yet men have found ways of escaping from it. No, no, gentlemen. Fort Knox is a myth like other myths. Shall I proceed to the plan?"

Billy Ring hissed through his teeth, like a Japanese, when he talked. He said harshly, "Listen, shamus, mebbe ya didn't know it, but the Third Armoured is located at Fort Knox. If that's a myth, why don't the Russkis come and take the United States the next time they have a team over here playing ice-hockey?"

Goldfinger smiled thinly. "If I may correct you without weakening your case, Mr Ring, the following is the order of battle of the military units presently quartered at Fort Knox. Of the Third Armoured Division, there is only the Spearhead, but there are also the 6th Armoured Cavalry Regiment, the 15th Armour Group, the 160th Engineer Group and approximately half a division from all units of the United States Army currently going through the Armoured Replacement Training Centre and Military Human Research Unit No 1. There is also a considerable body of men associated with Continental Armoured Command Board No 2, the Army Maintenance Board and various activities connected with the Armoured Centre. In addition there is a police force consisting of twenty officers and some four hundred enlisted men. In short, out of a total population of some sixty thousand, approximately twenty thousand are combat troops of one sort or another."

"And who's going to say boo to them?" jeered Mr Jack Strap through his cigar. Without waiting for an answer he disgustedly tore the tattered stump out of his mouth and mashed it to fragments in the ash-tray.

Next to him Miss Pussy Galore sucked her teeth sharply

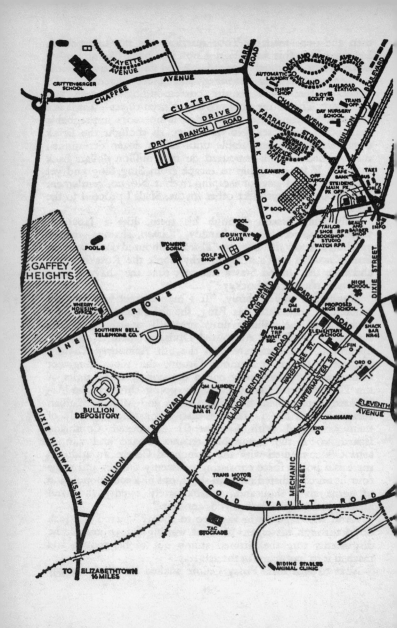

with the incisiveness of a parrot spitting. She said, "Go buy yourself some better smokes, Jacko. That thing smells like burning wrestlers' trunks."

"Shove it, Puss," said Mr Strap inelegantly.

Miss Galore was determined to have the last word. She said sweetly, "Know what, Jacko? I could go for a he-man like you. Matter of fact I wrote a song about you the other day. Care to hear its title? It's called 'If I had to do it all over again, I'd do it all over you'."

A bray of laughter came from Mr Midnight, a high giggle from Mr Ring. Goldfinger tapped lightly for order. He said patiently, "Now hear me through, please, gentlemen." He got up and walked to the blackboard and pulled a roll map down over it. It was a detailed town map of Fort Knox including the Godman Army Airfield and the roads and railway tracks leading into the town. The committee members on the right of the table swivelled their chairs. Goldfinger pointed to the Bullion Depository. It was down on the left-hand corner enclosed in a triangle formed by the Dixie Highway, Bullion Boulevard and Vine Grove Road. Goldfinger said, "I will show you a detailed plan of the depository in just a moment." He paused. "Now, gentlemen, allow me to point out the main features of this fairly straightforward township. Here"—he ran his finger from the top centre of the map down through the town and out beyond the Bullion Depository—"runs the line of the Illinois Central Railroad from Louisville, thirty-five miles to the north, through the town and on to Elizabethtown eighteen miles to the south. We are not concerned with Brandenburg Station in the centre of the town, but with this complex of sidings adjoining the Bullion Vault. That is one of the loading and unloading bays for the bullion from the Mint in Washington. Other methods of transport to the vault, which are varied in no particular rotation for security reasons, are by truck convoy down the Dixie Highway or by freight plane to Godman Airfield. As you can see, the vault is isolated from these routes and stands alone without any natural cover whatsoever in the centre of approximately fifty acres of grassland. Only one road leads to the vault, a fifty-yard driveway through heavily armed gates on Bullion Boulevard. Once inside the armoured stockade, the trucks proceed on to this circular road which runs round the vault to the rear entrance where the bullion is unloaded. That circular road, gentlemen, is manufactured out of steel plates or flaps. These plates are on hinges and in an emergency the entire steel surface of the road can be raised hydraulically to create a second internal stockade of steel. Not so obvious to the eye, but known to me, is that an underground delivery tunnel runs below the plain between Bullion Boulevard and Vine Grove Road. This serves as an additional means of access to the vault through steel doors that lead from the wall of the tunnel to the first sub-ground floor of the depository."

Goldfinger paused and stood away from the map. He looked round the table. "All right, gentlemen. There is the vault and those are the main approaches to it with the exception of its front door which is purely an entrance to the reception hall and offices. Any questions?"

There were none. All eyes were on Goldfinger, waiting. Once again the authority of his words had gripped them. This man seemed to know more about the secrets of Fort Knox than had ever been released to the outside world.

Goldfinger turned back to the blackboard and pulled down a second map over the first. This was the detailed plan of the Gold Vault. Goldfinger said, "Well, gentlemen, you can see that this is an immensely solid two-storey building somewhat like a square, two-layered cake. You will notice that the roof has been stepped for bomb protection, and you will observe the four pill boxes on the ground at the four corners. These are of steel and are connected with the interior of the building. The exterior dimensions of the vault are a hundred and five by a hundred and twenty-one feet. The height from ground level is forty-two feet. The construction is of Tennessee granite, steel-lined. The exact constituents are: sixteen thousand cubic feet of granite, four thousand cubic yards of concrete, seven hundred and fifty tons of reinforcing steel and seven hundred and sixty tons of structural steel. Right? Now, within the building, there is a two-storey steel and concrete vault divided into compartments. The vault door weighs more than twenty tons and the casing of the vault is of steel plates, steel I-beams and steel cylinders laced with hoopbands and encased in concrete. The roof is of similar construction and is independent of the roof of the building. A corridor encircles the vault at both levels and gives access both to the vault and to the offices and storerooms that are housed in the outer wall of the building. No one person is entrusted with the combination to the door of the vault. Various senior members of the depository staff must separately dial combinations known only to each of them. Naturally the building is equipped with the latest and finest protective devices. There is a strong guard-post within the building and immensely powerful reinforcements are at all times available from the Armoured Centre less than a mile distant. Do you follow me? Now, as to the actual content of the vault—these amount, as I said earlier, to some fifteen billion dollars' worth of standard mint bars one thousand fine. Each bar is double the size of the one before you and contains four hundred Troy ounces, the avoirdupois weight being some twenty-seven and a half pounds. These are stored without wrappings in the compartments of the vault." Goldfinger glanced round the table. "And that, gentlemen and madam," he concluded flatly, "is all I can tell you, and all I think we need to know, about the nature and contents of Fort Knox Depository. Unless there are any questions at this stage, I will proceed to a brief explanation of how this depository may be penetrated and its contents seized."

There was silence. The eyes round the table were rapt, intent. Nervously, Mr Jack Strap took a medium-sized cigar out of his vest pocket and stuffed it in the corner of his mouth.

Pussy Galore said sternly, "If you set fire to that thing I swear I'll kayo you with my gold brick." She took a threatening hold of the bar.

"Take it easy, kid," said Mr Strap out of the corner of his mouth.

Mr Jed Midnight commented decisively, "Mister, if you can heist that joint, you got yourself a summum cum laude. Go ahead and tell. This is either a bust or the Crime de la Crime."

Goldfinger said indifferently, "Very well, gentlemen. You shall hear the plan." He paused and looked carefully round the table and into each pair of eyes in turn. "But I hope you understand that total security must now prevail. What I have said so far, if repeated, would be taken for the maunderings of a lunatic. What I am about to say will involve all of us in the greatest peace-time conspiracy in the history of the United States. May I take it that we are all bound by an oath of absolute secrecy?"

Almost instinctively, Bond watched the eyes of Mr Helmut Springer from Detroit. While affirmatives in various tones of voice came from the others, Mr Springer veiled his eyes. His portentous "You have my solemn word" rang hollow. To Bond, the candour was as false as a second-hand motor salesman's. Casually he drew a short straight minus line beside Mr Springer's name on the agenda.

"Very well then." Goldfinger returned to his seat at the table. He sat down, picked up his pencil and began talking to it in a thoughtful, conversational voice. "First, and in some ways most difficult, is the question of disposal. One billion dollars of gold bullion weighs approximately one thousand tons. To transport this amount would require one hundred ten-ton trucks or some twenty six-wheel heavy industry road transporters. I recommend the latter vehicles. I have a list of the charter companies who hire out this type of vehicle and I recommend that, if we are to be partners, you should proceed immediately after this meeting to contracting with the relevant companies in your territories. For obvious reasons you will all wish to engage your own drivers and this I must leave in your hands. No doubt"—Mr Goldfinger allowed himself the ghost of a smile—"the Teamsters' Union will prove a fruitful source for reliable men and you will perhaps consider recruiting ex-drivers from the Negro Red Ball Express that served the American armies during the war. However, these are details requiring exact planning and co-ordination. There will also be a traffic control problem and no doubt you will make arrangements among yourselves for sharing out the available roads. Transport aircraft will be a subsidiary source of mobility and arrangements will be made to keep open the north-south runway on the Godman Airfield. Your subsequent disposal of the bullion will, of course, be your own affair. For my part"—Goldfinger looked coolly round the table—"I shall initially be using the railroad and, since I have a bulkier transport problem, I trust you will allow me to reserve this means of egress for my own." Goldfinger did not wait for comment. He continued in an even tone: "Compared with this problem of transport, the other arrangements will be relatively simple. To begin with, on D–1, I propose to put the entire population, military and civilian, of Fort Knox temporarily out of action. Exact arrangements have been made and only await my signal. Briefly, the town is supplied with all drinking and other water-supplies by two wells and two filter plants yielding just under seven million gallons per day. These are under the control of the Post Engineer. This gentleman has been pleased to accept a visit from the Superintendent and Deputy Superintendent of the Tokyo Municipal Waterworks who wish to study the workings of a plant of this size for installation in a new suburb planned for the environs of Tokyo. The Post Engineer has been much flattered by this request and the Japanese gentlemen will be accorded all facilities. These two gentlemen, who are, of course, members of my staff, will be carrying on their persons relatively small quantities of a highly concentrated opiate devised by the German chemical warfare experts for just this purpose during the last war. This substance disseminates rapidly through a volume of water of this magnitude, and, in its consequent highly diluted form, has the effect of instant but temporary narcosis of any person drinking half a tumbler of the infected water. The symptoms are a deep and instant sleep from which the victim awakens much refreshed in approximately three days. Gentlemen—" Goldfinger held out one hand palm upwards—"in the month of June in Kentucky I consider it out of the question that a single resident is able to go through twenty-four hours without consuming half a glass of water. There may perhaps be a handful of confirmed alcoholics on their feet on D-Day, but I anticipate that we shall enter a town in which virtually the entire population has fallen into a deep sleep where they stand."

"What was that fairytale?" Miss Galore's eyes were shining with the vision.

"*Puss in Boots*," said Mr Jack Strap in a surly voice. "Go ahead, mister. This is good. How do we get into the town?"

"We come in," said Goldfinger, "on a special train that will have left New York City on the night of D–1. There will be approximately one hundred of us and we shall be attired as Red Cross workers. Miss Galore will, I hope, provide the necessary contingent of nurses. It is to fill this minor but important role that she has been invited to this meeting."

Miss Galore said enthusiastically, "Wilco, Roger, over and out! My girls'll look sweet in starch. Whaddya say, Jacko?" She leant sideways and nudged Mr Strap in the ribs.

"I say they'd look better in cement overcoats," said Mr Strap impatiently. "Whaddya have to keep on butting in for? Keep going, mister."

"At Louisville, thirty-five miles from Fort Knox, I myself and an assistant will ask to be allowed to ride in the leading diesel. We shall have delicate instruments. We shall say that it will be necessary for us to sample the air as we approach Fort Knox for, by this time, news of the mysterious affliction that has struck down the inhabitants will have reached the outer world and there is likely to be some panic in the surrounding area, and indeed in the country as a whole. Rescue planes may be expected to approach shortly after our arrival at dawn and an early task will be to man the control tower at Godman Airfield, declare the base closed and re-route all planes to Louisville. But, to go back for a moment, shortly after leaving Louisville, my assistant and I will dispose of the driver and fireman by as humane methods as are possible" (I bet, thought Bond) "and I shall personally bring the train—I may say that I have the requisite knowledge of these locomotives—through Fort Knox to the bullion sidings alongside the depository." Goldfinger paused. He looked with slow, grave eyes round the circle. Satisfied with what he saw, he continued in the same even tone. "By this time, gentlemen and madam, your transport convoys should be arriving. The traffic controller will dispose them in the neighbourhood of the depository according to a pre-arranged plan, the airport staff will proceed by truck to Godman Airfield and take over, and we shall enter the depository, paying no heed to the sleeping bodies with which the landscape will be—er—decorated. Right?"

Mr Solo's dark eyes burned across the table. He said softly, "Sure, is right so far. Now mebbe you—" he blew out his cheeks and gave a quick hard puff towards Goldfinger—"like this and the twenty-ton door he fall down. Yes?"

"Yes," said Goldfinger equably. "Almost exactly like that." He rose and went to the table under the blackboard, lifted up the big ungainly carton and carried it carefully back and placed it on the table in front of him. It seemed to be very heavy.

He sat down and continued, "While ten of my trained assistants are making preparations for the vault to be opened, stretcher teams will enter the depository and remove to safety as many of the inmates as can be located." Bond thought he noticed a treacherous purr underlying Goldfinger's next words. "I am sure you will all agree, gentlemen and madam, that all unnecessary loss of life should be avoided. Thus far, I hope you notice that there have been no casualties with the exception of two employees of the Illinois Central Railroad who have received sore heads." Goldfinger didn't wait for comment but went on. "Now," he reached out and placed his hand on the carton, "when you, gentlemen, and your associates have needed weapons, other than the conventional small arms, where have you found them? At military establishments, gentlemen. You have purchased sub-machine guns and other heavy equipment from quartermaster storekeepers at nearby military bases. You have achieved this by the use of pressure, blackmail or money. I have done the same. Only one weapon would be powerful enough to blast open the Bullion Vault at Fort Knox and I obtained one, after much seeking, from a certain allied military base in Germany. It cost me exactly one million dollars. This, gentlemen, is an atomic warhead designed for use with the Corporal Intermediate Range Guided Missile."

"Cheesus Kerist." Jed Midnight's hands reached for the edge of the table beside Bond and gripped it.

All the faces round the table were pale. Bond could feel the skin taut over his own tensed jaw. To break his tension he reached inside his coat pocket for the Chesterfields and lit one. He slowly blew out the flame and put the lighter back in his pocket. God Almighty! What had he got himself into? Bond looked back down the vista of his knowledge of Goldfinger. The first meeting with the naked brown body on the roof of the Floridiana Cabana Club. The casual way he had rapped Goldfinger's knuckles. The interview with M. The meeting at the bank at which it had been a question of tracking down a gold smuggler— admittedly a big one and one who worked for the Russians —but still only a man-sized criminal, someone Bond had taken trouble to beat at golf and then had pursued coolly, efficiently, but still as only one more quarry like so many others. And now! Now it was not a rabbit in the rabbit hole, not even a fox, it was a king cobra—the biggest, most deadly inhabitant of the world! Bond sighed wearily. Once more into the breach, dear friends! This time it really was St George and the dragon. And St George had better get a move on and do something before the dragon hatched the little dragon's egg he was now nesting so confidently. Bond smiled tautly. Do what? What in God's name was there he could do?

Goldfinger held up his hand. "Gentlemen and madam, believe me, this object is an entirely harmless lump of machinery. It is not armed. If I hit it with a hammer it would not explode. Nothing can make it explode until it is armed and that will not happen until The Day."

Mr Billy Ring's pale face was shiny with sweat. The words trembled slightly as they hissed out through the false grin. "Mister, what . . . what about this thing they call—er—fall-out?"

"Fall-out will be minimal, Mr Ring, and extremely localized. This is the latest model—the so-called 'clean' atomic bomb. But protection suits will be issued to the squad that first enters the ruins of the building. They will form the first in the human chain that will remove the gold and pass it to the waiting trucks."

"Flying debris, Mister? Chunks of concrete and steel and so forth?" Mr Midnight's voice came from somewhere in his stomach.

"We shall take shelter behind the outer steel stockade of the depository, Mr Midnight. All personnel will wear ear-plugs. There may be minor damage to some of the trucks, but that hazard must be accepted."

"Da sleeping guys?" Mr Solo's eyes were greedy. "Mebbe dey jess sleeps a liddle longer?" Mr Solo obviously didn't worry too much about the sleeping guys.

"We shall move as many as possible to safety. We must, I am afraid, accept minor damage to the town. I estimate that casualties among the population will approximately equal three days' toll on the roads of Fort Knox. Our operation will merely serve to keep road accident statistics at a steady level."

"Damn nice of us." Mr Midnight's nerves had now recovered.

"Any more questions?" Goldfinger's voice was bland.

He had read out the figures, estimated the prospects for the business. Now it was time to put the meeting to the vote. "Details remain to be worked out exactly. In that, my staff here"—he turned first to Bond and then to Miss Masterton—"will be assisting me. This room will be our operations room to which you will all have access by day or by night. The code word for the project is 'Operation Grand Slam', which will always be used in referring to the project. May I suggest that those of you who wish to participate should brief one, and only one, of your most trusted lieutenants. Other staff can be trained for their functions as if this were a run-of-the-mill bank robbery. On D – 1 a slightly wider briefing of staff will be necessary. I know I can rely on you, gentlemen and madam, if you decide to participate, to treat this whole project as an operation of war. Inefficiency or insecurity will of course have to be dealt with decisively. And now, gentlemen and madam, I will ask you to reply on behalf of your respective organizations. Which of you wishes to enter this race? The prize is gigantic. The risks are minimal. Mr Midnight?" Goldfinger turned his head an inch to the right. Bond saw the wide open X-ray gaze devour his neighbour. "Yes?" There was a pause. "Or no?"

CHAPTER 19

SECRET APPENDIX

"MR GOLD," Jed Midnight pronounced sonorously, "you are undoubtedly the greatest thing in crime since Cain invented murder and used it on Abel." He paused and added emphatically, "I shall count it an honour to be associated with you in this enterprise."

"Thank you, Mr Midnight. And you, Mr Ring?"

Bond was doubtful about Mr Billy Ring. He had scrawled plusses against all the names except Ring and Helmut Springer. To Mr Ring he had allotted a nought, to Springer a minus sign. He had come to his conclusions by watching eyes, mouths, hands, but nothing had been betrayed by The

Grinner's unwavering false smile. The wink in his right eye had been as steady on the pulse-beat as a metronome and he had kept his hands below the table.

Now Billy Ring brought his hands up from below the table and formed a cat's cradle with them on the green baize in front of him. For a moment he watched the two thumbs twirling, then he raised his nightmare face to Goldfinger's. The tic in his right eye had stopped. The two rows of teeth began to operate like a ventriloquist's dummy. "Mister—" he found difficulty with his b's, m's and p's and produced them by bringing his upper lip down over his teeth like a horse does when it takes sugar out of your hand—"long time now my friends and I been back in legal. What I mean, the old days of leaving corpses strewn all over the landscape went out with the 'forties. Me and my associates, we do all right with the girls, the hemp, and the racetrack, and when we're short there's our good friends the Unions to slip us the odd fin. Ya see, mister—" The Grinner opened his hands and then put them back into the cradle—"we figger the old days are gone. Big Jim Colossimo, Johnny Torrio, Dion O'Bannion, Al Capone—where are those guys today, huh? Mister, they're pushing up the morning glory by the fence. Mebbe you weren't around in the days when we used to hide up between fights in Little Bohemia up behind Milwaukee? Well, siree, in those days, people were shooting at each other so fast you'd often need a programme to tell the act from the spectators. So all right, people got tired of it—those that hadn't already got tired to death, if you get my meaning—and when the 'fifties come along and I take over the team, it's unanimous that we get out of the fireworks business. And now what, mister? Now you come along and put it to me that me and my friends assist you to let off the biggest fizzbang in history! So what do I figger to say to your proposition, Mister—er—Whoosis? Well, I tell you, mister. Everybody's got his price, see?—and for a billion dollars it's a deal. We'll put away the marbles and bring out the sling-shots. We're in."

"Grinner, you sure take one hell of a long time to say yes," commented Mr Midnight sourly.

Goldfinger said cordially, "Thank you for your most interesting statement, Mr Ring. I am very happy to welcome you and your associates. Mr Solo?"

Mr Solo prefaced his reply by reaching into his coat pocket and taking out a battery shaver. He switched it on. The room filled with the noise of angry bees. Mr Solo leant his head back and began running the machine thoughtfully up the right side of his face while his uptilted eyes sought decision in the ceiling. Suddenly he switched the razor off, put it down on the table in front of him and jerked his head down and forward like a snake striking. The black gun-muzzles of his eyes pointed threateningly across the table at Goldfinger and moved slowly from feature to feature of the big moon-face. Half Mr Solo's own face now looked naked. The other half was dark with the Italian swarthiness that comes from an uncontrollable beard growth. Bond guessed that he probably had to shave every three or four hours. Now Mr Solo decided to speak. He spoke in a voice that brought chill into the room. He said softly, "Mister, I been watching you. You are a very relaxed man for someone who speaks such big things. Last man I knew was so much relaxed he got himself totally relaxed by a quick burst of the chopper. Okay, okay." Mr Solo sat back. He spread open palms in reluctant surrender. "So I come in, yes. But mister—" there was a pause for emphasis—"either we get that billion or you get dead. Is okay with you?"

Goldfinger's lips bent ironically. "Thank you, Mr Solo. Your conditions are quite acceptable. I have every wish to stay alive. Mr Helmut Springer?"

Mr Springer's eyes looked deader than ever. He said pompously, "I am still giving the matter my full consideration. Pray consult my colleagues while I deliberate."

Mr Midnight commented impatiently, "Same old Hell. Waits for what he calls inspiration. He's guided—messages from the Almighty on the angels' wavelength. I guess he hasn't heard a human voice in twenty years."

"And Mr Strap?"

Mr Jack Strap crinkled his eyes at Goldfinger. He said smoothly, "Mister, I figure you know the odds and you surely pay the best since one of our machines at Vegas got the trots and gave continuous jackpots. I guess if we provide the muscles and the guns this caper'll pay off. You can count me in." Mr Strap turned off the charm. His eyes, now frightening again, turned, with Goldfinger's, to Miss Pussy Galore.

Miss Galore veiled her violet eyes so as not to have to look at either of them. She said indifferently to the room at large, "Business ain't been so brisk in my corner of the woods." She tapped with long, silver-painted finger-nails on the gold bar before her. "Mind you, I won't say I'm overdrawn at the bank. Let's put it I'm just a shade under-deposited. Yup. Sure I'll come in. Me and my gals got to eat."

Goldfinger allowed himself a half-smile of sympathy. "That is excellent news, Miss Galore. And now," he turned to face across the table, "Mr Springer, might we ask if you have made up your mind?"

Slowly Mr Springer rose to his feet. He gave the controlled yawn of an opera goer. He followed the yawn with a small belch. He took out a fine linen handkerchief and patted his lips. His glazed eyes moved round the table and finally rested on Goldfinger. Slowly his head moved from side to side as if he was trying to exercise fibrositis in his neck muscles. He said gravely, like a bank manager refusing a loan, "Mr Gold, I fear your proposal would not find favour with my colleagues in Detroit." He gave a little bow which included everyone. "It only remains for me to thank you for a most interesting occasion. Good afternoon, gentlemen and madam." In the chilly silence, Mr Springer tucked his handkerchief carefully into the left-hand cuff of his immaculate pin-stripe, turned and walked softly to the door and let himself out.

The door closed with a sharp click. Bond noticed Goldfinger's hand slip casually below the table. He guessed that Oddjob was getting his signal. Signal for what?

Mr Midnight said nastily, "Glad he's out. He's strictly a four-ulcer man. Now then—" he got up briskly and turned to Bond—"how about a little drink?"

They all rose and gathered round the buffet. Bond found himself between Miss Pussy Galore and Tilly Masterton. He offered them champagne. Miss Galore looked at him coldly and said, "Move over, Handsome. Us girls want to talk secrets. Don't we, yummy?" Miss Masterton blushed and then turned very pale. She whispered adoringly, "Oh yes please, Miss Galore."

Bond smiled sourly at Tilly Masterton and moved down the room.

Jed Midnight had witnessed the snub. He got close to Bond and said earnestly, "Mister, if that's your doll, you better watch her. Pussy gets the girls she wants. She consumes them in bunches—like grapes, if you follow me." Mr Midnight sighed wearily. "Cheesus how they bore me, the lizzies! You'll see, she'll soon have that frail parting her hair three ways in front of the mirror."

Bond said cheerfully, "I'll watch out. There's nothing much I can do. She's an independent sort of a girl."

"That so?" said Mr Midnight with a spark of interest. "Well mebbe I can help to break it up." He straightened his tie. "I could go for that Masterton. She's sure got natural resources. See you around." He grinned at Bond and moved off down the room.

Bond was having a quiet square meal off caviar and champagne and thinking how well Goldfinger had handled the meeting when the door at the end of the room opened and one of the Koreans hurried in and went up to Goldfinger. Goldfinger bent his head to the whispered words. His face became grave. He rapped a fork on his glass of Saratoga Vichy.

"Gentlemen and madam." He looked sadly round the group. "I have received bad news. Our friend Mr Helmut Springer has met with an accident. He fell down the stairs. Death was instantaneous."

"Ho, ho!" Mr Ring's laugh was not a laugh. It was a hole in the face. "And what does that Slappy Hapgood, his torpedo, have to say about it?"

Goldfinger said gravely, "Alas, Mr Hapgood also fell down the stairs and has succumbed to his injuries."

Mr Solo looked at Goldfinger with new respect. He said softly, "Mister, you better get those stairs fixed before me and my friend Giulio come to use them."

Goldfinger said seriously, "The fault has been located. Repairs will be put in hand at once." His face grew thoughtful. "I fear these accidents may be misconstrued in Detroit."

Jed Midnight said cheerfully, "Don't give it a thought, mister. They love funerals up there. And it'll take a load off their minds. Old Hell wouldn't have lasted much longer. They been stoking the fires under him these twelve months." He appealed to Mr Strap who stood next to him. "Am I right, Jacko?"

"Sure, Jed," said Mr Strap sagely. "You got the score. Mr Helmut M. Springer had to be hit."

"Hit"—mobese for murder. When Bond at last got to bed that night, he couldn't wipe the word out of his mind. Oddjob had got the signal, a double ring, and Springer and his guard had got hit. There had been nothing Bond could have done about it—even if he had wanted to, and Mr Helmut Springer meant nothing to him, probably richly deserved to be hit anyway—but now some 59,998 other people were going to get hit unless he, and only he, could do something about it.

When the meeting of paramount hoods had broken up to go about their various duties, Goldfinger had dismissed the girl and kept Bond in the room. He told Bond to take notes and then for more than two hours went over the operation down to the smallest detail. When they came to the doping of the two reservoirs (Bond had to work out an exact timetable to ensure that the people of Fort Knox would all be 'under' in good time) Bond had asked for details of the drug and its speed of action.

"You won't have to worry about that."

"Why not? Everything depends on it."

"Mr Bond." Goldfinger's eyes had a faraway, withdrawn look. "I will tell you the truth because you will have no opportunity of passing it on. From now, Oddjob will not be more than a yard from your side and his orders will be strict and exact. So I can tell you that the entire population of Fort Knox will be dead or incapacitated by midnight on D-1. The substance that will be inserted in the water supply, outside the filter plant, will be a highly concentrated form of GB."

"You're mad! You don't really mean you're going to kill sixty thousand people!"

"Why not? American motorists do it every two years."

Bond stared into Goldfinger's face in fascinated horror. It couldn't be true! He couldn't mean it! He said tensely, "What's this GB?"

"GB is the most powerful of the Trilone group of nerve poisons. It was perfected by the Wehrmacht in 1943, but never used for fear of reprisals. In fact, it is a more effective instrument of destruction than the hydrogen bomb. Its disadvantage lies in the difficulty of applying it to the populace. The Russians captured the entire German stocks at Dyhernfurth on the Polish frontier. Friends of mine were able to supply me with the necessary quantities. Introduction through the water supply is an ideal method of applying it to a densely populated area."

Bond said, "Goldfinger, you're a lousy, —— bastard."

"Don't be childish. We have work to do."

Later, when they had got to the problem of transporting the tons of gold out of the town, Bond had had one last try. He said, "Goldfinger, you're not going to get this stuff away. Nobody's going to get their hundred tons of gold out of the place—let alone five hundred. You'll find yourself tearing down the Dixie Highway in a truck with a few gold bars loaded with gamma rays and the American Army on your tail. And you'll have killed sixty thousand people for that? The thing's farcical. Even if you do get a ton or two away, where the hell do you think you're going to hide it?"

"Mr Bond." Goldfinger's patience was infinite. "It just happens that a Soviet cruiser of the *Sverdlovsk* class will be visiting Norfolk, Virginia, on a goodwill cruise at that time. It sails from Norfolk on D+1. Initially by train and then by transporter convoy, my gold will arrive on board the cruiser by midnight on D-Day. I shall sail in the cruiser for Kronstadt. Everything has been carefully planned, every possible hitch has been foreseen. I have lived with this operation for five years. Now the time has come for the performance. I have tidied up my activities in England and Europe. Such small debris as remains of my former life can go to the scavengers who will shortly be sniffing on my trail. I shall be gone. I shall have emigrated and, Mr Bond, I shall have taken the golden heart of America with me. Naturally"—Goldfinger was indulgent—"this unique performance will not be immaculate. There has not been enough time for rehearsals. I need these clumsy gangsters with their guns and their men, but I could not bring them into the plan until the last moment. They will make mistakes. Conceivably they will have much trouble getting their own loot away. Some will be caught, others killed. I couldn't care less. These men are amateurs who were needed, so to speak, for the crowd scenes. They are extras, Mr Bond, brought in off the streets. What happens to them after the play is of no interest to me whatsoever. And now, on with the work. I shall need seven copies of all this by nightfall. Where were we . . . ?"

So in fact, reflected Bond feverishly, this was not only a Goldfinger operation with SMERSH in the background. SMERSH had even got the High Praesidium to play. This was Russia versus America with Goldfinger as the spearhead! Was it an act of war to steal something from another country? But who would know that Russia had the gold? No one, if the plan went off as Goldfinger intended. None of the gangsters had an inkling. To them Goldfinger was just another of them, another gangster, slightly larger than life-size. And Goldfinger's staff, his drivers for the golden convoy to the coast? Bond himself, and Tilly Masterton? Some would be killed, including him and the girl. Some, the Koreans for instance, would no doubt sail in the cruiser. Not a trace would be left, not a witness. It was modern piracy with all the old-time trimmings. Goldfinger was sacking Fort Knox as Bloody Morgan had sacked Panama. There was no difference except that the weapons and the techniques had been brought up to date.

And there was only one man in the whole world who could stop it. But how?

The next day was an unending blizzard of paper-work. Every half-hour a note would come in from Goldfinger's operations room asking for schedules of this, copies of that, estimates, timetables, lists of stores. Another typewriter was brought in, maps, reference books—anything that Bond requisitioned. But not once did Oddjob relax the extreme care with which he opened the door to Bond's knock, not once did his watchful eyes wander from Bond's eyes, hands, feet when he came into the room to bring meals or notes or supplies. There was no question of Bond and the girl being part of the team. They were dangerous slaves and nothing else.

Tilly Masterton was equally reserved. She worked like a machine—quick, willing, accurate, but uncommunicative. She responded with cool politeness to Bond's early attempts to make friends, share his thoughts with her. By the evening, he had learnt nothing about her except that she had been a successful amateur ice-skater in between secretarial work for

Unilevers. Then she had started getting star parts in ice-shows. Her hobby had been indoor pistol and rifle shooting and she had belonged to two marksman clubs. She had few friends. She had never been in love or engaged. She lived by herself in two rooms in Earls Court. She was twenty-four. Yes, she realized that they were in a bad fix. But something would turn up. This Fort Knox business was nonsense. It would certainly go wrong. She thought Miss Pussy Galore was 'divine'. She somehow seemed to count on her to get her out of this mess. Women, with a sniff, were rather good at things that needed finesse. Instinct told them what to do. Bond was not to worry about her. She would be all right.

Bond came to the conclusion that Tilly Masterton was one of those girls whose hormones had got mixed up. He knew the type well and thought they and their male counterparts were a direct consequence of giving votes to women and 'sex equality'. As a result of fifty years of emancipation, feminine qualities were dying out or being transferred to the males. Pansies of both sexes were everywhere, not yet completely homosexual, but confused, not knowing what they were. The result was a herd of unhappy sexual misfits— barren and full of frustrations, the women wanting to dominate and the men to be nannied. He was sorry for them, but he had no time for them. Bond smiled sourly to himself as he remembered his fantasies about this girl as they sped along the valley of the Loire. Entre Deux Seins indeed!

At the end of the day, there was a final note from Gold-finger:

Five principals and myself will leave La Guardia Airport tomorrow at 11 am in chartered plane flown by my pilots for aerial survey of Grand Slam. You will accompany. Masterton will remain. G.

Bond sat on the edge of his bed and looked at the wall. Then he got up and went to the typewriter. He worked for an hour, typing, single-spaced, on both sides of the sheet, exact details of the operation. He folded the sheet, rolled it to a small cylinder about the size of his little finger and sealed it carefully with gum. Next he typed on a slip of paper:

URGENT AND VITAL. REWARD OF FIVE THOUSAND DOLLARS IS GUARANTEED WITH NO QUESTIONS ASKED TO THE FINDER

Bond rolled this message round the cylinder, wrote $5000 REWARD in red ink on the outside, and stuck the little package down the centre of three inches of Scotch tape. Then he sat down again on the edge of the bed and carefully strapped the free ends of the Scotch tape down the inside of his thigh.

CHAPTER 20

JOURNEY INTO HOLOCAUST

"MISTER, Flying Control is buzzing us. Wants to know who we are. They say this is restricted air."

Goldfinger got up from his seat and went forward into the cockpit. Bond watched him pick up the hand microphone. His voice came back clearly over the quiet hum of the ten-seater Executive Beechcraft. "Good morning. This is Mr Gold of Paramount Pictures Corporation. We are carrying out an authorized survey of the territory for a forthcoming 'A' picture of the famous Confederate raid of 1861 which resulted in the capture of General Sherman at Muldraugh Hill. Yes, that's right. Cary Grant and Elizabeth Taylor in the lead. What's that? Clearance? Sure we've got clearance. Let me see now" (Goldfinger consulted nothing) "—yes, here it is. Signed by Chief of Special Services at the Pentagon. Sure, the Commanding Officer at the Armoured Centre will have a copy. Okay and thanks. Hope you'll enjoy the picture. 'Bye."

Goldfinger wiped the breezy expression off his face, handed over the microphone and came back into the cabin. He braced his legs and stood looking down at his passengers. "Well, gentlemen and madam, do you think you've seen enough? I think you'll agree it's all pretty clear and conforms with your copies of the town plan. I don't want to go much lower than six thousand. Perhaps we could make one more circuit and be off. Oddjob, get out the refreshments."

There was a mumble of comment and questions which Goldfinger dealt with one by one. Oddjob got up from Bond's side and walked down to the rear. Bond followed him and, under his hard, suspicious stare, went into the little lavatory and locked the door.

He sat down calmly and thought. There hadn't been a chance on the way down to La Guardia. He had sat with Oddjob in the back of an unobtrusive Buick saloon. The doors had been locked on them by the driver and the windows tightly closed. Goldfinger had ridden in front, the partition closed behind him. Oddjob had sat slightly sideways, his horn-ridged hands held ready on his thighs like heavy tools. He had not taken his eyes off Bond until the car had driven round the boundary to the charter hangars and come up alongside the private plane. Sandwiched between Goldfinger and Oddjob, Bond had had no alternative but to climb up the steps into the plane and take his seat with Oddjob beside him. Ten minutes later, the others had arrived. There was no communication with them except an exchange of curt greetings. They were all different now—no smart remarks, no unnecessary talk. These were men who had gone to war. Even Pussy Galore, in a black Dacron macintosh with a black leather belt, looked like some young S.S. guardsman. Once or twice in the plane she had turned and looked at Bond rather thoughtfully. But she hadn't answered his smile. Perhaps she just couldn't understand where Bond fitted in, who he was. When they got back to La Guardia there would be the same routine. It was now or never. But where? Among the leaves of lavatory paper? But they might be disturbed too soon or not for weeks. Would the ash-tray be emptied? Possibly not. But one thing would.

There was a rattle at the door-handle. Oddjob was getting restless. Perhaps Bond was setting fire to the plane. Bond called, "Coming, ape." He got up and lifted the seat. He tore the little package off the inside of his thigh and transferred it to the underside of the fore-edge of the seat. The seat would have to be lifted to get at the Elsan and that would certainly be looked to as soon as the plane got back to the hangar. The $5000 REWARD stared back at him boldly. Not even the most hasty cleaner could miss it. So long as no one preceded the cleaner. But Bond didn't think any of the passengers would lift the seat. The little compartment was too cramped to stand comfortably in. He softly put the seat down, ran some water in the basin, washed his face and smoothed his hair and walked out.

Oddjob was waiting angrily. He pushed past Bond, looked carefully round the lavatory and came out again, shutting the door. Bond walked back to his seat. Now the SOS was in the bottle and the bottle had been committed to the waves. Who would be the finder? How soon?

Everyone, down to the pilot and co-pilot, went to the blasted little lavatory before they got back on the ground. As each one came out, Bond expected to feel the cold nose of a gun in his neck, the harsh suspicious words, the crackle of the paper being unfolded. But at last they were back in the Buick and speeding over the Triborough into uptown Manhattan and then down the river on the parkway and in through the well-guarded doors of the warehouse and back to work.

Now it was a race—a race between Goldfinger's calm, unhurried, efficient machine and the tiny gunpowder trail Bond had lit. What was going on outside? During every hour of the next three days Bond's imagination followed what might be happening—Leiter telling his chief, the conference, the quick flight down to Washington, the FBI and Hoover, the Army, the President. Leiter insisting that Bond's conditions be adhered to, that no suspicious moves be made, no inquiries started, that no one moved an inch except according to some master plan that would operate on the day and get the whole gang into the bag so that not one of them escaped. Would they accept Bond's conditions or would they not dare take the chance? Had they talked across the Atlantic with M? Had M insisted that Bond should be somehow pulled out? No, M would see the point. He would agree that Bond's life must be disregarded. That nothing must jeopardize the big clean-up. They would have to get the two 'Japanese', of course, somehow beat out of them the code message Goldfinger would be waiting for on D-1.

Was that how it was going, or was it all a shambles? Leiter away on another assignment. "Who is this 007? What does it stand for? Some crazy loon. Hi, Smith, check on this, could you? Get down to the warehouse and take a look. Sorry, mister, no five grand for you. Here's car fare back to La Guardia. Afraid you've been hoaxed."

Or, worse still, had none of these things happened? Was the plane still standing in a corner of the field, unserviced?

Night and day, the torment of thoughts went through Bond's head while the work got cleared and the hours ticked by and the deadly machine whirred quietly on. D—1 came and flashed by in a last fever of activity. Then, in the evening, came the note from Goldfinger.

First phase of operation successful. Entrain as planned at midnight. Bring copies of all maps, schedules, operation orders. G.

In close formation, with Bond and Tilly Masterton— he in a white surgeon's coat, she dressed as a nurse—wedged in the middle, the Goldfinger contingent marched swiftly through the almost empty Concourse of Pennsylvania station and down to the waiting Special. Everyone, including Goldfinger, was wearing the conventional white garb and armbands of a medical field force and the dim platform was crowded with the ghostly waiting figures of the posses from the gangs. The silence and tension was appropriate for an emergency force hurrying to the scene of a disaster, and the stretcher and decontamination suits being loaded into the compartments added drama to the scene. The Superintendent was talking quietly with the senior physicians in the shape of Midnight, Strap, Solo and Ring. Nearby stood Miss Galore with a dozen pale-faced nurses who waited with eyes bent as if they stood beside an open grave. Without makeup, their exotic hair-do's tucked into dark blue Red Cross caps, they had been well rehearsed. They were giving an excellent performance—dutiful, merciful, dedicated to the relief of human suffering.

When the Superintendent saw Goldfinger and his party approaching he hurried up. "Dr Gold?" his face was grave. "I'm afraid the news coming through isn't too good. Guess it'll all be in the papers tonight. All trains held at Louisville, no reply from the depot at Fort Knox. But we'll get you through all right. God Almighty, Doctor! What's going on down there? People coming through from Louisville are talking about the Russians spraying something from the air. Of course"—the Superintendent looked keenly at

Goldfinger—"I'm not believing *that* kind of stuff. But what is it? Food poisoning?"

Goldfinger's face was solemn. He said in a kindly voice, "My friend, that's what we've got to find out. That's why we're being rushed down. If you want me to make a guess, but mark you it's only a guess, it's a form of sleeping sickness—trypanosomiasis we call it."

"That so?" the Superintendent was impressed by the sound of the malady. "Well, believe you me, Doctor, we're all mighty proud of you and your folks of the Emergency Force." He held out his hand, Goldfinger took it. "Best of luck, Doc; and now, if you'll get your men and the nurses on board, I'll have this train on its way just as quick as may be."

"Thank you, Superintendent. My colleagues and I will not forget your services." Goldfinger gave a short bow. His contingent moved on.

"Board!"

Bond found himself in a Pullman with Tilly Masterton across the aisle and the Koreans and Germans all around them. Goldfinger was in the front of the car talking cheerfully with his satraps. Miss Pussy Galore strolled by. She ignored the upturned face of Tilly Masterton but gave Bond the usual searching glance. There was a banging of doors being closed. Pussy Galore stopped and rested an arm on the back of the seat in front of Bond. She looked down at him. "Hullo, Handsome. Long time no see. Uncle doesn't seem to let you off the lead much."

Bond said, "Hullo, Beautiful. That outfit suits you fine. I'm feeling rather faint. How about doing a bit of nursing?"

The deep violet eyes examined him carefully. She said softly, "You know what, Mister Bond? I got a feeling there's something phoney about you. I got instincts, see? Just what are you and that doll"—she jerked her head back—"doing in this outfit?"

"We do all the work."

The train began to move. Pussy Galore straightened herself. She said, "Mebbe you do. But if any little thing goes wrong with this caper, for my money it'll be Handsome who knows why. Get me?"

She didn't wait for Bond's answer, but moved on down and joined the Chiefs of Staff meeting.

It was a confused, busy night. Appearances had to be kept up before the inquisitive, sympathetic eyes of the conductors. Last-minute conferences up and down the train had to wear the appearance of serious medical conclaves—no cigar smoking, no swearing, no spitting. Jealousies and competition between the gangs had to be kept under rigid control. The cold superiority of the Mafia, particularly vis-à-vis Jack Strap and his soft, easy living crowd from the West, might have led to gunplay if the chiefs hadn't been ready for trouble and constantly on the lookout for it. All these minor psychological factors had been foreseen by Goldfinger and prepared for. The women from the Cement Mixers were carefully segregated, there was no drinking and the gang chiefs kept their men occupied with further exact briefings, dummy exercises with maps and lengthy discussions about their escape plans with the gold. There was casual spying on each other's plans and Goldfinger was often called in to judge who should have which routes to the Mexican border, to the desert, to Canada. To Bond it was amazing that a hundred of the toughest crooks in America, on edge with excitement and greed, could be kept as quiet as they were. It was Goldfinger who had achieved the miracle. Apart from the calm, dangerous quality of the man, it was the minuteness of the planning and the confidence he exuded that calmed the battle nerves and created some sort of a team-spirit among the rival mobs.

As the iron gallop of the train stretched itself out through the flat lands of Pennsylvania, gradually the passengers fell into an uneasy, troubled sleep. But not Goldfinger or Oddjob. They remained awake and watchful and soon Bond gave up any idea he might have had of using one of his hidden knives on Oddjob and making a bid for freedom when the train slowed through a station or on an up-gradient.

Bond dozed fitfully, wondering, imagining, puzzling over the Superintendent's words. The Superintendent had certainly thought they were the truth, knew that Fort Knox was in emergency. Was his news from Louisville the truth or part of the giant cover plan that would be necessary to get every member of the conspiracy in the bag? If it was a cover plan, how meticulously had it been prepared? Would someone slip up? Would there be some ghastly bungle that would warn Goldfinger in time? Or if the news was true, if the poison had been successful, what did there remain for Bond to do?

Bond had made up his mind on one score. Somehow, in the excitement of H-Hour, he would get close to Goldfinger and cut his throat with one of his hidden knives. How much would that achieve apart from an act of private vengeance? Would Goldfinger's squad accept another man's order to arm the warhead and fire it? Who would be strong enough, cool enough to take over? Mr Solo? Probably. The operation would perhaps be half successful, they would get away with plenty of gold—except Goldfinger's men who would be lost without him to lead them. And in the meantime, whatever else Bond could now do, had sixty thousand people already died? Was there anything he could have done to prevent that? Had there ever been a chance to kill Goldfinger? Would it have done any good to make a scene at Pennsylvania Station? Bond stared at his dark reflection in the window, listened to the sweet ting of the grade-crossing bells and the howl of the windhorn clearing their way, and shredded his nerves with doubts, questions, reproaches.

CHAPTER 21

THE RICHEST MAN IN HISTORY

SLOWLY THE red dawn broke over the endless plain of black grass that gradually turned to the famous Kentucky blue as the sun ironed out the shadows. At six o'clock the train began to slacken speed and soon they were gliding gently through the waking suburbs of Louisville to come to rest with a sigh of hydraulics in the echoing, almost deserted station.

A small, respectful group was awaiting them. Goldfinger, his eyes black-ringed with lack of sleep, beckoned to one of the Germans, picked up his authoritative little black bag and stepped down on to the platform. There was a short, serious conclave, the Louisville Superintendent doing the talking and Goldfinger interjecting a few questions and nodding gravely at the answers. Goldfinger turned wearily

back to the train. Mr Solo had been deputed to take his report.
He stood at the open door at the end of the Pullman. Bond
heard Goldfinger say sorrowfully, "I am afraid, Doctor, the
situation is as bad as we feared. I will now go forward to the
leading diesel with this," he held up the black bag, "and
we will proceed slowly into the infected area. Would you
please tell all personnel to be prepared to put on their masks?
I have masks for the driver and fireman. All other railway personnel will leave the train here."

Mr Solo nodded solemnly. "Right, Professor." He closed
his door. Goldfinger walked off down the platform followed
by his German strong-arm man and the respectful, head-
shaking group.

There was a short pause and then silently, almost reverently,
the long train whispered its way out of the station leaving
the little group of officials, now reinforced by four rather
shamefaced conductors, with hands raised in benediction.

Thirty-five miles, half an hour, to go! Coffee and dough-
nuts were brought round by the nurses, and (Goldfinger
thought of everything) for those whose nerves needed it,
two grains of dexedrine. The nurses were pale, silent. There
were no jokes, no smart remarks. The train was electric
with tension.

After ten minutes there was a sudden slackening of speed
and a sharp hiss from the brakes. Coffee was spilled. The
train almost stopped. Then there was a jerk and it gathered
speed again. A new hand had taken over on the dead man's
handle.

A few minutes later, Mr Strap came hurrying through
the train. "Ten minutes to go! On your toes, folks! Squads
A, B and C get their equipment on. Everything's going
fine. Stay calm. Remember your duties." He hurried through
to the next compartment and Bond heard the voice repeating its message.

Bond turned to Oddjob. "Listen, you ape, I'm going to
the lavatory and probably Miss Masterton will too." He
turned to the girl. "What about it, Tilly?"

"Yes," she said indifferently, "I suppose I'd better."

Bond said, "Well, go ahead."

The Korean beside the girl looked inquiringly at Oddjob.
Oddjob shook his head.

Bond said, "Unless you leave her alone I'm going to

start a fight. Goldfinger won't like that." He turned to the girl. "Go ahead, Tilly. I'll see to these apes."

Oddjob uttered a series of barks and snarls which the other Korean seemed to understand. The guard got up and said, "Okay, but not locking the door." He followed the girl down the Pullman and stood and waited for her to come out.

Oddjob carried out the same routine with Bond. Once inside, Bond took off his right shoe, slid out the knife and slipped it down inside the waist-band of his trousers. One shoe would now have no heel, but no one was going to notice that this morning. Bond washed himself. The face in the mirror was pale and the blue-grey eyes dark with tension. He went out and back to his seat.

Now there was a distant shimmer away to the right and a hint of low buildings rising like a mirage in the early morning ground mist. They slowly defined themselves as hangars with a squat control tower. Godman Field! The soft pounding howl of the train slackened. Some trim modern villas, part of a new housing development, slid by. They seemed to be unoccupied. Now, on the left, there was the black ribbon of Brandenburg Station Road. Bond craned. The gleaming modern sprawl of Fort Knox looked almost soft in the light mist. Above its jagged outline the air was clear as crystal—not a trace of smoke, no breakfasts cooking! The train slowed to a canter. On Station Road there had been a bad motor accident. Two cars seemed to have met head on. The body of a man sprawled half out of a smashed door. The other car lay on its back like a dead beetle. Bond's heart pounded. The main signal box came and went. Over the levers something white was draped. It was a man's shirt. Inside the shirt the body hung down, its head below the level of the window. A row of modern bungalows. A body clad in singlet and trousers flat on its face in the middle of a trim lawn. The lines of mown grass were beautifully exact until, near the man, the mower had written an ugly flourish and had then come to rest on its side in the newly turned earth of the border. A line of washing that had broken when the woman had grasped it. The woman lay in a white pile at one end of the sagging string of family underclothes, cloths and towels. And now the train was moving at walking pace into the town and everywhere, down every street, on every sidewalk, there were the sprawling figures—singly, in clumps, in rocking-chairs on the porches, in the middle of intersections where the traffic lights still unhurriedly ticked off their coloured signals, in cars that had managed to pull up and in others that had smashed into shop windows. Death! Dead people everywhere. No movement, no sound save the click of the murderer's iron feet as his train slid through the graveyard.

Now there was bustle in the carriages. Billy Ring came through grinning hugely. He stopped by Bond's chair. "Oh boy!" he said delightedly, "old Goldie certainly slipped them the Micky Finn! Too bad some people were out for a ride when they got hit. But you know what they say about omelettes: can't make 'em without you break some eggs, right?"

Bond smiled tightly. "That's right."

Billy Ring made his silent O of a laugh and went on his way.

The train trundled through Brandenburg Station. Now there were scores of bodies—men, women, children, soldiers. The platform was scribbled with them, faces upwards to the roof, down in the dust, cradled sideways. Bond searched for movement, for an inquisitive eye, for a twitching hand. Nothing! Wait! What was that? Thinly through the closed window there came a soft, mewing wail. Three perambulators stood against the ticket office, the mothers collapsed beside them. Of course! The babies in the perambulators would have drunk milk, not the deadly water.

Oddjob got to his feet. So did the whole of Goldfinger's team. The faces of the Koreans were indifferent, unchanged, only their eyes flickered constantly like nervous animals. The Germans were pale, grim. Nobody looked at anyone else. Silently they filed towards the exit and lined up, waiting.

Tilly Masterton touched Bond's sleeve. Her voice trembled. "Are you sure they're only asleep? I thought I saw some sort of . . . sort of froth on some of the lips."

Bond had seen the same thing. The froth had been pink. He said, "I expect some of them were eating sweets or something when they fell asleep. You know what these Americans are—always chewing something." He softly mouthed the next words. "Stay away from me. There may be shooting." He looked hard at her to see she understood.

She nodded dumbly, not looking at him. She whispered

out of the corner of her mouth, "I'm going to get near Pussy. She'll look after me."

Bond gave her a smile and said "Good", encouragingly.

The train clicked slowly over some points and slid to rest. There came one blast of the diesel's windhorn. The doors swung open and the different groups piled out on to the platform of the Bullion Depository siding.

Now everything went with military precision. The various squads formed up in their battle order—first an assault group with sub-machine guns, then the stretcher-bearers to get the guard and other personnel out of the vault (surely an unnecessary refinement now, thought Bond) then Goldfinger's demolition team—ten men with their bulky tarpaulin-covered package—then a mixed group of spare drivers and traffic-control men, then the group of nurses, now all armed with pistols, who were to stay in the background with a heavily armed reserve group that was to deal with any unexpected interference from anybody who, as Goldfinger had put it, "might wake up".

Bond and the girl had been included in the Command Group which consisted of Goldfinger, Oddjob and the five gang leaders. They were to be stationed on the flat roofs of the two diesel locomotives which now stood, as planned, beyond the siding buildings and in full view of the objective and its approaches. Bond and the girl were to handle the maps, the timetables and the stop-watch, and Bond was to watch out for fumbles and delays and bring them at once to Goldfinger's attention to be rectified by walkie-talkie with the squad leaders. When the bomb was due to be fired, they would take shelter behind the diesels.

There came a double blast from the windhorn and, as Bond and the girl climbed to their position on the roof of the first diesel, the assault squad, followed by the other sections, doubled across the twenty yards of open ground between the railway and Bullion Boulevard. Bond edged as close as he could to Goldfinger. Goldfinger had binoculars to his eyes. His mouth was close to the microphone strapped to his chest. But Oddjob stood between them, a solid mountain of flesh, and his eyes, uninterested in the drama of the assault, never flickered from Bond and the girl.

Bond, under cover of scanning his plastic map-case and keeping an eye on the stop-watch, measured inches and angles. He glanced at the next-door group of the four men and the woman. They were gazing, in frozen attention, at the scene before them. Now Jack Strap said excitedly, "They're through the first gates." Bond, putting half his mind to work on his own plans, took a quick look at the battlefield.

It was an extraordinary scene. In the centre stood the huge squat mausoleum, the sun glinting off the polished granite of its walls. Outside the big open field in which it stood, the roads—the Dixie Highway, Vine Grove and Bullion Boulevard—were lined with trucks and transporters two deep with the recognition flags of the gangs flying from the first and last vehicle of each convoy. Their drivers lay piled up outside the shelter of the surrounding guard wall of the vault while, through the main gate, poured the tidy disciplined squads from the train. Outside this world of movement there was absolute stillness and silence as if the rest of America was holding its breath at the committal of this gigantic crime. And outside lay the bodies of the soldiers, sprawling where they had fallen—the sentries by their pill boxes, still clutching their automatic pistols, and, inside the protecting wall, two ragged squads of soldiers in battledress. They lay in vague, untidy heaps, some bodies athwart or on top of their neighbours. Outside, between Bullion Boulevard and the main gate, two armoured cars had crashed into each other and now stood locked, their heavy machine guns pointing, one at the ground and the other at the sky. A driver's body sprawled out of the turret of one of the vehicles.

Desperately Bond looked for a sign of life, a sign of movement, a hint that all this was a careful ambush. Nothing! Not a cat moved, not a sound came out of the crowded buildings that formed a backdrop to the scene. Only the squads hurried about their tasks or now stood waiting in their planned dispositions.

Goldfinger spoke quietly into his microphone. "Last stretcher out. Bomb squad ready. Prepare to take cover."

Now the covering troops and the stretcher-bearers were hurrying for the exit, getting down under cover of the guard wall. There would be five minutes' delay to clear the area before the bomb squad, now waiting bunched at the main gate, would go in.

Bond said efficiently, "They're a minute ahead of time."

Goldfinger looked past Oddjob's shoulder. The pale eyes were aflame. They stared into Bond's. Goldfinger's mouth twisted into a harsh snarl. He said through his teeth, "You see, Mr Bond. You were wrong and I was right. Ten more minutes and I shall be the richest man in the world, the richest man in history! What do you say to that?" His mouth spat out the words.

Bond said equably, "I'll tell you after those ten minutes are up."

"Will you?" said Goldfinger. "Maybe." He looked at his watch and spoke rapidly into his microphone. The Goldfinger squad loped slowly through the main gate, their heavy burden slung from four shoulders in a cradle of webbing.

Goldfinger looked past Bond at the group on the roof of the second diesel. He called out triumphantly, "Another five minutes, gentlemen, and then we must take cover." He turned his eyes on Bond and added softly, "And then we will say goodbye, Mr Bond. And thank you for the assistance you and the girl have given me."

Out of the corner of his eye, Bond saw something moving—moving in the sky. It was a black, whirling speck. It reached the top of its trajectory, paused and then came the ear-splitting crack of a maroon signal.

Bond's heart leapt. A quick glance showed him the ranks of dead soldiers springing to life, the machine guns on the locked armoured cars swinging to cover the gates. A loudspeaker roared from nowhere, "Stand where you are. Lay down your arms." But there came a futile crackle of fire from one of the rearguard covering party and then all hell broke loose.

Bond seized the girl round the waist and jumped with her. It was a tenfoot drop to the platform. Bond broke his fall with his left hand and hoisted the girl to her feet with a jerk of his hip. As he began to run, close to the train for cover, he heard Goldfinger shout, "Get them and kill them." A splatter of lead from Goldfinger's automatic whipped at the cement to his left. But Goldfinger would have to shoot left handed. It was Oddjob that Bond feared. Now, as Bond tore down the platform with the girl's hand in his, he heard the lightning scuffle of the running feet.

The girl's hand tugged at him. She screamed angrily, "No, No. Stop! I want to stay close to Pussy. I'll be safe with her."

Bond shouted back, "Shut up, you little fool! Run like hell!" But now she was dragging at him, checking his speed. Suddenly she tore her hand out of his and made to dart into an open Pullman door. Christ, thought Bond, that's torn it! He whipped the knife out of his belt and swirled to meet Oddjob.

Ten yards away Oddjob hardly paused in his rush. One hand whipped off his ridiculous, deadly hat, a glance to take aim and the black steel half-moon sang through the air. Its edge caught the girl exactly at the nape of the neck. Without a sound she fell backwards on to the platform in Oddjob's path. The hurdle was just enough to put Oddjob off the flying high kick he had started to launch at Bond's head. He turned the kick into a leap, his left hand cutting the air towards Bond like a sword. Bond ducked and struck upwards and sideways with his knife. It got home somewhere near the ribs but the momentum of the flying body knocked the knife out of his hand. There was a tinkle on the platform. Now Oddjob was coming back at him, apparently unharmed, his hands outstretched and his feet splayed back ready for another leap or a kick. His blood was up. The eyes were red and there was a fleck of saliva at the open, panting mouth.

Above the boom and rattle of the guns outside the station, three blasts sounded on the diesel's windhorn. Oddjob snarled angrily and leapt. Bond dived at full length sideways. Something hit him a gigantic blow on the shoulder and sent him sprawling. Now, he thought as he hit the ground, now the death stroke! He scrambled clumsily to his feet, his neck hunched into his shoulders to break the impact. But no blow came and Bond's dazed eyes took in the figure of Oddjob flying away from him up the platform.

Already the leading diesel was on the move. Oddjob got to it and leapt for the footplate. For a moment he hung, his legs scrabbling for a foothold. Then he had disappeared into the cabin and the huge streamlined engine gathered speed.

Behind Bond the door of the quartermaster's office burst open. There was the hammer of running feet and a yell

"Santiago!"—St James, the battle-cry of Cortez that Leiter had once jokingly allotted to Bond.

Bond swivelled. The straw-haired Texan, clad in his wartime Marine Corps battledress, was pounding up the platform followed by a dozen men in khaki. He carried a one-man bazooka by the steel hook he used for a right hand. Bond ran to meet him. He said, "Don't shoot my fox, you bastard. Give over." He snatched the bazooka out of Leiter's hand and threw himself down on the platform, splaying out his legs. Now the diesel was two hundred yards away and about to cross the bridge over the Dixie Highway. Bond shouted "Stand clear!" to get the men out of line of the recoil flash, clicked up the safe and took careful aim. The bazooka shuddered slightly and the ten-pound armour-piercing rocket was on its way. There was a flash and a puff of blue smoke. Some bits of metal flew off the rear of the flying engine. But then it had crossed the bridge and taken the curve and was away.

"Not bad for a rookie," commented Leiter. "May put the rear diesel out, but those jobs are twins and he can make it on the forward engine."

Bond got to his feet. He smiled warmly into the hawk-like, slate-grey eyes. "You bungling oaf," he said sarcastically, "why in hell didn't you block that line?"

"Listen, shamus. If you've got any complaints about the stage management you can tell them to the President. He took personal command of this operation and it's a honey. There's a spotter plane overhead now. They'll pick up the diesel and we'll have old Goldilocks in the hoosegow by midday. How were we to know he was going to stay aboard the train?" He broke off and thumped Bond between the shoulderblades. "Hell, I'm glad to see you. These men and I were detailed off to give you protection. We've been dodging around looking for you and getting shot at by both sides for our pains." He turned to the soldiers. "Ain't that right, men?"

They laughed. "Sure is, Cap'n."

Bond looked affectionately at the Texan with whom he had shared so many adventures. He said seriously, "Bless you, Felix. You've always been good at saving my life. It was darn nearly too late this time. I'm afraid Tilly Masterton's had it." He walked off up the train with Felix at his heels.

The little figure still lay sprawled where she had fallen. Bond knelt beside her. The broken-doll angle of the head was enough. He felt for her pulse. He got up. He said softly, "Poor little bitch. She didn't think much of men." He looked defensively at Leiter. "Felix, I could have got her away if she'd only followed me."

Leiter didn't understand. He put his hand on Bond's arm and said, "Sure kid. Take it easy." He turned to his men. "Two of you carry the girl into the QM's office over there. O'Brien, you go for the ambulance. When you've done that, stop over at the Command post and give 'em the facts. Say we've got Commander Bond and I'll bring him right over."

Bond stood and looked down at the little empty tangle of limbs and clothes. He saw the bright, proud girl with the spotted handkerchief round her hair in the flying TR3. Now she had gone.

High up over his head a whirling speck soared into the sky. It reached the top of its flight and paused. There came the sharp crack of the maroon. It was the cease-fire.

CHAPTER 22

THE LAST TRICK

IT WAS two days later. Felix Leiter was weaving the black Studillac fast through the lanes of dawdling traffic on the Triborough bridge. There was plenty of time to catch Bond's plane, the evening BOAC Monarch to London, but Leiter enjoyed shaking up Bond's low opinion of American cars. Now the steel hook that he used for a right hand banged the gear lever into second and the low black car leapt for a narrow space between a giant refrigerator truck and a mooning Oldsmobile whose rear window was almost obscured by holiday stickers.

Bond's body jerked back with the kick of the 300 b.h.p. and his teeth snapped shut. When the manoeuvre was completed, and the angry hooting had vanished behind them, Bond said mildly, "It's time you graduated out of the Kiddicar class and bought yourself an express carriage. You want to get cracking. This pedalling along ages one. One of these days you'll stop moving altogether and when you stop moving is when you start to die."

Leiter laughed. He said, "See that green light ahead? Bet I can make it before it goes red." The car leapt forward as if it had been kicked. There was a brief hiatus in Bond's life, an impression of snipe-like flight and of a steel wall of cars that somehow parted before the whiplash of Leiter's triple klaxons, a hundred yards when the speedometer touched ninety and they were across the lights and cruising genteelly along in the centre lane.

Bond said calmly, "You meet the wrong traffic cop and that Pinkerton card of yours won't be good enough. It isn't so much that you drive slowly, it's holding back the cars behind they'll book you for. The sort of car you need is a nice elderly Rolls Royce Silver Ghost with big plate-glass windows so you can enjoy the beauties of nature"— Bond gestured towards a huge automobile junk heap on their right. "Maximum fifty and it can stop and even go backwards if you want to. Bulb horn. Suit your sedate style. Matter of fact there should be one on the market soon—Goldfinger's. And by the same token, what the hell's happened to Goldfinger? Haven't they caught up with him yet?"

Leiter glanced at his watch and edged into the outside lane. He brought the car down to forty. He said seriously, "Tell you the truth, we're all a bit worried. The papers are needling us, or rather Edgar Hoover's crowd, like hell. First they had a gripe at the security clamp-down on you. We couldn't tell them that wasn't our fault and that someone in London, an old limey called M, had insisted on it. So they're getting their own back. Say we're dragging our feet and so forth. And I'm telling you, James"—Leiter's voice was glum, apologetic—"we just haven't a clue. They caught up with the diesel. Goldfinger had fixed the controls at thirty and had let it run on down the line. Somewhere he and the Korean had got off and probably this Galore girl and the four hoods as well because they've vanished too. We found his truck convoy, of course, waiting on the east-bound highway out of Elizabethville. But never a driver. most probably scattered, but somewhere there's Goldfinger and a pretty tough team hiding up. They didn't get to the *Sverdlovsk* cruiser at Norfolk. We had a plain-clothes guard scattered round the docks and they report that she sailed to schedule without any strangers going aboard. Not a cat's been near that warehouse on East River, and no one's shown at Idlewild or the frontiers—Mexico and Canada. For my money, that Jed Midnight has somehow got them out to Cuba. If they'd taken two or three trucks from the convoy and driven like hell they could have got down to Florida, somewhere like Daytona Beach, by the early hours of D+1. And Midnight's darn well organized down there. The Coast Guards and the Air Force have put out all they've got, but nothing's shown yet. But they could have hidden up during the day and got over to Cuba during the night. It's got everybody worried as hell and it's no help that the President's hopping mad."

Bond had spent the previous day in Washington treading the thickest, richest red carpet. There had been speeches at the Bureau of the Mint, a big brass lunch at the Pentagon, an embarrassing quarter of an hour with the President, and the rest of the day had been hard work with a team of stenographers in Edgar Hoover's suite of offices with a colleague of Bond's from Station A sitting in. At the end of that, there had been a brisk quarter of an hour's talk with M on the Embassy transatlantic scrambler. M had told him what had been happening on the European end of the case. As Bond had expected, Goldfinger's cable to Universal Export had been treated as emergency. The factories at Reculver and Coppet had been searched and extra evidence of the gold smuggling racket had been found. The Indian Government had been warned about the Mecca plane that was already en route for Bombay and that end of the operation was on the way to being cleaned up. The Swiss Special Brigade had quickly found Bond's car and had got on to the route by which Bond and the girl had been taken to America, but there, at Idlewild, the FBI had lost the scent. M seemed pleased with the way Bond had handled Operation Grand Slam, but he said the Bank of England were worrying him about Goldfinger's twenty million pounds in gold. Goldfinger had assembled all this at the Paragon Safe Deposit Co in New York but had withdrawn it on D−1. He and his men had driven it away in a covered truck. The Bank of England had ready an Order in Council to impound the gold when it was found and there would then be a case to prove that it had been smuggled out of England, or at least that it was originally smuggled gold whose value had been increased by various doubtful means. But this was now being handled by the US Treasury and the FBI and, since M had no jurisdiction in America, Bond had better come home at once and help tidy things up. Oh yes—at the end of the conversation M's voice had sounded gruff—there had been a very kind request to the PM that Bond should be allowed to accept the American Medal of Merit. Of course M had had to explain via the PM that the Service didn't go in for those sort of things—particularly from foreign countries, however friendly they were. Too bad, but M knew that this was what Bond would have expected. He knew the rules. Bond had said yes of course and thank you very much and he'd take the next plane home.

Now, as they motored quietly down the Van Wyck Expressway, Bond was feeling vaguely dissatisfied. He didn't like leaving ragged ends to a case. None of the big gangsters had been put in the bag and he had failed in the two tasks he had been given, to get Goldfinger and get Goldfinger's bullion. It was nothing but a miracle that Operation Grand Slam had been broken. It had been two days before the Beechcraft had been serviced and the cleaner who found the note had got to Pinkerton's only half an hour before Leiter was due to go off to the Coast on a big racing scandal. But then Leiter had really got cracking—to his chief, then to the FBI and the Pentagon. The FBI's knowledge of Bond's record, plus contact with M through the Central Intelligence Agency, had been enough to get the whole case up to the President within an hour. After that it had just been a case of building up the gigantic bluff in which all the inhabitants of Fort Knox had participated in one way or another. The two 'Japanese' had been taken easily enough and it was confirmed by Chemical Warfare that the three pints of GB carried as gin in their briefcases would have been enough to slay the entire population of Fort Knox. The two men had been quickly and forcibly grilled into explaining the form of the all clear cable to Goldfinger. The cable had been sent. Then the Army had declared emergency. Road and rail and air blocks had turned back all traffic to the Fort Knox area with the exception of the gangster convoys which had not been hindered. The rest was play-acting right down to the pink froth and the squalling babies which it was thought would add nice touches of verisimilitude.

Yes, it had all been very satisfactory so far as Washington was concerned, but what about the English end? Who in America cared about the Bank of England's gold? Who cared that two English girls had been murdered in the course of this business? Who really minded that Goldfinger was still at liberty now that America's bullion was safe again?

They idled across the drab plain of Idlewild, past the ten-million-dollar steel and cement skeletons that would one day be an adult airport, and pulled up outside the make-shift huddle of concrete boxes that Bond knew so well. Already the well mannered iron voices were reaching out to them. "Pan American World Airways announces the departure of its President Flight PA 100", "Transworld Airways calling Captain Murphy. Captain Murphy, please." And the pear-shaped voweis and fluted diction of BOAC, "BOAC announces the arrival of its Bermudan Flight BA 491. Passengers will be disembarking at gate number neyne."

Bond took his bag and said goodbye to Leiter. He said, "Well, thanks for everything, Felix. Write to me every day."

Leiter gripped his hand hard. He said, "Sure thing, kid. And take it easy. Tell that old bastard M to send you back over soon. Next visit we'll take some time off from the razzmatazz. Time you called in on my home state. Like to have you meet my oil-well. 'Bye now."

Leiter got into his car and accelerated away from the arrival bay. Bond raised his hand. The Studillac dry-skidded out on to the approach road. There was an answering glint from Leiter's steel hook out of the window and he was gone.

Bond sighed. He picked up his bag and walked in and over to the BOAC ticket counter.

Bond didn't mind airports so long as he was alone in them. He had half an hour to wait and he was quite content to wander through the milling crowds, have a bourbon and soda at the restaurant and spend some time choosing something to read at the bookstore. He bought Ben Hogan's *Modern Fundamentals of Golf* and the latest Raymond Chandler and sauntered along to the Souvenir Shop to see if he could find an amusing gimmick to take back to his secretary.

Now there was a man's voice on the BOAC announcing system. It called out a long list of Monarch passengers who were required at the ticket counter. Ten minutes later Bond was paying for one of the latest and most expensive ball-point pens when he heard his own name being called. "Will Mr James Bond, passenger on BOAC Monarch flight No 510 to Gander and London, please come to the BOAC ticket counter. Mr James Bond, please." It was obviously that infernal tax form to show how much he had earned during his stay in America. On principle Bond never went to the Internal Revenue Office in New York to get clearance and he had only once had to argue it out at Idlewild. He went out of the shop and across to the BOAC counter. The official said politely, "May I see your health certificate, please, Mr Bond?"

Bond took the form out of his passport and handed it over.

The man looked at it carefully. He said, "I'm very sorry, sir, but there's been a typhoid case at Gander and they're insisting that all transit passengers who haven't had their shots in the last six months should be topped up. It's most annoying, sir, but Gander's very touchy about these things. Too bad we couldn't have managed a direct flight, but there's a strong head-wind."

Bond hated inoculations. He said irritably, "But look here, I'm stuffed with shots of one kind or another. Been having them for twenty years for one damned thing or another!" He looked round. The area near the BOAC departure gate seemed curiously deserted. He said, "What about the other passengers? Where are they?"

"They've all agreed, sir. Just having their shots now. It won't take a minute, sir, if you'll come this way."

"Oh well." Bond shrugged his shoulders impatiently. He followed the man behind the counter and through a door to the BOAC station manager's office. There was the usual white-clothed doctor, a mask over the bottom of his face, the needle held ready. "Last one?" he asked of the BOAC official.

"Yes, Doctor."

"Okay. Coat off and left sleeve up, please. Too bad they're so sensitive up at Gander."

"Damned sight too bad," said Bond. "What are they afraid of? Spreading the black death?"

There came the sharp smell of the alcohol and the jab of the needle.

"Thanks," said Bond gruffly. He pulled down his sleeve and made to pick his coat up from the back of the chair. His hand went down for it, missed it, went on down, down towards the floor. His body dived after the hand, down, down, down . . .

All the lights were on in the plane. There seemed to be plenty of spare places. Why did he have to get stuck with a passenger whose arm was hogging the central arm-rest. Bond made to get up and change his seat. A wave of nausea swept over him. He closed his eyes and waited. How extraordinary! He was never air-sick. He felt the cold sweat on his face. Handkerchief. Wipe it off. He opened his eyes again and looked down at his arms. The wrists were bound to the arms of his chair. What had happened? He had had his shot and then passed out or something. Had he got violent? What the hell was all this about? He glanced to his right and then stared, aghast. Oddjob was sitting there. Oddjob! Oddjob in BOAC uniform!

Oddjob glanced incuriously at him and reached for the steward's bell. Bond heard the pretty ding-dong back in the pantry. There was the rustle of a skirt beside him. He looked up. It was Pussy Galore, trim and fresh in the blue uniform of a stewardess! She said, "Hi, Handsome." She gave him the deep, searching look he remembered so well from when? From centuries ago, in another life.

Bond said desperately, "For Christ's sake, what's going on? Where did you come from?"

The girl smiled cheerfully, "Eating caviar and drinking champagne. You Britishers sure live the life of Reilly when you get up twenty thousand feet. Not a sign of a Brussels sprout and if there's tea I haven't got around to it yet. Now, you take it easy. Uncle wants to talk to you." She sauntered up the aisle, swinging her hips, and disappeared through the cockpit door.

Now nothing could surprise Bond. Goldfinger, in a BOAC captain's uniform that was rather too large for him, the cap squarely on the entre of his head, closed the cockpit door behind him and come down the aisle.

He stood and looked grimly down at Bond. "Well, Mr Bond. So Fate wished us to play the game out. But this time, Mr Bond, there cannot possibly be a card up your sleeve. Ha!" The sharp bark was a mixture of anger, stoicism and respect. "You certainly turned out to be a snake in my pastures." The great head shook slowly. "Why I kept you alive! Why I didn't crush you like a beetle! You and the girl were useful to me. Yes, I was right about that. But I was mad to have taken the chance. Yes, mad." The voice dropped and went slow. "And now tell me, Mr Bond. How did you do it? How did you communicate?"

Bond said equally, "We will have a talk, Goldfinger. And I will tell you certain things. But not until you have taken off these straps and brought me a bottle of bourbon, ice, soda water and a packet of Chesterfields. Then, when you have told me what I wish to know, I will decide what to tell you. As you say, my situation is not favourable, or at least it doesn't appear to be. So I have nothing to lose and if you want to get something out of me it will be on my own terms."

Goldfinger looked gravely down. "I have no objection to your conditions. Out of respect for your abilities as an opponent, you shall spend your last journey in comfort. Oddjob"—the voice was sharp. "Ring the bell for Miss Galore and undo those straps. Get into the seat in front. There is no harm he can do at the rear of the plane but he is not to approach the cockpit door. If need be, kill him at once, but I prefer to get him to our destination alive. Understood?"

"Arrgh."

Five minutes later Bond had what he wanted. The tray in front of him was down and on it were his whisky and cigarettes. He poured himself a stiff bourbon. Goldfinger was seated in the chair across the aisle, waiting. Bond picked up his drink and sipped it. He was about to take a deeper drink when he saw something. He put the glass carefully down without disturbing the little round paper coaster that had stuck to the bottom of his glass. He lit a cigarette, picked up his drink again and removed the ice-cubes and put them back in the ice bucket. He drank the whisky down almost to the end. Now he could read the words through the bottom of the glass. He carefully put the glass down without disturbing the coaster. The message had read, 'I'm with you. XXX. P.'

Bond turned and made himself comfortable. He said, "Now then, Goldfinger. First of all, what's going on, how did you get this plane, where are we heading?"

Goldfinger crossed one leg over the other. He gazed away from Bond, up the aisle. He said in a relaxed, conversational tone, "I took three trucks and drove across country to the vicinity of Cape Hatteras. One of the trucks contained my personal hoard of gold bullion. The other two contained my drivers, spare personnel and those gangsters. I required none of them except Miss Galore. I kept a nucleus of the staff I would need, paid off the others with huge sums and dispersed them gradually along the route. At the coast I held a meeting with the four gang leaders in a deserted place, having left Miss Galore under some pretext with the trucks. I shot the four men in my usual fashion—one bullet for each. I went back to the trucks and explained that the four men had chosen money and independent action. I was now left with six men, the girl and the bullion. I hired a plane and flew to Newark, New Jersey, the crates of gold being passed off as lead for X-ray plates. From there I proceeded alone to a certain address in New York from which I talked with Moscow by radio and explained the mishap to Operation Grand Slam. In the course of the talk I mentioned your name. My friends, whom I believe you know," Goldfinger looked hard at Bond, "pass under the generic name of SMERSH. They recognized the name of Bond and told me who you were. I at once understood a great deal of what had previously been hidden from me. SMERSH said they would greatly like to interview you. I pondered the matter. In due course I conceived the plan which you now see in operation. Posing as a friend of yours, I had no difficulty in finding out the flight on which you were booked. Three of my men were formerly of the Luftwaffe. They assured me there would be no difficulty in flying this plane. The rest was mere detail. By cool bluffing, impersonation and the use of a certain amount of force, all the BOAC personnel at Idlewild, the crew of this plane and the passengers were given the necessary injections from which they will now be recovering. We changed clothes with the unconscious crew, the bullion was loaded on the plane, you were dealt with and carried out on a stretcher and in due course the new BOAC crew, with their stewardess, boarded the plane and we took to the air."

Goldfinger paused. He lifted a hand resignedly. "Of course there were small hitches. We were told to 'follow taxiway Alpha to runway four', and it was only by following a KLM plane that we were successful. The Idlewild routine was not easy to master and we must have seemed somewhat clumsy and inexperienced, but, Mr Bond, with assurance, strong nerves and a gruff, intimidating manner it is never difficult to override the Civil Service mentality of what, after all, are minor employees. I understand from the wireless operator that a search for this plane is under way. They were already questioning us before we were out of VHF range at Nantucket. Then the Distant Early Warning system queried us on high frequency. That did not disturb me. We have enough fuel. We have already had clearance from Moscow for East Berlin, Kiev or Murmansk. We shall take whichever route the weather dictates. There should be no trouble. If there is, I shall talk my way out of it on the radio. No one is going to shoot down a valuable BOAC plane. The mystery and confusion will protect us until we are well within Soviet territory and then, of course, we shall have disappeared without trace."

To Bond there had been nothing fantastic, nothing impossible about Goldfinger since he had heard the details of Operation Grand Slam. The theft of a Stratocruiser, as Goldfinger had explained it, was preposterous, but no more so than his methods of smuggling gold, his purchase of an atomic warhead. When one examined these things, while they had a touch of magic, of genius even, they were logical exercises. They were bizarre only in their magnitude. Even the tiny manoeuvre of cheating Mr Du Pont had been quite brilliantly contrived. There was no doubt about it, Goldfinger was an artist—a scientist in crime as great in his field as Cellini or Einstein in theirs.

"And now, Mr Bond of the British Secret Service, we made a bargain. What have you to tell me? Who put you on to me? What did they suspect? How did you manage to interfere with my plans?" Goldfinger sat back, placed his hands across his stomach and looked at the ceiling.

Bond gave Goldfinger a censored version of the truth. He mentioned nothing about SMERSH or the location of the postbox and he said nothing about the secrets of the Homer, a device that might be new to the Russians. He concluded, "So you see, Goldfinger, you only just got away. But for Tilly Masterton's intervention at Geneva, you'd have been in the bag by now. You'd be sitting picking your teeth in a Swiss prison waiting to be sent to England. You underestimate the English. They may be slow, but they get there. You think you'll be pretty safe in Russia? I wouldn't be too sure. We've got people even out of there before now. I'll give you one last aphorism for your book, Goldfinger: 'Never go a bear of England.' "

CHAPTER 23

T.L.C. TREATMENT

THE PLANE throbbed on, high above the weather, over the great moonlit landscape. The lights had been turned out. Bond sat quietly in the darkness and sweated with fear at what he was going to do.

An hour before, the girl had brought him dinner. There was a pencil hidden in the napkin. She had made some tough remarks for the benefit of Oddjob and gone away. Bond had eaten some scraps of food and drunk a good deal of bourbon while his imagination hunted round the plane wondering what he could conceivably do to force an emergency landing at Gander or somewhere else in Nova Scotia. As a last resort, could he set fire to the plane? He toyed with the idea, and with the possibility of forcing the entrance hatch open. Both ideas seemed impracticable and suicidal. To save him the trouble of pondering over them, the man whom Bond had seen before at the BOAC ticket counter, one of the Germans, came through and stopped by Bond's chair.

He grinned down at Bond. "BOAC takes good care of you, isn't it? Mister Goldfinger thinks you might have foolish notions. I am to keep an eye on the rear of the plane. So just sit back and enjoy the ride, isn't it?"

When Bond didn't answer, the man went on back to the rear section.

Something was nagging at Bond's mind, something connected with his previous thoughts. That business about forcing the hatch. Now what was it that had happened to that plane, flying over Persia back in '57? Bond sat for a while and stared with wide, unseeing eyes at the back of the seat in front of him. It might work! It just conceivably might!

Bond wrote on the inside of the napkin, '*I'll do my best. Fasten your seat belt. XXX. J.*'

When the girl came to take his tray Bond dropped the napkin and then picked it up and handed it to her. He held her hand and smiled up into the searching eyes. She bent to pick up the tray. She kissed him quickly on the cheek. She straightened herself. She said toughly, "I'll see you in my dreams, Handsome," and went off to the galley.

And now Bond's mind was made up. He had worked out exactly what had to be done. The inches had been measured, the knife from his heel was under his coat and he had twisted the longest end of his seat belt round his left wrist. All he needed was one sign that Oddjob's body was turned away from the window. It would be too much to expect Oddjob to go to sleep, but at least he could make himself comfortable. Bond's eyes never left the dim profile he could see reflected in the Perspex oblong of the window of the seat in front, but Oddjob sat stolidly under the reading light he had prudently kept burning, his eyes staring at the ceiling, his mouth slightly open and his hands held ready and relaxed on the arms of his chair.

One hour, two hours. Bond began to snore, rhythmically, drowsily, he hoped hypnotically. Now Oddjob's hands had moved to his lap. The head nodded once and pulled itself up, shifted to get more comfortable, turned away from the piercing eye of light in the wall, rested on its left cheek away from the window!

Bond kept his snores exactly even. Getting under the Korean's guard would be as difficult as getting past a hungry mastiff. Slowly, inch by inch, he crouched forward on the balls of his feet and reached with his knife hand between the wall and Oddjob's seat. Now his hand was there. Now the needle-sharp tip of the dagger was aimed at the centre of the square inch of Perspex he had chosen. Bond grasped the end of his seat belt tightly in his hand, drew the knife back two inches and lunged.

Bond had had no idea what would happen when he cut through the window. All he knew from the Press reports of the Persian case was that the suction out of the pressurized cabin had whirled the passenger next to the window out through the window and into space. Now, as he whipped back his dagger, there was a fantastic howl, almost a scream of air, and Bond was sucked violently against the back of Oddjob's seat with a force that tore the end of the seat belt from his hand. Over the back of the seat he witnessed a miracle. Oddjob's body seemed to elongate towards the howling black aperture. There was a crash as his head went through and his shoulders hit the frame. Then, as if the Korean's body was toothpaste, it was slowly, foot by foot, sucked with a terrible whistling noise through the aperture. Now Oddjob was out to his waist. Now the huge buttocks stuck and the human paste moved only inch by inch. Then, with a loud boom, the buttocks got through and the legs disappeared as if shot from a gun.

After that came the end of the world. With an appalling crash of crockery from the galley, the huge plane stood on its nose and dived. The last thing Bond knew before he blacked out was the high scream of the engines through the open window and a fleeting vision of pillows and rugs whipping out into space past his eyes. Then, with a final desperate embrace of the seat in front, Bond's oxygen-starved body collapsed in a sear of lung pain.

The next thing Bond felt was a hard kick in the ribs. There was a taste of blood in his mouth. He groaned. Again the foot smashed into his body. Painfully he dragged himself to his knees between the seats and looked up through a red film. All the lights were on. There was a thin mist in the cabin. The sharp depressurization had brought the air in the cabin down below the dew-point. The roar of the engines through the open window was gigantic. An icy wind seared him. Goldfinger stood over him, his face fiendish under the yellow light. There was a small automatic dead steady in his hand. Goldfinger reached back his foot and kicked again. Bond lit with a blast of hot rage. He caught the foot and twisted it sharply, almost breaking the ankle. There came a scream from Goldfinger and a crash that shook the plane. Bond leapt for the aisle and threw himself sideways and down on to the heap of body. There was an explosion that burned the side of his face. But then his knee thudded into Goldfinger's groin and his left hand was over the gun.

For the first time in his life, Bond went berserk. With his fists and knees he pounded the struggling body while again and again he crashed his forehead down on to the glistening face. The gun came quavering towards him again. Almost indifferently Bond slashed sideways with the edge of his hand and heard the clatter of metal among the seats. Now Goldfinger's hands were at his throat and Bond's at Goldfinger's. Down, down went Bond's thumbs into the arteries. He threw all his weight forward, gasping for breath. Would he black out before the other man died? Would he? Could he stand the pressure of Goldfinger's strong hands? The glistening moon-face was changing. Deep purple showed through the tan. The eyes began to flicker up. The pressure of the hands on Bond's throat slackened. The hands fell away. Now the tongue came out and lolled from the open mouth and there came a terrible gargling from deep in the lungs. Bond sat astride the silent chest and slowly, one by one, unhinged his rigid fingers.

Bond gave a deep sigh and knelt and then stood slowly up. Dazedly he looked up and down the lighted plane. By the galley, Pussy Galore lay strapped in her seat like a heap of washing. Farther down, in the middle of the aisle, the guard lay spreadeagled, one arm and the head at ridiculous angles. Without a belt to hold him when the plane dived, he must have been tossed at the roof like a rag doll.

Bond brushed his hands over his face. Now he felt the burns on his palm and cheeks. Wearily he went down on his knees again and searched for the little gun. It was a Colt ·25 automatic. He flicked out the magazine. Three rounds left and one in the chamber. Bond half walked, half felt his way down the aisle to where the girl lay. He unbuttoned her jacket and put his hand against her warm breast. The heart fluttered like a pigeon under his palm.

He undid the seat belt and got the girl face down on the floor and knelt astride her. For five minutes he pumped rhythmically at her lungs. When she began to moan, he got up and left her and went on down the aisle and took a fully loaded Luger out of the dead guard's shoulder holster. On the way back past the shambles of the galley he saw an unbroken bottle of bourbon rolling gently to and fro among the wreckage. He picked it up and pulled the cork and tilted it into his open mouth. The liquor burned like disinfectant. He put the cork back and went forward. He stopped for a minute outside the cockpit door, thinking. Then, with a gun in each hand, he knocked the lever down and went through.

The five faces, blue in the instrument lights, turned towards him. The mouths made black holes and the eyes glinted white. Here the roar of the engines was less. There was a smell of fright-sweat and cigarette smoke. Bond stood with his legs braced, the guns held unwavering. He said, "Goldfinger's dead. If anyone moves or disobeys an order I shall kill him. Pilot, what's your position, course, height and speed?"

The pilot swallowed. He had to gather saliva before he could speak. He said, "Sir, we are about five hundred miles east of Goose Bay. Mr Goldfinger said we would ditch the plane as near the coast north of there as we could get. We were to reassemble at Montreal and Mr Goldfinger said we would come back and salvage the gold. Our ground speed is two hundred and fifty miles per hour and our height two thousand."

"How much flying can you do at that altitude? You must be using up fuel pretty fast."

"Yes, sir. I estimate that we have about two hours left at this height and speed."

"Get me a time signal."

The navigator answered quickly, "Just had one from Washington, sir. Five minutes to five am. Dawn at this level will be in about an hour."

"Where is Weathership Charlie?"

"About three hundred miles to the north-east, sir."

"Pilot, do you think you can make Goose Bay?"

"No, sir, by about a hundred miles. We can only make the coast north of there."

"Right. Alter course for Weathership Charlie. Operator, call them up and give me the mike."

"Yes, sir."

While the plane executed a wide curve, Bond listened to the static and broken snatches of voice that sounded from the amplifier above his head.

The operator's voice came softly to him, "Ocean Station Charlie. This is Speedbird 510. G-ALGY calling C for Charlie, G-ALGY calling Charlie, G-ALGY . . ."

A sharp voice broke in. "G-ALGY give your position. G-ALGY give your position. This is Gander Control. Emergency. G-ALGY . . ."

London came over faintly. An excited voice began chattering. Now voices were coming at them from all directions. Bond could imagine the fix being quickly co-ordinated at all flying control stations, the busy men under the arcs working on the big plot, telephones being lifted, urgent voices talking to each other across the world. The strong signal of Gander Control smothered all other transmissions. "We've located G-ALGY. We've got them at about 50 N by 70 E. All stations stop transmitting. Priority. I repeat, we have a fix on G-ALGY . . ."

Suddenly the quiet voice of C for Charlie came in. "This is Ocean Station Charlie calling Speedbird 510. Charlie calling G-ALGY. Can you hear me? Come in Speedbird 510."

Bond slipped the small gun into his pocket and took the offered microphone. He pressed the transmitter switch and talked quietly into it, watching the crew over the oblong of plastic.

"C for Charlie this is G-ALGY Speedbird hi-jacked last evening at Idlewild. I have killed the man responsible and partly disabled the plane by depressurizing the cabin. I have the crew at gunpoint. Not enough fuel to make Goose so propose to ditch as close to you as possible. Please put out line of flares."

A new voice, a voice of authority, perhaps the captain's, came over the air. "Speedbird this is C for Charlie. Your message heard and understood. Identify the speaker. I repeat identify the speaker over."

Bond said and smiled at the sensation his words would cause, "Speedbird to C for Charlie. This is British Secret

Service agent Number 007, I repeat Number 007. Whitehall Radio will confirm. I repeat check with Whitehall Radio over."

There was a stunned pause. Voices from round the world tried to break in. Some control, presumably Gander, cleared them off the air. C for Charlie came back, "Speedbird this is C for Charlie alias the Angel Gabriel speaking okay I'll check with Whitehall and Wilco the flares but London and Gander want more details ..."

Bond broke in, "Sorry C for Charlie but I can't hold five men in my sights and make polite conversation just give me the sea conditions would you and then I'm going off the air till we come in to ditch over."

"Okay Speedbird I see the point wind here force two sea conditions long smooth swell no broken crests you should make it okay I'll soon have you on the radar and we'll keep constant watch on your wavelength have whisky for one and irons for five waiting good luck over."

Bond said, "Thanks C for Charlie add a cup of tea to that order would you I've got a pretty girl on board this is Speedbird saying over and out."

Bond released the switch and handed the microphone to the radio officer. He said, "Pilot, they're putting down flares and keeping constant watch on our wavelength. Wind force two, long smooth swell with no broken crests. Now take it easy and let's try and get out of this alive. As soon as we hit the water I'll get the hatch open. Until then if anyone comes through the cockpit door he gets shot. Right?"

The girl's voice sounded from the door behind Bond. "I was just coming to join the party but I won't now. Getting shot doesn't agree with me. But you might call that man back and make it two whiskies. Tea makes me hiccup."

Bond said, "Pussy, get back to your basket." He gave a last glance round the cockpit and backed out of the door.

Two hours, two years, later Bond was lying in the warm cabin in Weathership Charlie listening dreamily to an early morning radio programme from Canada. Various parts of his body ached. He had got to the tail of the plane and made the girl kneel down with her head cradled in her arms on the seat of a chair. Then he had wedged himself in behind and over her and had held her life-jacketed body tightly in his arms and braced his back against the back of the seat behind him.

She had been nervously making facetious remarks about the indelicacy of this position when the belly of the Stratocruiser had thudded into the first mountain of swell at a hundred miles an hour. The huge plane skipped once and then crashed nose first into a wall of water. The impact had broken the back of the plane. The leaden weight of the bullion in the baggage compartment had torn the plane in half, spewing Bond and the girl out into the icy swell, lit red by the line of flares. There they had floated, half stunned, in their yellow life-jackets until the lifeboat got to them. By then there were only a few chunks of wreckage on the surface and the crew, with three tons of gold round their necks, were on their way down to the bed of the Atlantic. The boat hunted for ten minutes but when no bodies came to the surface they gave up the search and chugged back up the searchlight beam to the blessed wall of iron of the old frigate.

They had been treated like a mixture of royalty and people from Mars. Bond had answered the first, most urgent questions and then it had all suddenly seemed to be too much for his tired mind to cope with. Now he was lying luxuriating in the peace and the heat of the whisky and wondering about Pussy Galore and why she had chosen shelter under his wing rather than under Goldfinger's.

The connecting door with the next cabin opened and the girl came in. She was wearing nothing but a grey fisherman's jersey that was decent by half an inch. The sleeves were rolled up. She looked like a painting by Vertes. She said, "People keep on asking if I'd like an alcohol rub and I keep on saying that if anyone's going to rub me it's you, and if I'm going to be rubbed with anything it's you I'd like to be rubbed with." She ended lamely, "So here I am."

Bond said firmly, "Lock that door, Pussy, take off that sweater and come into bed. You'll catch cold."

She did as she was told, like an obedient child.

She lay in the crook of Bond's arm and looked up at him. She said, not in a gangster's voice, or a Lesbian's, but in a girl's voice, "Will you write to me in Sing Sing?"

Bond looked down into the deep blue-violet eyes that were no longer hard, imperious. He bent and kissed them lightly. He said, "They told me you only liked women."

She said, "I never met a man before." The toughness came back into her voice. "I come from the South. You know the definition of a virgin down there? Well, it's a girl who can run faster than her brother. In my case I couldn't run as fast as my uncle. I was twelve. That's not so good, James. You ought to be able to guess that."

Bond smiled down into the pale, beautiful face. He said, "All you need is a course of TLC."

"What's TLC?"

"Short for Tender Loving Care treatment. It's what they write on most papers when a waif gets brought in to a children's clinic."

"I'd like that." She looked at the passionate, rather cruel mouth waiting above hers. She reached up and brushed back the comma of black hair that had fallen over his right eyebrow. She looked into the fiercely slitted grey eyes. "When's it going to start?"

Bond's right hand came slowly up the firm, muscled thighs, over the flat soft plain of the stomach to the right breast. Its point was hard with desire. He said softly, "Now." His mouth came ruthlessly down on hers.

About the author

Ian Fleming was born in 1908 and educated at Eton. After a brief period at Sandhurst, he went abroad to further his education. In 1931, having failed to get an appointment in the Foreign Office, he joined Reuters News Agency. During the Second World War, he was Personal Assistant to the Director of Naval Intelligence at the Admiralty, rising from the rank of Lieutenant to Commander. His wartime experiences provided him with a first-hand knowledge of secret operations.

After the war he became Foreign Manager of Kemsley Newspapers and built his house, Goldeneye, in Jamaica. There at the age of 42 he wrote CASINO ROYALE, the first of the James Bond novels. By the time of his death in 1964, Fleming's fourteen Bond adventures had sold more than 40 million copies and the cult of James Bond was internationally established.